SCATTERED ASHES

Scott Nicholson

SCOTT NICHOLSON

SCATTERED ASHES

SCOTT NICHOLSON

DARK REGIONS PRESS

Publication History:

originals: "The Rocking Chair", "Sewing Circle", "The Endless Bivouac" 2008
"Silver Run" in *Legends of the Mountain State*, Oct. 2007
"The Night Is An Ally" in *A Dark And Deadly Valley*, Feb. 2007
"Work In Progress" in *Crimewave #9*, Dec. 2006
"Last Writes" (co-written with Edgar Allan Poe) in the Cemetery Dance anthology *Poe's Lighthouse*, May 2006
"She Climbs A Winding Stair" in *The Book of Dark Wisdom #9*, May 2006
"Dog Person" in *Cemetery Dance Magazine #56*, Summer 2006.
"The Weight of Silence" in the *Corpse Blossoms* anthology, Dec. 2005
"Watermelon" in *Cemetery Dance Magazine #51*, Spring 2005
"In The Family" in *The Third Alternative #41*, March 2005
"Playmates" (aka "October Girls") in e-book *New Voices From Kensington*, 2002.
"You'll Never Walk Alone" in *The Book of Final Flesh*, May 2003
"Penance" in *Black October #3*, October 2002. E-versions available at FictionWise
"The Hounds of Love" in *The Book Of More Flesh*, October 2002
"Murdermouth" in anthology *The Book of All Flesh*, October 2001.
"Scarecrow Boy" in *Chiaroscuro*, July 2001
"The Meek" in the CD-ROM anthology *EXTREMES II*, February, 2001
"Sung Li" in *At The Brink of Madness #3*, October 1999.
"The Timing Chains of the Heart" in *E-SCAPE #8*, June 1998

ISBN:-10 1-888993-64-2
ISBN-13: 978-1-888993-64-6

Dark Regions Press
PO Box 1264
Colusa, CA 95932

CONTENTS

THE HORROR OF IT ALL

BY JONATHAN MAYBERRY

Horror is a scary word.

Especially to people in the horror industry.

To readers it's a great word—full of dark promise and wicked delights. To the largest of the mainstream publishers and most chain bookstores, 'horror' is a bad, bad word. Horror books don't sell. You hear that all the time. Horror is just gore and exploitation. You hear that, too.

Often it's true. Except when it's not.

Here's the thing. Once upon a time 'horror' was a nice word that was used to embrace a broad genre of spooky tales ranging from classic ghost stories to vampires to all sorts of creatures that go bump in the nighttime of our imagination. Horror tales didn't have to be supernatural; of course, Edgar Allen Poe proved that with his psychological thrillers that gouged barbs into our paranoia and private fears. Horror could overlap with other genre—science fiction (you want to tell me *Alien* wasn't a horror flick?), speculative fiction (Richard Matheson's 1954 classic novel *I Am Legend*, nicely bridged the gap between 'what if?' and 'what the hell's that!'), mystery (Robert Bloch nailed that one with *Psycho*), fantasy (Lovecraft's Cthulhu mythos), Fantastique Populaire (Alexandre Dumas brought werewolves into the modern age of fiction with his 1848 story *Le Meneur de Loups* (The Leader Of

5

Wolves), comedy (start with *Abbott & Costello Meet Frankenstein,* keep going through *Young Frankenstein* and put the pedal all the way down with *Shaun of the Dead*), and even social commentary (*Night, Dawn* and *Day of the Dead*).

Horror has been the framework and vehicle for centuries of great storytelling. Millennia if you factor in the ancient myths of dragons, Cyclopes, revenants, ghouls, mummies, and other beasts going all the way back to *The Epic of Gilgamesh*—the oldest surviving piece of writing, which is rife with monsters.

So why is it a bad word?

The short answer is 'marketing'. In 1978 *Halloween* hit movie houses like a bloody tsunami. Eerie, unnerving, horrific, terrifying. *Halloween* was everything good horror should be. And it *was* a horror film. Michael Myers was an unkillable embodiment of evil. Good job John Carpenter. If there had been no sequels and if a lot of folks hadn't taken an incidental aspect of the movie and build an entire genre on it, the word 'horror' might still be safe for polite conversation within the publishing world. But a lot of folks in Hollywood who are not and never have been aficionados of horror or even *readers* of horror, went on to focus on the big fricking knife that Michael Myers carried and the plot device of his killing several people in inventive ways. The weapon and the method are not core to the story. The unstoppable nature of evil and the struggle between overwhelming threat and the natural impulse to survive *are* what the movie was all about. Those are tropes of the horror genre. But Hollywood can never be accused grasping the subtleties of theme and structure; hence the Slasher movie genre was born.

Most of the Slasher flicks—and the natural off-shoots, the Slasher novels—were, as I said, not written by horror writers. They are pre-packaged tripe whose purpose is to tantalize with young flesh and then indulge in ultraviolence that has no thematic value and no artistic flair. They're mind candy of the least nutritious kind.

The Slasher films collided with another horror sub-genre—the Serial Killer film. There are good and even great novels and movies about serial kills. Bloch's *Psycho,* Thomas Harris' *Red Dragon* and *Silence of the Lambs*, Jack Ketchum's *Off Season* are examples for the sub-genre in print; the film versions of most of these are terrific, and there are horrifying entries like *Henry, Portrait of a Serial Killer.* But the genre was truly born out of films like *Last House on the Left* and *The Texas Chainsaw Massacre*, and despite their huge fan followings, neither is a horror film. *Chainsaw* is probably the more debatable of the two since there are real moments of tension; but it's been spoiled by sequels and remakes that are so overtly exploitive that many viewers have stepped back from the genre in disgust.

In the late '90s and early 21st Century we saw the rise of yet another genre that polluted the word horror: torture porn. Films like *Hostel, Saw* and their many imitators are shock cinema. They're disturbing to be sure, but perspective makes true horror aficionados wonder at just what is attracting the audiences. The films are sexist and misogynistic in the extreme. The torture seems to be the point of the film rather than an element of a larger and more genuinely frightening tale. The technique appears to be shock rather than suspense.

Good horror is built on suspense. Shock has it moments, but it isn't, and should never be, the defining characteristic of the genre.

Here's the bottom line. Slasher, Serial Killer and Torture flicks have all been marketed as 'horror'. Go to Blockbuster or check Netflix…that's where they are.

Discerning audiences, those who enjoy the suspense and subtlety of true horror storytelling were repelled, and they also moved away from *all* horror because to modern audiences horror equals graphic and relentless violence.

Horror took it in the back.

It doesn't help that many of the most popular authors of horror novels—folks like Stephen King, Dean Koontz, Robert McCammon, Peter Straub—don't consider themselves to be horror authors. They prefer to be known as authors of 'suspense' or 'thrillers' or other more marketable genre labels,

I can't blame them. My own horror novels, the Pine Deep Trilogy (Ghost Road Blues, Dead Man's Song and Bad Moon Rising) were released as 'supernatural thrillers'. One of my best friends, L. A. Banks sees her vampire and werewolf novels published as 'paranormal romances'. The list goes on.

7

So, is horror dead?

Nope.

The book you're holding is proof of that.

Some writers have managed to hold the line against the propagandized war against 'horror'. Scott Nicholson's been at the forefront of that phalanx for years. He writes horror novels. He writes horror short stories. He writes horror. Make no mistake.

Sure, Scott can spin a mystery or a thriller with the best of them. He's a true writer and true writers can write in any damn genre they pick. But what sets Scott's horror fiction apart—or, perhaps, raises it as an example—is that it *is* horror. It's subtle, layered, textured, suspenseful and pretty god damn scary. There are shocks, sure; but you won't find one cheap shot in this whole collection. There's blood, too—Scott's not afraid of getting his hands dirty when it comes to violence. But those are elements he selects with care from a large toolbox of delicate instruments. Like all *true* horror writers, Scott is a craftsman who knows how to build a story on character and plot nuance, and then tweak this and twist that so that the story begins to quietly sink its claws into the reader.

Scattered Ashes is a wonderfully creepy, powerful and inventive collection of horror tales that will open doors in your mind— to let things out, and to let things in.

This is a book of horror tales from someone who understands— and loves—the genre. A lot of folks joke about having to leave the lights on when they read horror. Go ahead, try it. It won't help. This is a different kind of darkness: older, more devious, and if you're reading this then the darkness was already there inside you, waiting for a nightmare wizard to set it free.

—Jonathan Maberry
Multiple Bram Stoker Award-winning author of *PATIENT ZERO* and *ZOMBIE CSU;* and co-creator/consulting producer for *On The Slab* (ABC Disney)

TIMING CHAINS OF THE HEART

eather on leather, glove on shift ball, the faint smell of oil in the air. Wide-tread rubber clinging desperately to asphalt, a ton-and-a-half of steel-and-chrome stud machine that could grab and growl in five gears, not counting reverse. It was great to be alive.

J.D. Jolley peered at the strip of black ribbon that rolled out in front of his headlights. The ribbon disappeared into the larger strip of night. Night hid the rest of the world, and that was fine with J.D. The world was nothing but litter along the highway, as far as he was concerned.

He pumped the accelerator once, then again, steadily, listening to the thrush of exhaust. A lot of muscle drivers stomped, but J.D. never stomped. You had to treat a '69 Camaro like a lady. With tenderness, compassion, lots of foreplay if you wanted a smooth ride.

"You're purring like a kitten in a kettle tonight, Cammie," J.D. said, patting the dashboard. "Warm as a manifold cover and wet as a water pump. What say we get it on?"

The moon was out, weakly grinning down on his left shoulder through the clouds. No matter how far he drove, the moon never seemed to move. It was one of those things about the world that J.D. accepted without a second thought. Hell, that was up there in the sky, and the moon didn't have a damned inch of asphalt. Maybe if those pencil-necked engineers ever came up with solo rockets, he'd take another study of the heavens. But until then, the sky was nothing but wind resistance.

He hung his arm out the window. A good little back-breeze played against his elbow. Ought to add a couple of miles per hour. He was shooting for one-forty tonight.

This was his favorite stretch of road, a nice straight three miles of open country. The local cops never patrolled out here for the simple reason that the only traffic was farm tractors and cattle trucks and the occasional riding lawn mower. The few farmhouses in the area were back from the highway, buffered by wide green and brown fields lined with barbed wire. Nobody to bother but the big-eyed cows, and they were practically kneeling in awe.

J.D. pressed the clutch and slid the Camaro into first gear. He clenched his left hand on the steering wheel. A lot of muscle guys had those faggy vinyl wraps on their steering wheels, but J.D. liked the natural factory feel. Same way with his women.

The back seat practically needed reconditioning, he'd worked the shock absorbers so much. A '69 Camaro drew the babes. They couldn't resist the sleek curves and classic lines, not to mention the throbbing under the hood. True, it was a lower class of women, but hell, one was pretty much the same as another when their legs were splayed out the back window.

So women were allowed in his meat wagon. But not on his midnight runs. Those were reserved strictly for him and his Cammie, a bond that was far more sacred than any relationship of mere flesh. This love was truer than motherly and was right up there with religious love. This was a man and his car racing against themselves.

For that same reason, he never dragged in the Saturday night specials with the hot rodders. There was a brisk betting business going on in this two-factory Iowa town because there wasn't much else to get excited about if you didn't invest in hog futures. The local cops were under orders to steer clear of the four-lane east of town when the muscleheads fired up their engines. But solo riders like J.D. were cracked faster than a powder-dry engine block.

10

If they did blue-light him out here, he could easily outrun them. They had those little pussyfoot cruisers that whined if they even got within sniffing distance of triple digits. They were driving damned imports, made in Korea even if the label said American. Ought to be a law against that.

J.D. closed his eyes and gave the gas pedal a little boot leather. His bucket seat shivered and he shivered with it, even though it was April. He was joining with the car. The spoiler was his open and gasping mouth, the carburetor throat was sucking oxygen, his crankcase belly was growling, hungry for petroleum, and the tires itched like his moist toes. The muffler was backfiring brimstone.

He popped the clutch at the same moment he popped open his eyelids. The asphalt squealed in agony as he left a fifty-foot scar up its spine. He straddled the dotted white line as he power-shifted into second, leaving another mist of scalded rubber hanging in the air behind him. J.D. glanced at the tachometer, saw that he was at 7,000 RPM, and he booted into third. Cammie was already at sixty and they'd not yet begun to party.

This was better than sex. This was red-eyed adrenaline, a spark in the old plug, a rush that made the small hairs on the back of J.D.'s neck stand up and dance. Fence posts blurred past both quarter panels as the Camaro's grill chewed up moths and the slipstream set the sawgrass swaying along the ditches. The G-force pressed J.D. against the seat. An excited sweat gathered under his eyes and his tongue felt like a gasket between the valve covers of his teeth.

He squinted at the small fuzzy dot ahead where the headlights petered out, at the murky oblivion that was always his destination. He was getting there, he felt it in his bones, he glanced down and saw the needle tacking toward one-ten and his bowels had gone zero-gravity. He was reaching down to glide into fourth when he saw the pale shape, a small figure that grew large too soon, from nothing to five-feet-six in only three seconds, and J.D. barely had time to see the face in the sweep of headlights.

Later he would tell himself that there was no way he could have observed all that detail in a fraction of a second. It was his imagination that must have painted the portrait. Eyes like a spotlighted deer's, wide and brown, impossibly deep. Eyebrows frantically climbing the white slope of forehead. Mouth open, choking on a scream that could fill the Holland Tunnel.

It was a glancing blow. J.D. didn't remember doing it, but he must have nudged the wheel slightly and his virgin-tight rack-and-pinion responded instantly. Otherwise the Camaro would have bucked and rolled, tumbling through the shin-high corn and strewing vital organs and steaming spare parts across the stubbled fields. At over a hundred, mistakes got amplified. But in that over-driven moment, J.D. was more car than man, high octane in his blood as he manipulated the automobile back onto course.

His foot had instantly left the accelerator but he had resisted the impulse to lock down on the brakes. The braking instinct was natural, but the resulting fishtail would have had J.D. ending up with a drive shaft necktie. The muffler growled as he downshifted and when he reached sixty he began working the brake pedal. He pulled to the side of the road and felt his heart beating in time to the idling pistons.

"Damn, Cammie," he said, when at last he was able to take a breath. "That was a close one."

He left the engine running while he opened the door and stood up, disoriented from the abrupt change in motion. He walked to the front of the car and knelt at the right fender. There was a crumple in the panel and the headlight chrome was dented and hanging loose. He took off his glove and ran a gentle hand along the fender and a few chips of candy-apple red paint flaked onto the shoulder of the road. He saw a smudge on the bumper and wiped at it.

Blood.

He looked back up the highway, but under the veiled moon, he couldn't see anything on the pavement. J.D. got behind the wheel and shifted into reverse.

"I'm so sorry, Cammie," he whimpered. The closest thing he'd ever had to tears tried to collect in his eyes. "It was just an accident."

He held the horses in check as he backed up, keeping the revolutions steady. The crankshaft turned quietly in its pit of golden thirty-weight. He'd damaged her flesh, but he could take care with her heart. J.D. pushed the gas pedal gently as he cut a U-turn and drove up the road.

He killed the engine when he reached the body, but left his headlights on. The first exhalation of night fog swirled in the low-beams as he loomed over the figure.

She was wearing a dress. The cotton was tattered, but it was a pretty dress, butterfly yellow, the kind that should have been easy to see at night. Her slim legs were sticking out below the hem at an obtuse angle, a scuffed sandal dangling from one big toe. The other foot was completely bare, a red sock of blood where the skin had peeled away.

Her arms were accordioned under her chest and she was face-down. Her hair was brown, and the big curls fluttered in the breeze. A pool of crimson was spreading out from under her belly. She was leaking like a busted oil pan.

He touched her skin where the dress had slid down one creamy shoulder. This was a dairy girl, J.D. was positive. Must have crept out her window and met some little boy blue behind a haystack. Come blow your horn. She had no business being out on the road at that time of night.

He turned her over and wished he hadn't. That split-second portrait before the accident had been of a pleasant face, one with round cheekbones and plump ruby lips and strong nostrils. But this, this was like a bag of beef soup that had been dropped on the highway from a helicopter. This was roadkill.

"You shouldn'ta been out so late," J.D. whispered. "Now look what you gone and done to yourself."

He glanced at one white exposed breast that had managed to avoid visible harm. Then he let her roll forward again. Her bones rattled like lug nuts in a hub cap.

"Now what am I going to do with you?" he said, licking his lips. He looked both ways but there were no headlights in sight.

"Can't leave you out here, that's for sure. Might get yourself run over, and then where would you be?"

That, plus J.D. didn't want his ass behind bars for second degree murder. A few speeding tickets were one thing, but this deal meant some hard time. At state prison, a pretty boy like him would be up on the blocks in no time, and the grease monkeys wouldn't wait for every twenty thousand miles to give him a lube job, either.

He stood up and looked around. He could slide her into the ditch, but that would be leaving things up to luck. She might be found before morning if some gap-toothed farmer came out early to get an early squeeze of swollen udder. And who knew what the forensics boys would come up with? He thought of the paint flakes up the road. They could look into those little microscopes and say whatever they wanted to, and the cops had been after him for years.

"Nope. Can't leave you here."

He walked behind the Camaro and unlocked the trunk. He unrolled a tarp that was stowed in one corner. He didn't want to mess up his trunk carpet. He took off his leather jacket and tossed it on the passenger seat, but he kept his gloves on.

The night smelled of cow manure and car exhaust and sweet, coppery body fluids. Cammie's engine ticked as it cooled. He patted her on the hood as he went past. Then he stooped and lifted the broken body.

It hung like a rag doll, with too many universal joints in the arms and legs. It was light, too, as if all its gears and cogs had slipped out. He put her in the trunk, hearing the largest chunk of her skull ding off the wheel well. He walked up the road until he found the other sandal, then he tossed it in and closed the trunk.

He drove back to town without breaking fifty-five. It was raining by the time he hit the outskirts.

Mama must not have heard him come in. She was already gone when he woke up, down checking side stitches on boxer shorts for five-and-a-quarter plus production. He was glad he'd slept through her coffee and butter toast. That made another half-dozen hundred questions she'd never get around to bugging him with.

He winced when he saw Cammie in daylight. There was a dimple on top of the fender and the chrome striping was peeling

14

away from the side panel, damage he hadn't noticed the night before. He drove down to the shop and pulled into the middle bay.

Floyd was smoking a cigarette and wiping his hands on a greasy orange rag. Floyd owned the shop, and liked to let everyone know it. He glowered at J.D. with oil-drop eyes.

"Yo, Jayce," he said. "What you doing here so early?"

"Got a ding on the shoulder. Need you to hammer it out."

"Had you a little bender, did you? Demolition derby with a mailbox?"

Floyd snickered and then started coughing. He pulled his cigarette out of his mouth and spat a wad of phlegm onto the greasy concrete floor.

"Just get me a rubber mallet, wouldja?"

"Sure, I'll help. Thanks for asking," Floyd said.

"You don't have to be a smart-ass."

"And you don't have to work here if you don't want to."

Floyd could be a real pain in the plug hole. But he was a body-work pro. He'd worked the pits for Bobby Allison about twenty years back. When he got down to business, he was an artist, and steel and fiberglass and primer were his media.

And J.D. could tell Floyd loved Cammie almost as much as he did. They pounded out the dents and replaced the headlight frame and put on the primer coat before they started taking care of the customer's cars. Then at lunch, Floyd feathered out a coat of red so that it blended with the color of the rest of the car's body.

J.D. was up to his elbows in an automatic transmission when he saw Floyd put down his airbrush and step back to admire his work.

"That's gooder than snuff," he proclaimed. J.D. nodded in appreciation. The quarter panel didn't have so much as a shadow in it.

"Preesh, Floyd. Nobody can fix them like you do," J.D. said.

"Nope. Throw me your keys, Jayce. I need to change my plugs, and I left my good ratchet in your trunk yesterday."

"Hey, buddy. After all you've done for me? You got to be kidding. Let me do it."

Floyd frowned around the black fingerprints on his cigarette butt. Floyd didn't like other people tinkering under the hood of his '57 Chevy. But J.D. moved quickly, before Floyd could say no.

J.D. popped the trunk and there she was, Miss American Pie. Mincemeat pie. The blood had clotted and dried and she was starting to smell a little. Her left arm was draped over the toolbox. As he moved it away, he noticed that it had stiffened a little from rigor mortis.

He clattered around in the toolbox and found the ratchet. He was about to slam the lid when he saw that her eyes were open. Damned things weren't open last night, he was positive. Her eyes didn't sparkle at all. They were staring at him.

"What's the matter, J.D.?"

J.D. gulped and slammed the trunk. "Nothing," he said, holding up the ratchet. "Found it."

"Make sure you gap the damned things right. Don't want you screwing up my gas mileage."

"You got it, Floyd."

J.D. drove out to the trailer park after work to pick up Melanie, his Thursday girl. He thought he heard a noise in the rear end as he pulled into the gravel driveway. Transfer case was groaning a little. He'd have to check it out later. He honked his horn and the trailer door opened.

Melanie slid in the passenger side and J.D. watched her rear settle into the bucket seat. She smiled at him. She was a big-boned redhead with lots of freckles, but her aqua eye shadow was so thick it quivered when she blinked.

"What you want to do, J.D.?"

He looked out the window. In the next yard, two brats were playing with a broken Easy-Bake oven. "Ride around, I reckon."

"Ride around? That's all you ever want to do."

"What else is there to do? Would you rather sit around the trailer park with your thumb up your ass?"

Melanie pouted. She was a first-class pouter. J.D. had told her that her lip drooped so low you could drive up on it and swap out your oil filter.

"Okay," she said after a moment. "Let's go circle the burger joint."

That wasn't a bad idea. Everybody hung out at the burger joint, the muscleheads and the dope peddlers and the zombie teens. And that meant everybody would see that the Camaro was unscratched. J.D. didn't have a damn thing to hide.

Later, after they'd split two burgers and a six-pack of Pabst Blue Ribbon, J.D. had driven out to their favorite dirt back road. The sun was just going down by the time he'd sweet-talked Melanie into the back seat. He was wrestling with her double-hook D-cup when she suddenly tensed underneath him.

"Joo hear that?" she whispered. J.D. heard only crickets and the slight squeaking of leaf springs.

"Hear what?"

"A scratching, like. On metal."

J.D. looked up. He always parked away from the trees out on these country roads. Damned branches would claw the hell out of a custom paint job. He saw nothing but the gangly shadows of the far underbrush.

"I don't hear nothing, babe. Now, where were we?"

"There it went again. Sounds like it's coming from the trunk."

"Bullshit."

"Sounds like a squirrel running around in there."

J.D. strained his ears. He heard the faint rattle of tools. Then, fingernails on metal.

He sat up suddenly.

"What the hell, J.D.?"

"Nothing. Better get you back to town, is all."

Melanie whimpered. She was as good at whimpering as she was at pouting.

"But J.D., I thought—"

"Not tonight, I got . . . work to do."

She whined all the way back into town, but J.D. didn't hear her. All he could hear were the low moans coming from the trunk and the sound of fists banging like rubber mallets off the trunk lid.

After J.D. dropped off Melanie, he pulled out behind Floyd's garage and looked around the auto graveyard. Here was where Detroit's mistakes came to die. Pontiacs draped over Plymouths while Chryslers sagged on cinder blocks. A school bus slept in its bed of briars. A couple of Studebakers decayed beside the high wooden fence, and a dozen junk jeeps were lined in rows like dead soldiers awaiting body bags. The few unbroken headlights were like watching eyes, but they would be the only witnesses.

Back here, Miss American Mincemeat Pie could rust in peace.

He stepped out among the bones of cars, gang-raped engines, and jagged chassis. The moon was glaring down, all of last night's clouds now long-hauled to the east. J.D. gripped the trunk key between his sweaty fingers.

"Open it, J.D.," said the voice. It was a young, hollow voice, with the kind of drawn-out accent a country girl might have. The long syllables reverberated inside the tin can of the trunk space.

J.D. looked around the junkyard.

"Stick it in, muscleboy," the voice taunted. "You know you want to."

He unlatched the trunk and it opened with a rush of foul air.

She sat up and arched her back.

"Cramped in here," she said. The moon shone fully on her, like a spotlight. The raw flesh of her face was tinged green, and her eyes were ringed with black. She reached up to smooth her hair and her arm hung like a broken clutch-spring.

"You . . . y-you're dead." But that was dumb. He knew machines didn't die, they only got rebuilt.

"Now, do I look dead?"

J.D. didn't know what to say. It wasn't the kind of thing he could look up in the troubleshooting section of his owner's manual.

"Still got a few miles left on me," she said, tugging at the strap of her dress that had slipped too low over her mottled chest. Her eyes were wide but as dull as Volkswagen hubcaps. "Besides, all I need is a little body work and I'll be good as new."

"What's the big idea, screwing up my date like that?" J.D. angled his head so he could look at her out of the corners of his eyes.

"Your cheating days are over, rough rider. You've only got room in your heart for one girl now."

"Whatchoo talking about? And why did you dump over my toolbox?" J.D. couldn't be sure, but it looked like radiator fluid was leaking from her eyes.

"A lady's always in search of that one good tool. What say we get it on?"

"No. I'm going to stuff you behind the seat of that Suburban over there, and you're going to stay until you're both a collector's item."

"J.D., is that any way to treat a lady?"

"Well, you ought to be glad I think enough of you to leave you in a Chevy. There's plenty of Datsuns out here."

She shook her head, and tattered meat swung below her face. "I don't think so, muscleboy."

Her finger flexed like a carb linkage as she beckoned him closer.

J.D. couldn't help himself. He was as captivated as he'd been by his first *Hot Rod* magazine. She smelled of gasoline and grave dirt, hot grease and raw sex. She'd oozed out all over the spare tire. He'd never get his trunk clean.

"I think we're ready for a midnight run." She slid her mangled tongue over her teeth.

He leaned over the back bumper. He felt a cold limp hand slide behind his Mark Martin belt buckle. She put the mashed blackberries of her lips to his ear.

"And from now on, I ride up front," she whispered, and her words came out with no breath.

Three months, and J.D. was dragging.

The summer heat was wearing on him, and he'd lost twenty of his hundred-and-forty pounds. But it was even worse for her. She had gone from pink to green to gray and still the meat clung stubbornly to her bones.

He hid her during the day, in a self-storage garage he rented. Floyd had given him hell at first, asking him why he walked all the time these days, was he afraid of putting another dent in Cammie or what. But lately Floyd had quit the ribbing. This morning Floyd said J.D. looked like he'd been run all night by the hounds of hell.

"Something like that," J.D. wanted to say, but he'd promised to keep the affair a secret.

And that evening, as he'd done every night since he'd picked up his new passenger, he carried a five-gallon can of gas to the garage and filled up the Camaro.

And when the sun slid behind the flat Midwestern horizon and midnight raised its oil-soaked rags, he backed the car out and pointed it toward the street.

"Where to tonight, Cammie?" he asked, as if he had to ask.

She grinned at him. She was always grinning, now that her face was mostly skull. "The usual, muscleboy."

He drove out to that three-mile stretch of open black road and idled. Oblivion beckoned beyond the yellow cones of the headlights.

"One-sixty-five tonight," she said.

He gulped and nodded. One-sixty-five. He could do it. Probably.

Not that he had any choice. He could damage her flesh, but couldn't break the timing chains of love.

"Okay, Cammie," he said to her.

As J.D. stomped the accelerator and jerked his foot off the clutch, he wondered if this would be the night of consummation. Would she let him release the steering wheel as he wound into fifth gear, making them truly one, all blood and twisted metal and spare parts?

He glanced at her. There was no sign of requited love in the dim holes of her skull. She was as cold as a machine, unforgiving, more metal than bone, more petroleum than blood.

She was going to ride shotgun forever, as the odometer racked up miles and miles of endless highway.

If only he could please her. But he was afraid that he was nothing to her, just a vapor in the combustion chambers of her heart.

He shifted into fourth.

DOG PERSON

The final breakfast was scrambled eggs, crisp bacon, grits with real butter. Alison peeled four extra strips of bacon from the slab. On this morning of all mornings, she would keep the temperature of the stove eye just right. She wasn't the cook of the house, but Robert had taught her all about Southern cuisine, especially that of the Blue Ridge Mountains. Before they met, her breakfast consisted of a cup of what Robert teasingly called a "girly French coffee" and maybe a yogurt. He'd introduced her to the joys of an unhealthy start to the morning, along with plenty of other things, the best of the rest coming after sundown.

Even after two years, Alison wasn't as enthusiastic about the morning cholesterol infusion as Robert was. Or his dog. About once a week, though, she'd get up a half-hour early, drag the scarred skillet from beneath the counter, and peel those slick and marbled pieces of pig fat. The popping grease never failed to mark a red spot or two along her wrist as she wielded the spatula. But she wouldn't gripe about the pain today.

Robert would be coming down any minute. She could almost picture him upstairs, brushing his teeth without looking in the mirror. He wouldn't be able to meet his own eyes. Not with the job that awaited him.

Alison cracked six eggs in a metal bowl and tumbled them with a whisk until the yellow and white were mingled but not fully mixed. The grits bubbled and burped on the back burner. Two slices of bread stood in the sleeves of the toaster, and the coffee maker gurgled as the last of its heated water sprayed into the basket. Maxwell House, good old all-American farm coffee.

She avoided looking in the pantry, though the louvered doors were parted. The giant bag of Kennel Ration stood in a green trash can. On the shelf above was a box of Milk Bones and rows of canned dog food. Robert had a theory that hot dogs and turkey bologna were cheaper dog treats than the well-advertised merchandise lines, but he liked to keep stock on hand just in case. That was Robert; always planning ahead. But some things couldn't be planned, even when you expected them.

Robert entered the room, buttoning the cuffs on his flannel shirt. The skin beneath his eyes was puffed and lavender. "Something smells good."

She shoveled the four bacon strips from the skillet and placed them on a double layer of paper towels. "Only the best today."

"That's sweet of you."

"I wish I could do more."

"You've done plenty." ·

Robert moved past her without brushing against her, though the counter ran down the center of the kitchen and narrowed the floor space in front of the stove. Most mornings, he would have given her an affectionate squeeze on the rear and she would have threatened him with the spatula, grinning all the while. This morning he poured himself a cup of coffee without asking if she wanted one.

She glanced at Robert as he bent into the refrigerator to get some cream. At thirty-five, he was still in shape, the blue jeans snug around him and only the slightest bulge over his belt. His brown hair showed the faintest streaks of gray, though the lines around his eyes and mouth had grown visibly deeper in the last few months.

He wore a beard but he hadn't shaved his neck in a week. He caught her looking.

Alison turned her attention back to the pan. "Do you want to talk about it?"

"Not much to say." He stirred his coffee, tapped his spoon on the cup's ceramic rim, and reached into the cabinet above the sink. He pulled the bottle of Jack Daniels into the glare of the morning sun. Beyond the window, sunlight filtered through the red and golden leaves of maple trees that were about to enter their winter sleep.

Robert never drank before noon, but Alison didn't comment as he tossed a splash into his coffee. "I made extra bacon," she said. "A special treat."

Robert nodded, his eyes shot with red lightning bolts. He had tossed all night, awakening her once at 3 a.m. when his toenails dug into her calf. He must have been dreaming of days with Sandy Ann, walking by the river, camping in the hollows of Grandfather Mountain, dropping by the animal shelter to volunteer for a couple of hours.

Alison moved the grits from the heat and set them aside. The last round of bacon was done, and she drained some of the bacon grease away and poured the eggs. The mixture lay there round and steaming like the face of a cartoon sun. She let the eggs harden a bit before she moved them around. A brown skin covered the bottom of the skillet.

"Nine years is a lot," she said. "Isn't that over seventy in people years?"

"No, it's nine in people years. Time's the same for everybody and everything."

Robert philosophy. A practical farm boy. If she had been granted the power to build her future husband in a Frankenstein laboratory, little of Robert would have been in the recipe. Maybe the eyes, brown and honest with flecks of green that brightened when he was aroused. She would have chosen other parts, though the composite wasn't bad. The thing that made Robert who he was, the spark that juiced his soul, was largely invisible but had shocked Alison from the very first exposure.

She sold casualty insurance, and Robert liked to point out she was one of the "Good Hands" people. Robert's account had been assigned to her when a senior agent retired, and during his first appointment to discuss whether to increase the limit on his home-owner's policy, she'd followed the procedure taught in business school, trying to sucker him into a whole-life policy. During the con-versation, she'd learned he had no heirs, not even a wife, and she explained he couldn't legally leave his estate to Sandy Ann. One follow-up call later, to check on whether he would get a discount on his auto liability if he took the life insurance, and they were dating.

The first date was lunch in a place that was too nice and dressy for either of them to be comfortable. The next week, they went to a movie during which Robert never once tried to put his arm around her shoulder. Two days later, he called and said he was never going to get to know her at this rate so why didn't she just come out to his place for a cook-out and a beer? Heading down his long gravel drive between hardwoods and weathered outbuildings, she first met Sandy Ann, who barked at the wheels and then leapt onto the driver's side door, scratching the finish on her new Camry.

Robert laughed as he pulled the yellow Labrador retriever away so Alison could open her door. She wasn't a dog person. She'd had a couple of cats growing up but had always been too busy to make a long-term pet commitment. She had planned to travel light, though the old get-married-two-kids-house-in-the-suburbs had nig-gled at the base of her brain once or twice as she'd approached thirty. It turned out she ended up more rural than suburban, Robert's sperm count was too low, and marriage was the inevitable result of exposure to Robert's grill.

She plunged the toaster lever. The eggs were done and she arranged the food on the plates. Her timing was perfect. The edges of the grits had just begun to congeal. She set Robert's plate before him. The steam of his coffee carried the scent of bourbon.

"Where's the extra bacon?" he asked.

"On the counter."

"It'll get cold."

"She'll eat it."

"I reckon it won't kill her either way." Robert sometimes

poured leftover bacon or hamburger grease on Sandy Ann's dry food even though the vet said it was bad for her. Robert's justification was she ate rotted squirrels she found in the woods, so what difference did a little fat make?

"We could do this at the vet," Alison said. "Maybe it would be easier for everybody, especially Sandy Ann." Though she was really thinking of Robert. And herself.

"That's not honest. I know you love her, too, but when you get down to it, she's my dog. I had her before I had you."

Sandy Ann had growled at Alison for the first few weeks, which she found so unsettling that she almost gave up on Robert. But he convinced her Sandy Ann was just slow to trust and would come around in time. Once, the dog nipped at her leg, tearing a hole in a new pair of slacks. Robert bought her a replacement pair and they spent more time in Alison's apartment than at the farm. Alison bought the groceries and let him cook, and they did the dishes together.

The first time Alison spent the night at the farm, Sandy Ann curled outside Robert's door and whined. He had to put the dog outside so they could make love. They were married four months later and Robert was prepared to take the dog with them on their honeymoon, an RV and backpacking trip through the Southwest. Only a desperate plea from Alison, stopping just short of threat, had persuaded Robert to leave Sandy Ann at a kennel.

"You got the eggs right," Robert said, chewing with his mouth open.

"Thank you."

He powdered his grits with pepper until a soft black carpet lay atop them. The dust was nearly thick enough to make Alison sneeze. He worked his fork and moved the grits to his mouth, washing the bite down with another sip of the laced coffee.

"Maybe you can wait until tomorrow," Alison said. She didn't want to wait another day, and had waited months too long already, but she said what any wife would. She bit into her own bacon, which had grown cool and brittle.

"Tomorrow's Sunday." Robert wasn't religious but he was peculiar about Sundays. It was a holdover from his upbringing as the son of a Missionary Baptist. Though Robert was a house painter by trade, he'd kept up the farming tradition. The government was buying out his tobacco allocation and cabbage was more of a hobby than a commercial crop. Robert raised a few goats and a beef steer, but they were more pets than anything. She didn't think Robert would slaughter them even if they stood between him and starvation. He wasn't a killer.

"Sunday might be a better day for it," she said.

"No." Robert nibbled a half-moon into the toast. "It's been put off long enough."

"Maybe we should let her in."

"Not while we're eating. No need to go changing habits now."

"She won't know the difference."

"No, but I will."

Alison drew her robe tighter across her body. The eggs had hardened a little, the yellow gone an obscene greenish shade.

Sandy Ann had been having kidney and liver problems and had lost fifteen pounds. The vet said they could perform an operation, which would cost $3,000, and there would still be no guarantee of recovery. Alison told Robert it would be tough coming up with the money, especially since she'd given up her own job, but she would be willing to make the necessary sacrifices. Robert said they would be selfish to keep the dog alive if it was suffering.

"Want some more grits?" she asked. Robert shook his head and finished the coffee. She looked at the fork in his hand and saw that it was quivering.

Sandy Ann ran away when Alison moved in. Robert stayed up until after midnight, going to the door and calling its name every half-hour. He'd prowled the woods with a flashlight while Alison dozed on the couch. Sandy Ann turned up three days later in the next town, and Robert said if he hadn't burned his phone number into the leather collar, the dog might have been lost forever.

Sandy Ann was mostly Lab, with a little husky mix that gave its eyes a faint gray tint in certain light. The dog had been spayed before Robert got it at the pound. Robert's mother had died that year, joining her husband in their Baptist heaven and leaving the farm to their sole heir. Sandy Ann had survived thirty-seven laying hens, two sows, a milk cow, one big mouser tomcat that haunted the barn, and a Shetland pony.

Until today.

Alison's appetite was terrible even for her. Three slices of bacon remained on her plate. She pushed them onto a soiled paper napkin for the dog.

"Four's enough," Robert said.

"I thought you could give her one piece now."

"It's not like baiting a fish. A dog will follow bacon into hell if you give it half a chance."

Robert finished his plate and took the dishes to the sink. She thought he was going to enter the cabinet for another shot of bourbon, but he simply rinsed the dishes and stacked them on top of the dirty skillet. His hair seemed to have become grayer at the temples and he hunched a little, like an old man with calcium deficiency.

"I'd like to come," she said.

"We've been through that."

"We're supposed to be there for each other. You remember April eighth?"

"That was just a wedding. This is my dog."

Alison resented Sandy Ann's having the run of the house. The carpets were always muddy and no matter how often she vacuumed, dog hair seemed to snow from the ceiling. The battle had been long and subtle, but eventually Sandy Ann became an outdoor dog on all but the coldest days. The dog still had a favorite spot on the shotgun side of Robert's pick-up, the vinyl seat cover scratched and animal-smelling. Alison all but refused to ride in the truck, and they took her Camry when they were out doing "couple things."

"Do you want to talk about it?" Alison asked. She had tried to draw him out. In the early days, Robert had been forthcoming about everything, surprising her with his honesty and depth of feeling. Despite the initial attraction, she had thought him a little rough around the edges. She'd been raised in a trailer park but had attended Wake Forest University and so thought she had escaped her breeding. But Robert reveled in his.

"Nothing left to say. Maybe later."

"We can go down to the farmer's market when you get back. Maybe we can get some sweet corn for dinner. And I've been looking for a philodendron for the living room."

"I won't feel like it."

"Robert, I know it's hard. Talk to me."

"I am talking."

"Really. Don't shut me out."

"Never have."

She slammed her fist on the table, causing her flatware to jump and clatter. "Damn it, don't be so stoic. You're allowed to grieve."

Robert wiped his hands on the kitchen towel that hung from the refrigerator handle. "Thanks for breakfast."

He went past her to the hall. She heard him open the closet door and rummage on the upper shelf. One of the snow skis banged against the doorjamb. She had convinced Robert to try skiing, and they'd spent a weekend at Wintergreen in Virginia. He'd twisted his ankle on the first run. He said skiing was a rich kid's sport and it had served him right to try and escape his breeding.

Robert came back to the kitchen, the rifle tucked against his right shoulder. A single bullet made a bulge in his pocket, the shape long and mean.

"Have you decided where to bury her?" Alison had always thought of Sandy Ann as an "it," and had to consciously use the feminine pronoun. Alison wanted to show she cared, whether her husband appreciated it or not.

"She's not that heavy, or I'd do it near where I was going to bury her. I'm figuring behind the barn. She loved to lay in the shade back there."

Alison hated the back of the barn. It was full of barbed wire and blackberry vines, and once she'd seen a snake slither through the tall weeds. The garden lay beyond it, and she tended a bed of marigolds there, but she associated shadows with unseen reptiles. Sandy Ann would sometimes watch from the edge of the garden while Alison worked, but the two rarely communicated when Robert wasn't around, though Alison often left bacon for it by the back steps.

The grease from breakfast coated Alison's throat, and her chest ached. Robert went through the back door onto the porch. Alison followed him, trading the heavy smells of the kitchen for the tart, dry October morning. The mountains were vibrant in their dying glory, umber, burgundy, ochre.

Sandy Ann was sleeping in a hollowed-out place under the steps. The dog lifted its head at the sound of their feet. It must have smelled the bacon in Robert's hand, because its dusty nose wiggled and Sandy Ann dragged itself into the yard.

The sun glinted in the tears that ran down Robert's cheeks. "Good girl," he said, giving the dog a piece of bacon. The dog swallowed it without chewing and ran its rough tongue over its lips, ears lifting a little in anticipation of more. Robert moved the bacon to his rifle hand and scratched the dog on top of the head.

"Come on, girl, let's take a walk." He headed toward the woods.

Sandy Ann looked back at Alison, eyes dim and hiding pain, brown crust in their corners. She held out the bacon in her hand. Unlike the other pieces she had fed it, this one wasn't sprinkled with rat poison. The dog licked its lips once more, exhaled a chuffing sigh, then followed Robert, the yellow tail swinging gently like a piece of frozen rope.

Robert led the way across the yard, holding the bacon aloft so the dog could smell it. He and Sandy Ann went through a crooked gate and Robert leaned the rifle against the fence while he fastened the latch. He looked back at the porch. Alison waved and bit into her own bacon.

They started again, both of them stooped and limping. They reached the trees, Robert's boots kicking up the brittle leaves, Sandy Ann laboring by his side. The last she saw of him was his plaid flannel shirt.

She should chase them. Maybe she could hold the bacon while Robert loaded the gun. After all, she had cooked it. And, in a way, she was replacing Sandy Ann. If Robert ever got another dog, it would be Alison's home and therefore it would be the dog that would have to adjust, not the other way around. She didn't think they would get another dog, not for a while.

Sandy Ann was just a dog, and Alison wasn't a dog person. She was the practical one in the relationship. She could have driven Sandy Ann to the vet, even at the risk of getting dog hair in her car. The vet would have drawn out a nice, clean needle and Sandy Ann could drift off to sleep, dreaming of fast squirrels and chunks of cooked meat and snacks by the back porch of home.

Maybe Robert needed the catharsis of violence. Perhaps that would be his absolution, though surely he couldn't view the dog's infirmity as his fault. After all, it would have aged no matter the owner. Sandy Ann, like all of them, would die and go to whatever heaven was nearest. Robert's way might be best after all. One split-second and then the pain would end.

Alison went inside and poured herself a half cup of coffee and sat at the kitchen table, looking through the window. The sunlight was soft on the stubbled garden. Some of the marigolds clung to a defiant life, their edges crinkled and brown. Collard leaves swayed in the breeze like the ears of small green puppies. The shovel stood by the barn, waiting.

Her coffee mug was to her lips when the shot sounded. The report echoed off the rocky slopes and the hard, knotty trees. Alison didn't know whether to smile or pout against the ceramic rim. The house was hers.

When Robert returned, she would have tears in her eyes. She would hug him and let him sag onto her, and she would lead him to the couch. She would remind him of all the great memories, and let him talk for hours about the dog's life. She would kneel before him and remove his boots and wipe the mud from them. He would have no appetite, but she would cook for him anyway, maybe something sweet, like a pie. If he wanted, he could have some more of the Jack Daniels. She would turn on the television and they would sit together, the two of them in their house.

Her house.

Alison finished her coffee. The remaining bacon was covered with a gray film of grease but she ate it anyway, her stomach finally unclenching.

She washed dishes, a chore she loathed. She rinsed the pans

with hot water. Later in the evening, she would vacuum, try to remove the last traces of Sandy Ann from the living room carpet.

Something clicked on the porch steps. She wondered if Robert had decided to come back to the house before he began digging. Either way, Alison would be there for him. She would shovel until she raised blisters if he would let her. Alison wiped her hands on her bathrobe and hurried to the door, blinking rapidly so her eyes would water.

The scratching sound was at the door now, as if Robert were wiping his boots on the welcome mat. She braced herself for Robert's crestfallen expression, the caved-in look of his eyes, the deep furrows at the corners of his mouth. She would never have inflicted such suffering if it weren't for the best.

Alison opened the door. On the porch, Sandy Ann stood on bowed legs, working her dry lips. The dog lifted a forlorn paw and dropped it with a click of nails. There were spatters of blood across the dog's snout.

One shot.

Robert couldn't have missed.

Not from so close.

Could he have...?

No, not Robert.

But it was the kind of choice Robert would make.

His only choice.

A dog person to the end.

"Robert?" she called, voice cracking, knowing there would be no answer.

Alison's ribs were a fist gripping the yolk of her heart. Her legs were grits, her head popping like hot grease on a griddle. Her spine melted like butter. She sagged against her house and slid to a sitting position. Sandy Ann whimpered, limped over, and ran a papery tongue against her cheek.

The dog's breath reeked of bacon and poison and unconditional love.

THE OCTOBER GIRLS

The evening was Halloween cool, the sun creeping toward the horizon. It would be dark soon, and the games would be over. Margaret could stay out as late as she wanted, but not Ellen. Ellen had a mom and a bed and a life to worry about.

"Come out," Ellen called.

The scraggly shrubbery trembled. Margaret was hiding under the window of the mobile home where Ellen lived. For an invisible person, Margaret wasn't so good at hide-and-seek, but she loved to play. Maybe you got that way when you were dead.

The mobile home vibrated with the noise of the vacuum cleaner. Mom was inside, cleaning up. Taking a break from beer and television. Maybe cooking a supper of sliced wieners in cheese noodles.

"I know you're in there," Ellen said.

She stooped and peered under the lowest brown leaves of the forsythia. Vines snaked through the shrubbery. In the summer, yellow flowers dangled from the tips of the vines. Ellen and Margaret would pull the white tendrils from the flowers, holding them to the sun so the sweet drops of honeysuckle fell on their tongues. They would laugh and hold hands and run into the woods, playing tag until night fell. Then they would follow the fireflies into darkness.

But only in the summer. Now it was autumn, with the leaves like kites and November rushing toward them from Tennessee. Now Ellen had school five mornings a week, homework, chores if Mom caught her. Not much time for games, so she and Margaret had to make the most of their time together.

The bushes shook again.

"Come out, come out," Ellen called, afraid that Mom would switch off the vacuum cleaner and hear her having fun.

Margaret's long blonde hair appeared in a gap between the bushes. A hand emerged, slender and pale and wearing a plastic ring that Ellen had gotten as a Crackerjack prize. The hand was followed by the red sleeve of Margaret's sweater. At last Ellen's playmate showed her face with its uneven grin.

"Peek-a-boo," Margaret said.

"Your turn to be 'it.'"

The vacuum cleaner suddenly switched off, and the silence was broken only by the brittle shivering of the trees along the edge of the trailer park. Ellen put her index finger to her lips to shush Margaret, then crawled into the bushes beside her. The trailer door swung open with a rusty creak.

Mom looked out, shading her eyes against the setting sun. Ellen ducked deeper into the shrubbery, where the dirt smelled of cat pee. Margaret stifled a giggle beside her. Everything was a game to Margaret. But Margaret wasn't the one who had to worry about getting her hide tanned, and Margaret could disappear if she wanted.

Mom had that look on her face, the red of anger over the pink of drunkenness. She stood in the doorway and chewed her lip. A greasy strand of hair dangled over one eye. Her fists were balled. The stench of burnt cheese powder and cigarettes drifted from the trailer.

"Ellen," Mom called, looking down the row of trailers to the trees. Mom hated Ellen's staying out late more than anything. Except maybe the special teachers at school.

Ellen tensed, hugging her knees to her chest.

"She looks really mad," Margaret whispered.

"No, she's probably just worried."

A thin rope of smoke drifted from the trailer door. "She burned supper," Margaret said.

"It's my fault. She's really going to whip me this time."

Mom called once more, then slammed the door closed. Margaret rolled her eyes and stuck her tongue out at the mobile home. Ellen laughed, though her stomach felt full of bugs.

"Let's go to my place," Margaret said.

"What if Mom sees me? She can see me, even if she can't see you."

Margaret started crawling behind the row of dying shrubbery. "Your mom won't find you there."

"She always finds me anywhere." Ellen hung her head, near tears.

Margaret crawled back and poked her in the side. "Don't be a gloomy Gus."

Ellen slapped Margaret's hand away. "I'm not no gloomy Gus."

"Why don't you let me get her? I can make her hurt like she makes you hurt."

Ellen folded her arms and studied Margaret's brown eyes. Margaret would do it. She was a good friend. And in her eyes, behind the sparkle, was a darkness buried deep. Maybe you looked at things that way when you were dead.

"No. It's better if we keep you secret," Ellen said. "I already got in trouble at school, telling the special teachers about you."

Margaret poked her in the ribs again. Ellen smiled this time.

"Follow me. Hurry," Margaret said.

Margaret scrambled ahead, staying low beneath the hedge. Ellen looked at the trailer door, checked for any sign of movement in the windows. Then she crawled after Margaret, the dead twigs sharp against the skin of her palms and knees.

From the end of the hedge, they dashed for the concealment of the forest. Ellen half expected to hear Mom's angry shout, telling her to get inside right this minute. But then they were under the trees and lost among the long shadows.

Margaret laughed with the exhilaration of escape. She ran between the oaks with their orange leaves, the silver birch, the sweet green pine, ignoring the branches and briars that tugged the fabric of her sweater. Ellen followed just as recklessly, her footsteps soft on the rotting loam of the forest floor.

The girls passed a clearing covered by crisp leaves. Margaret veered away to a path that followed the river. The air smelled of fish and wet stones. Ellen stumbled over a grapevine, and by the time she looked up, Margaret had disappeared.

Ellen looked around. A bird chittered in a high treetop. The sun had slipped lower in the sky. Purple and pink clouds hung in the west like rags on a clothesline. She was alone.

Alone.

The special teachers at school told Ellen it was worse to be alone than have invisible friends. "You can't keep playing all by yourself," they told her. "You have to learn to get along with others. You have to let go of the past."

When Ellen told the special teachers about what happened at home, the teachers' eyes got wide. They must have talked to Mom, because when Ellen got home that day, she got her hide tanned harder than ever. Someday Mom was going to lose her temper and do something really bad.

Ellen thought of Mom, with fists clenched and supper burnt, waiting back at the trailer. Ellen shivered. She didn't want to be alone.

She put her hands to her mouth. "Margaret!"

She heard a giggle from behind a stand of trees. The red sweater flashed and vanished. Margaret was playing another game, trying to make Ellen get lost by leading her deeper into the woods. Well, Ellen wasn't going to be scared.

And she wasn't going to cry. Sometimes the girls at school made her cry. They would stand around her in a circle and say she was in love with Joey Hogwood. Well, she hated Joey Hogwood, and she hated the girls. Ellen wished that Margaret still went to school so that she would have a friend to sit beside.

Margaret wouldn't want her to cry. Margaret would just pretend to be bad for a little while, then pop out from behind a tree and tag her and make her "It."

Laughter came down from the hill where the pines were thickest. To the left, a sea of kudzu vines choked the trees. A run-down chicken coop had been swallowed by the leaves, with only a few rotten boards showing under the green. That's where Margaret was hiding.

Ellen ran across the kudzu, the leaves tickling her calves above her socks. She could read Margaret like a book. That was the best thing about invisible playmates: they did what you wanted them to do.

Right now, Ellen wanted Margaret to go just over the hill, into the new part of the forest. She reached the pines and started down the slope. Half a dozen houses were sprinkled among the folds of the hill. A highway ran through the darkening valley, the few cars making whispers as they rolled back and forth. The headlights were like giant fireflies in the dusk.

"Margaret," Ellen called.

A giggle floated up from the highway. Margaret was there by the ditch, waving her arm. Ellen smiled to herself. Margaret wouldn't leave her. Ellen picked her way down the slope, almost slipping on the dewy fallen leaves, until she reached the ditch.

"Tag, you're 'It,'" Margaret said, touching Ellen's shoulder.

Margaret's golden-white hair blazed in the lights of an approaching car. She spun and raced across the highway, the roar of the engine drowning out Ellen's scream. The car passed right through Margaret, not slowing at all. The red eyes of the tail lights faded into darkness. Ellen hurried across the road.

"You're a crazy-brain," Ellen said.

Margaret shook her head, her hair swaying from side to side. "Am not."

"Are, too."

"You're still 'It,'" Margaret said, running away. The darkness was more solid now, the sun fading in slow surrender. Margaret climbed over the low stone wall that bordered the highway.

"Crazy-brain." Ellen scrambled over the wall after her, into the graveyard. The alabaster angels and crosses and markers were like ghosts in the night. Margaret had vanished.

"Margaret?"

Laughter echoed off the granite.

Invisible friends didn't disappear unless you allowed it. They didn't hurt you or scare you or make you cry, at least not on purpose. They didn't tease you about Joey Hogwood, or make you sit in a chair and listen to all the reasons why invisible friends couldn't exist.

"Come out, come out, wherever you are," Ellen said. She scrambled between the cold gravestones. The grass was damp and full of autumn, and the air smelled of fall flowers. A sharp curve of moon had sliced its way into the black sky.

Ellen found Margaret beside a church-white marker.

"Mom's going to be mad," Ellen said.

"She's just an old meanie."

"She's really going to kill me." Ellen sat in the grass beside Margaret and the dew soaked her dress.

"Don't go back," Margaret said.

"I have to go back."

Margaret folded her arms across her chest and stuck out her lower lip. "In the summer, we got to play until way late."

"It's not summer anymore," Ellen said, looking at the sky. Three stars were out.

"Is that why the fireflies are gone?"

Ellen laughed. "You're such a dummyhead."

The moon was higher now, pale on Margaret's face. Her eyes were dark hollows. "I'm not no dummyhead."

"Yes, you are," Ellen said, her voice sing-songy and shrill. "Margaret is a dummyhead, Margaret is a dummyhead."

Margaret leaned back against the marker. Her shoulders trembled and thin lines of tears tracked down her cheeks. Ellen stopped teasing. With invisible playmates, you always felt what they felt.

"I'm sorry," Ellen whispered.

Margaret was bone silent.

"Hey," Ellen said. "Now who's the gloomy Gus?"

She poked Margaret in the side, feeling the hard ridges of her friend's ribs. It was funny how invisible friends could be solid, if you thought of them that way.

"Sometimes it's hard to remember," Margaret said, sniffing. "You know. What it was like."

Ellen poked again. "It's not that great."

Margaret twitched and tried to hold back her smile. Then the laughter broke and she blinked away the last of her tears. They watched the moon for a while and listened to the rush of the passing cars.

"I miss summer," Margaret said.

"Me, too."

"You don't have to go back."

They could play hide-and-seek all night and never have to hide in the same place twice. A few gnarled trees clutched at the ground with their roots, perfect for climbing. Honeysuckle vines covered the walls and gates, waiting for summer when they would again sweeten the air. Best of all was the quiet. Here, no one ever yelled in anger.

But Ellen didn't belong here. Not yet.

"I'd better get home," Ellen said. "I'm going to get my hide tanned as it is."

Margaret tried a pouty face, then gave up. All playtimes had to end. Ellen waved good-bye and started back over the stone wall.

"See you tomorrow?" Margaret called after her.

Ellen turned and looked back, but her friend had already vanished.

Margaret's voice came from everywhere, nowhere. "It won't hurt."

"Promise?"

"Even if it did, I would tickle you and make you laugh."

"Good night."

Ellen paused at the edge of the highway and waited for the next car. She could step out before the driver even saw her. Margaret had promised it wouldn't hurt. But maybe dead people always said that.

A car came over the hill, its engine roaring like a great beast, the headlights prowling for prey. Ellen ducked into the ditch and waited. Five seconds away, maybe. One jump, a big bump, and then she could be with Margaret.

Her lungs grew hard and cold, she couldn't breathe, and the car was maybe three seconds away. She told herself it was only another game, just hopscotch. She tensed. Two seconds.

Margaret whispered in her ear. "I lied. It really does hurt."

One second, and the car whizzed past, its exhaust lingering like a sigh.

"See you tomorrow?" Margaret said, sitting on the stone fence, pale under the scant moon.

"I guess so."

"You get this way," Margaret said. "When you're dead, you want to play games all the time."

"I guess I'll find out someday."

Ellen crossed the highway and tried to drift through the trees the way Margaret could. But it was no use. She was too solid, too real, she belonged too much to the world with its hard wood and hard people and hard rules. If only she were someone's invisible play-mate.

But she wasn't. She forgot games, laughter, the red sweater that Margaret had been buried in. Her thoughts were of nothing but Mom and home.

Ellen moved onward through the night, only half-dead, not nearly dead enough.

MURDERMOUTH

If only they had taken my tongue.

With no tongue, I would not taste this world. The air in the tent is buttered by the mist from popcorn. Cigarette smoke drifts from outside, sweet with candy apples and the liquor that the young men have been drinking. The drunken ones laugh the hardest, but their laughter always turns cruel.

If they only knew how much I love them. All of them, the small boys whose mothers pull them by the collar away from the cage, the plump women whose hair reflects the torchlight, the men all trying to act as if they are not surprised to see a dead man staring at them with hunger dripping from his mouth.

"Come and see the freak," says the man who cages me, his hands full of dollar bills.

Freak. He means me. I love him.

More people press forward, bulging like sausages against the confines of their skin. The salt from their sweat burns my eyes. I wish I could not see.

But I see more clearly now, dead, than I ever did while breathing. I know this is wrong, that my heart should beat like a trapped bird, that my veins should throb in my temples, that blood

41

should sluice through my limbs. Or else, my eyes should go forever dark, the pounding stilled.

"He doesn't look all that weird," says a long-haired man in denim overalls. He spits brown juice into the straw that covers the ground.

"Seen one like him up at Conner's Flat," says a second, whose breath falls like an ill wind. "I hear there's three in Asheville, in freak shows like this."

The long-haired man doesn't smell my love for him. "Them scientists and their labs, cooking up all kinds of crazy stuff, it's a wonder something like this ain't happened years ago."

The second man laughs and points at me and I want to kiss his finger. "This poor bastard should have been put out of his misery like the rest of them. Looks like he wouldn't mind sucking your brains out of your skull."

"Shit, that's nothing," says a third, this one as big around as one of the barrels that the clowns use for tricks. "I seen a woman in Parson's Ford, she'd take a hunk out of your leg faster than you can say 'Bob's your uncle.'"

"Sounds like your ex-wife," says the first man to the second. The three of them laugh together.

"A one hundred percent genuine flesh-eater," says my barker. His eyes shine like coins. He is proud of his freak.

"He looks like any one of us," calls a voice from the crowd. "You know. Normal."

"Say, pardnuh, you wouldn't be taking us for a ride, would you?" says the man as big as a barrel.

For a moment, I wonder if perhaps some mistake has been made, that I am in my bed, dreaming beside my wife. I put my hand to my chest. No heartbeat. I put a finger in my mouth.

"I'm as true as an encyclopedia," says my barker.

"Look at the bad man, Mommy," says a little girl. I smile at her, my mouth wet with desire. She shrieks and her mother leans forward and picks her up. I spit my finger out and stare at it, lying there pale against the straw, slick and shiny beneath the guttering torches.

Several of the women moan, the men grunt before they can stop themselves, the children lean closer, jostle for position. One slips, a yellow-haired boy with tan skin and meat that smells like soap. For an instant, his hands grip the bars of the cage. He fights for balance.

I love him so much, I want to make him happy, to please him. I crawl forward, his human stink against my tongue as I try to kiss him. Too quickly, a man has yanked him away. A woman screams and curses first at him, then at me.

The barker beats at the bars with his walking stick. "Get back, freak."

I cover my face with my hands, as he has taught me. The crowd cheers. I hunch my back and shiver, though I have not been cold since I took my final breath. The barker pokes me with the stick, taunting me. Our eyes meet and I know what to do next. I pick my finger off the ground and return it to my mouth. The crowd sighs in satisfaction.

The finger has not much flavor. It is like the old chicken hearts the barker throws to me at night after the crowd has left. Pieces of flesh that taste of dirt and chemicals. No matter how much of it I eat, I still hunger.

The crowd slowly files out of the tent. In the gap beyond the door, I see the brightly-spinning wheels of light, hear the bigger laughter, the bells and shouts as someone wins at a game. With so much amusement, a freak like me cannot hope to hold their attention for long. And still I love them, even when they are gone and all that's left is the stench of their shock and repulsion.

The barker counts his money, stuffs it in the pocket of his striped trousers. "Good trick there, with the finger. You're pretty smart for a dead guy."

I smile at him. I love him. I wish he would come closer to the bars, so I could show him how much I want to please him. I pleased my last barker. He screamed and screamed, but my love was strong, stronger than those who tried to pull him away.

The barker goes outside the tent to try and find more people with money. His voice rings out, mixes with the organ waltzes and the hum of the big diesel engines. The tent is empty and I feel something in my chest. Not the beating, beating, beating like before I died. This is more like the thing I feel in my mouth and stomach. I need. I put my finger in my mouth, even though no one is watching.

The juggler comes around a partition. The juggler is called Juggles and he wears make-up and a dark green body stocking. His painted eyes make his face look small. "Hey, Murdermouth," he says.

I don't remember the name I had when I was alive, but Murdermouth has been a favorite lately. I smile at him and show him my teeth and tongue. Juggles comes by every night when the crowds thin out.

"Eating your own damned finger," Juggles says. He takes three cigarettes from a pocket hidden somewhere in his body stocking. In a moment, the cigarettes are in the air, twirling, Juggles' bare toes a blur of motion. Then one is in his mouth, and he leans forward and lights it from a torch while continuing to toss the other two cigarettes.

He blows smoke at me. "What's it like to be dead?"

I wish I could speak. I want to tell him, I want to tell them all. Being dead has taught me how to love. Being dead has shown me what is really important on this earth. Being dead has saved my life.

"You poor schmuck. Ought to put a bullet in your head." Juggles lets the cigarette dangle from his lips. He lights one of the others and flips it into my cage with his foot. "Here you go. Suck on that for a while."

I pick up the cigarette and touch its orange end. My skin sizzles and I stare at the wound as the smoke curls into my nose. I put the other end of the cigarette in my mouth. I cannot breathe so it does no good.

"Why are you so mean to him?"

It is she. Her voice comes like hammers, like needles of ice, like small kisses along my skin. She stands at the edge of the shadows, a shadow herself. I know that if my heart could beat it would go crazy.

"I don't mean nothing," says Juggles. He exhales and squints against the smoke, then sits on a bale of straw. "Just having a little fun."

"Fun," she says. "All you care about is fun."

44

"What else is there? None of us are going anywhere."

She steps from the darkness at the corner of the tent. The torch-light is golden on her face, flickering playfully among her chins. Her breath wheezes like the softest of summer winds. She is beautiful. My Fat Lady.

The cigarette burns between my fingers. The fire reaches my flesh. I look down at the blisters, trying to remember what pain felt like. Juice leaks from the wounds and extinguishes the cigarette.

"He shouldn't be in a cage," says the Fat Lady. "He's no different from any of us."

"Except for that part about eating people."

"I wonder what his name is."

"You mean 'was,' don't you? Everything's in the past for him."

The Fat Lady squats near the cage. Her breasts swell with the effort, lush as moons. She stares at my face, into my eyes. I crush the cigarette in my hand and toss it to the ground.

"He knows," she says. "He can still feel. Just because he can't talk doesn't mean he's an idiot. Whatever that virus was that caused this, it's a hundred times worse than being dead."

"Hell, if I had arms, I'd give him a hug," mocks Juggles.

"You and your arms. You think you're the only one that has troubles?" The Fat Lady wears lipstick, her mouth is a red gash against her pale, broad face. Her teeth are straight and healthy. I wish she would come closer.

"Crying over that Murdermouth is like pissing in a river. At least he brings in a few paying customers."

The Fat Lady stares deeply into my eyes. I try to blink, to let her know I'm in here. She sees me. She sees me.

"He's more human than you'll ever be," the Fat Lady says, without turning her head.

"Oh, yeah? Give us both a kiss and then tell me who loves you." He has pulled a yellow ball from somewhere and tosses it back and forth between his feet. "Except you better kiss me first because you probably won't have no lips left after him."

"He would never hurt me," she says. She smiles at me. "Would you?"

I try to think, try to make my mouth around the word. My throat. All my muscles are dumb, except for my tongue. I taste her perfume and sweat, the oil of her hair, the sex she had with someone.

Voices spill from the tent flap. The barker is back, this time with only four people. Juggles hops to his feet, balances on one leg while saluting the group, then dances away. He doesn't like the barker.

"Hello, Princess Tiffany," says the barker.

The Fat Lady grins, rises slowly, groans with the effort of lifting her own weight. I love all of her.

"For a limited time only, a special attraction," shouts the barker in his money-making voice. "The world's fattest woman and the bottomless Murdermouth, together again for the very first time."

The Fat Lady waves her hand at him, smiles once more at me, then waddles toward the opening in the tent. She waits for a moment, obliterating the bright lights beyond the tent walls, then enters the clamor and madness of the crowd.

"Too bad," says the barker. "A love for the ages."

"Goddamn, I'd pay double to see that," says one of the group.

"Quadruple," says the barker. "Once for each chin."

The group laughs, then falls silent as all eyes turn to me.

The barker beats on the cage with his stick. "Give them a show, freak."

I eat the finger again. It is shredded now and bits of dirt and straw stick to the knuckle. Two of the people, a man and a woman, hug each other. The woman makes a sound like her stomach is bad. Another man, the one who would pay double, says, "Do they really eat people?"

"Faster than an alligator," says my barker. "Why, this very one ingested my esteemed predecessor in three minutes flat. Nothing left but two pounds of bones and a shoe."

"Doesn't look like much to me," says the man. "I wouldn't be afraid to take him on."

He calls to the man with him, who wobbles and smells of liquor and excrement. "What do you think? Ten-to-one odds."

"Maynard, he'd munch your ass so fast you'd be screaming

'Mommy' before you knew what was going on," says the wobbling man.

Maynard's eyes narrow and he turns to the barker. "What do you say? I'll give you a hundred bucks. Him and me, five minutes."

My barker points the stick toward the tent ceiling. "Five minutes. In the cage with that thing?"

"I heard about these things," says the man. "Don't know if I believe it."

My mouth tastes his courage and his fear. He is salt and meat and brains and kidneys. He is one of them. I love him.

He takes the stick from the barker and pokes me in the shoulder.

"That's not sporting," says the barker. He looks at the man and woman, who have gone pale and taken several steps toward the door.

Maynard rattles the stick against the bars and pokes me in the face. I hear a tearing sound. The woman screams and the man shouts beside her, then they run into the night. Organ notes trip across the sky, glittering wheels tilt, people laugh. The crowd is thinning for the night.

Maynard fishes in his pocket and pulls out some bills. "What do you say?"

"I don't know if it's legal," says the barker.

"What do you care? Plenty more where he came from." Maynard breathes heavily. I smell poison spilling from inside him.

"It ain't like it's murder," says Maynard's drunken companion.

The barker looks around, takes the bills. "After the crowd's gone. Come back after midnight and meet me by the duck-hunting gallery."

Maynard reaches the stick into the bars, rakes my disembodied finger out of the cage. He bends down and picks it up, sniffs it, and slides it into his pocket. "A little return on my investment," he says.

The barker takes the stick from Maynard and wipes it clean on his trouser leg. "Show's over, folks," he yells, as if addressing a packed house.

"Midnight," Maynard says to me. "Then it's you and me, freak."

The wobbly man giggles as they leave the tent. The barker waits by the door for a moment, then disappears. I look into the torchlight, watching the flames do their slow dance. I wonder what the fire tastes like.

The Fat Lady comes. She must have been hiding in the shadows again. She has changed her billowy costume for a large robe. Her hair hangs loose around her shoulders, her face barren of make-up.

She sees me. She knows I can understand her. "I heard what they said."

I stick out my tongue. I can taste the torn place on my cheek. I grip the bars with my hands. Maybe tomorrow, I will eat my hands, then my arms. Then I can be like Juggles. Except you can't dance when you're dead.

Or maybe I will eat and eat when the barker brings me the bucket of chicken hearts. If I eat enough, I can be the World's Fattest Murdermouth. I can be one of them. I will take money for the rides and pull the levers and sell cotton candy.

If I could get out of this cage, I would show her what I could do. I would prove my love. If I could talk, I would tell her.

The Fat Lady watches the tent flap. Somewhere a roadie is working on a piece of machinery, cursing in a foreign language. The smell of popcorn is no longer in the air. Now there is only cigarette smoke, cheap wine, leftover hot dogs. The big show is putting itself to bed for the night.

"They're going to kill you," she whispers.

I am already dead. I have tasted my own finger. I should be eating dirt instead. Once, I could feel the pounding of my heart.

"You don't deserve this." Her eyes are dark. "You're not a freak."

My barker says a freak is anybody that people will pay money to see.

My tongue presses against my teeth. I can almost remember. They put me in a cage before I died. I had a name.

The Fat Lady wraps her fingers around the metal catch. From somewhere she has produced a key. The lock falls open and she whips the chain free from the bars.

"They're coming," she says. "Hurry."

I smell them before I see them. Maynard smells like Maynard, as if he is wearing his vital organs around his waist. The wobbling man reeks even worse of liquor. The barker has also been drinking. The three of them laugh like men swapping horses.

I taste the straw in the air, the diesel exhaust, the smoke from the torches, the cigarette that Juggles gave me, my dead finger, the cold gun in Maynard's pocket, the money my barker has spent.

I taste and taste and taste and I am hungry.

"Hey, get away from there," yells the barker. He holds a wine bottle in one hand.

The Fat Lady pulls on the bars. The front of the cage falls open. I can taste the dust.

"Run," says the Fat Lady.

Running is like dancing. Maybe people will pay money to see me run.

"What the hell?" says Maynard.

I move forward, out of the cage. This is my tent. My name is on a sign outside. If I see the sign, I will know who I am. If I pay money, maybe I can see myself.

"This ain't part of the deal," says Maynard. He draws the gun from his pocket. The silver barrel shines in the firelight.

The Fat Lady turns and faces the three men.

"I swear, I didn't know anything about this," says the barker.

"Leave him alone," says the Fat Lady.

Maynard waves the gun. "Get out of the way."

This is my tent. I am the one they came to see. The Fat Lady blocks the way. I stare at her broad back, at the dark red robe, her long hair tumbling down her neck. She's the only one who ever treated me like one of them.

I jump forward, push her. The gun roars, spits a flash of fire from its end. She cries out. The bullet cuts a cold hole in my chest.

I must die again, but at last she is in my arms.

If my mouth could do more than murder, it would say words.

I am sorry. I love you.

They take her bones when I am finished.

SUNG LI

here's a story behind every glass eye.

That's what Uncle Theodore says. He got his glass eye after a fight in the jungle. Said something called a "goop" got him with a piece of shrapnel. I asked him once and he told me that shrapnel was a jaggedy piece of metal. Anyway, he's the one who gave Sung Li to my Mom.

If it's true what he said about glass eyes, then Sung Li has two stories. Her eyes aren't really glass, but I like to pretend anyway. Maybe she'll let me tell you her other story, the one you don't know about yet. But maybe not, since all you want to do is talk about what happened last night.

Who's Sung Li? I already told that other police. But maybe they figured since you're a woman police, I'll tell the truth this time. So I'll tell you who Sung Li is, and maybe you'll believe me.

She's the China doll that lives on the second shelf in that little showcase on the top of the stairs. She usually just lays there. Daddy says that's what girls are supposed to do, anyway. Lay there and look pretty. At least that's what he always told me on Mom's library nights. And Mom says if you handle Sung Li, the value will go down.

Mom really loves that doll, maybe more than anything else in the showcase. Did you look yet? There's a silver tray that's got some writing on it under a picture of a sailboat. Up above that is an old book that's got cardboard poking through the corners and a little red ribbon tucked inside as a bookmark. There's some other things, too. Daddy's old bowling trophy, some dollars from where they don't know how to spell good, and that knife from Mexico that's made out of volcano stuff. But Sung Li is the main thing. All the rest is kind of placed around her like an afterthought.

Mom taught me the word "afterthought." She sometimes even calls me that. Her Little Afterthought. She smiles when she says that, but it's one of those crooked smiles where one side of your face gets wrinkly.

Except to put something inside, Mom only opens that showcase about once a month, when she takes one of those dusters that looks like the back end of a chicken. She runs that duster over the shelves and all that stuff in the showcase. I don't see why she bothers, because that old stuff in there just keeps making more dust. When the light's just right, when you hide behind the door and the sun is sneaking through that little crack between the hall and my bedroom, you can watch her. After she leaves, you can sit there and watch the little silver hairs spin and twirl and then settle down all over again.

But mostly I watch Sung Li. You ought to go up and see her. Maybe you will, after I finish telling her story.

She wears this little robe with flowers on it and she's got a cloth belt tied around her waist. The sleeves where her hands come out are really wide. She has tiny black shoes and pants that are the color of raw rice. But her frosty white face is what I really like to look at.

Her cheeks go way up high under her eyes, and they're sharp like a naked bone. Her eyebrows are real skinny and rounded. She has a nose that's almost invisible, just a little nip of whatever it is they make plates out of. Her lips are bright red and shiny, almost like they're wet. I know it's all paint, but I like to pretend about things like that.

She doesn't look much like me. Except for the eyes. Sometimes

I'll look into those black glass eyes of hers, the eyes that seem to soak up whatever light hits them. Then I'll run into the bathroom down the hall, quick before I forget, and look in the mirror at my own eyes. And for just a second, or however long I can go without blinking, I can pretend that I'm pretty like Sung Li.

You really think I'm pretty? Well, it's nice of you to say that, anyway. But I'm not pretty like Sung Li.

At night in bed I wrap the blankets around me and think about Sung Li. I take off my pillowcases and put them on my arms and pretend they're big sleeves. I stick my lips out a little, like I'm waiting for a secret kiss. I pretend I'm sitting on the middle shelf and people look at me and like me because I am pretty and have good value.

Maybe I wouldn't ever have learned Sung Li's story. But one day Daddy opened the case with his little key because he bought a carved gnome and wanted to put it in there. Mom was watching him, to make sure he didn't break anything. Daddy used to break things sometimes.

No, I don't need a tissue. Everybody keeps telling me that it's okay to cry, and they give me candy bars. But why should I cry? Sung Li is going to be okay.

Usually Mom sent me away whenever the case was opened. I think she was afraid I would pick up something and make its value go down. So I hid behind the door and looked through that crack near the hinges. I heard Daddy tell Mom that the gnome was a collector's item. It was an ugly old thing, with a thick beard and a sharp nose and a face that's all wrinkly like somebody who stayed in the bathtub too long. You can see it when you go up to look at Sung Li, if you want to.

Daddy took Sung Li out of the center space on the main shelf and put that knotty old gnome in her place. He put Sung Li on the bottom shelf and leaned her against my baby shoes. They're bronze now. They weren't bronze when I wore them.

I knew Sung Li was mad about being moved, maybe just because Daddy had touched her. Her eyes burned with all that light they had soaked up over the years. But Daddy didn't notice, he just hummed his little hum and tilted his head back to make sure the gnome was centered on the shelf. Then he closed the door and I saw Mom hide the key under the showcase.

After they were gone, I tiptoed to the case and felt under the bottom edge until I found the key. I heard the front door slam and then heard Daddy start his car and drive away, back to work or wherever he stayed all day until dark. Mom was messing with the laundry downstairs. I put the key in the lock and turned it. The whole front of the case opened up, and it squeaked like a door in a haunted house.

I reached out to touch Sung Li, and my hand was trembling. She was so pretty, even when she was mad about being moved. Her lips were shining in the little bit of sunshine. Then I couldn't help myself, I had to feel her smooth skin, even if it meant her value would go down and Mom would be mad at me. I touched her secret lips and they were cold, cold like a popsicle, cold like the sidewalk in winter when you lay the back of your head against it.

I felt her soft black hair that was smoothed behind her head. I touched her robe with all its folds and tiny stitches. I rubbed that little pinch of a nose. I picked her up.

I thought she would be made out of that hard stuff they make plates out of. But only her head was. The rest must have been stuffed with rags or cotton or something like that. When I picked her up with my hand around her skinny waist, her head flopped over and banged against the bronze shoes. The showcase rattled and I was afraid Mom would hear it even over the noise of the washer.

I quick put my hand around Sung Li's head. I felt a sharp pain. I pulled my fingers out from under her hair and there was blood on them. Her head had cracked.

My heart must have skipped at least two beats. I was afraid Mom would be mad because Sung Li's value had gone down and Daddy would give me one of his special spankings. And I was afraid that Sung Li wouldn't love me after that.

Isn't that funny, how you love somebody but you end up breaking them?

But Sung Li's eyes weren't mad anymore. They just looked off over my shoulder and soaked up the sunshine. That's when I heard Mom coming up the stairs. I leaned Sung Li back against the bronze shoes and closed the case.

I think I was breathing again by then because I could see fog on the glass. I put the key back in its hiding place, and that's when I remembered that I hadn't locked the case. But I thought maybe I could do that later, if Mom didn't notice that I'd messed with anything. It almost looked exactly the same as before. The crack in Sung Li's head was hidden by her hair.

But one thing I knew Mom would notice. The dust on the shelves. Daddy had been real careful when he set Sung Li there on the lower shelf. But I was in such a hurry to pick her up, I had wiped a clean trail where Sung Li's robe had brushed across the wood. And one thing I had learned from watching dust settle all those times, you just can't hurry dust.

My tummy felt like it had a stone in it. When Mom reached the hall, she asked me why I was so pale. She said I was as white as a China doll. She felt my forehead and said I might be getting a fever. She was so worried that she forgot to look in the case.

She tucked me in and then Daddy came later and tucked me in twice. After he left, I stared up at the ceiling in the dark and thought I could see Sung Li's eyes. Even when I thought I was asleep, I still saw those eyes. And my head hurt. And the eyes got bigger and bigger until they filled up everything. And then it was like I was looking through Sung Li's eyes. You know how you get a fever and things get mixed up?

That's how I was feeling. How could my eyes feel cold and glassy and big like that when I was asleep? But all I know is that Sung Li wanted me to look through her eyes.

Sung Li saw the edge of the shelf, she felt the cold of the bronze shoes against her back. But the robe was soft and snug around her body, the sleeves as loose as pillowcases. She stretched out and then she was standing, raising up on those wiggly legs and walking to the glass door.

She tripped over an ivory elephant that came up to her knees.

The elephant fell over and landed on some of Uncle Theodore's army medals. The noise was so loud, it would have woken me up if I hadn't been dreaming so heavily. Then Sung Li crawled over a toy metal train that was old and rusty. Curly flakes of paint stuck to her robe.

She pushed open the glass door to the showcase and jumped to the floor with something from the shelf, something that was dark. She landed on her little shoes, her head flopping up and down because it was so heavy. In my sleep, I heard a thumping and scratching down the hall, at my parents' door. Or maybe I was awake, because a dog was barking somewhere down the street.

Then I heard Daddy's breathing, sort of long and loud, not the short and fast way it gets on Mom's library nights. Sung Li felt the edge of the blanket that was hanging down to the floor. She pulled herself up, the volcano knife tucked under her arm, and the next thing I knew she was on Daddy's chest and rocking up and down like a boat on the ocean.

I don't know what happened after that, only I heard Mom screaming and I think I woke up and I was glad it was only a dream because I was scared. But Mom kept screaming and screaming, then I knew I was awake because my finger hurt where I had cut it.

I cut it on the crack in Sung Li's head, just like I told you. Not on the volcano knife. I never touched the volcano knife.

Anyway, Mom screamed and then my head was hurting again. I went down the hall and looked in their bedroom. Mom was sitting up in bed, her face all pink and she screamed some more. I guess somebody finally heard her and called the police.

The police I talked to before asked why I had blood all over my clothes. I told him it was because I tried to get Mom off the bed, away from what happened to Daddy. Maybe you don't believe me, either, and you'll make me keep telling Sung Li's story over and over, and about those library nights, and how my finger got cut.

But just go upstairs and look in the showcase. Then maybe you'll quit looking at me like I'm an afterthought. You'll see two things right off. I know, because I did, and I'm only a kid.

First, you'll see Sung Li right back in her old place in the center of the shelf, staring out with those cold glass eyes that aren't really glass at all, only that stuff they make plates out of. The ugly gnome is down on the bottom shelf, its face all chipped and scarred like the woodcarver got mad at the thing he was making.

And there's one other thing, something Sung Li couldn't cover up. I don't know how she got the blood off her clothes. And she somehow got the ivory elephant back in place and wiped off the knife that's made of volcano stuff. The knife's gone now. One of those other police took it away in a plastic bag.

But look on the shelf, and the second shelf, too. You'll see what gives her away. What she left behind on her way back to her old place in the showcase. Two little rows of dots in the dust, about the size of the ends of somebody's fingers.

Footprints. She couldn't fix that, and I know why.

I hid behind the door enough times to know that you just can't hurry dust.

Can we go see Sung Li now?

SILVER RUN

ilver Run #19 ain't much in the daytime. A little longer than a football field, it's about three miles from Cairo, West Virginia. Now, I don't rightly know what a "football field" is, but that's what I hear folks say when they lead tours through the tunnel. Walking tours, as if the rail's not good enough for them. O' course, they went and took up the rails some years back, hear they made this into some sort of state park. No appreciation for the Iron Horse, these modern folk.

I don't get out much, so I don't know the ways of the world, and I ain't got a lick of sense for time. Some days it seems I just opened my eyes after the train snipped me in half, when I looked toward the east mouth of the tunnel and saw a couple bits of myself being drug off by the undercarriage of the caboose, dribbling red everywhere. Other days it seems like I been here since the world was born, before these Appalachian hills rose up from the belly of the Earth and then settled down to the long, slow business of erosion. But maybe all days are the same anyway, when you get down to it.

I used to think so. And then she came along.

Pretty little thing, dressed up in her evening gown. You can see right though it, and if I wasn't old enough to nearly be her grandpap, I'd probably look more often. But you can see right through her as well, so I reckon there's nothing ungentlemanly in letting my eyes linger now and then. Even dead, a man's still a man.

She happened during one of the wars, I reckon. The wars all got mixed up for me, because all I remember is the real one, when the Yanks and Rebs went at it and Virginia got split up by Lincoln. I stayed out of that one, I was out in Missouri territory at the time, where the rail was just starting to catch on and Chinamen and Irish were dying by the dozens laying steel and spiking ties. I came back when the B & O line was booming, working the firebox and generally trying not to get tied down with women, card debts, and such, because I figured on heading to the Pacific Coast eventually. And I stayed clear of the women just fine until this latest one.

Well, I didn't really choose her like you might do a wife. And her gown ain't rightly a wedding dress, neither. For one thing, it's not white, it's sort of green like the leaves of a chestnut tree in April. At least when it has color. In the tunnel, color comes and goes, at least to folks like me and her.

That's a little peculiar, but you get used to it after awhile . And—

Tarnation. Here she comes now, so I reckon I'd best see what she wants.

"Have you seen my head?" she asks.

It's in ghost words, 'cause her lips don't move but her voice is in my ears. Maybe that's why normal folk, them still alive, never hear us when they walk through the tunnel. Some of them shiver and hoof it just a little faster, some look around at the slick masonry walls like they expect some secret message to be wrote in the slime.

"I done told you a thousand times, your head's on top of your shoulders where it belongs." She has a fine set of shoulders, smooth as rounded marble and the color of cream skimmed right off the top of the butter churn. Her head ain't no less a marvel, with her hair swooped up in a fancy bundle that only ladies in companion houses wore back in my day. During her time, though, it might have passed for normal ladylike dress-up.

She reaches up to touch her hair, and I can't really tell where her fingers end and the curly locks begin. Still, it's fetching as all get out. "I can't do a thing with it," she says.

I nod. I know my part so well that I don't really have to think it through. I'm like a stage actor or maybe the bass in a barbershop quartet, just delivering lines the way I ought. "You look just fine," I say, though her motion makes me lick my lips. Damned dry lips, what they wouldn't give for a touch of barrel-mash whiskey.

"They'll be coming soon," she says.

"They always do."

You'd think after all these years I'd know how to dress for the occasion. I never had a worry over it before she came along. I'd just hoof it around in my old wool pants and cotton shirt. The holes in my clothes never troubled me none, because there wasn't much difference between the hole and what it was supposed to be covering up. But I wouldn't know where to find clothes even if I wanted them.

There in the early days, before I settled down to this notion of just what "forever" means, I'd go off half-cocked. More rightly, I'd either be floating around three feet off the ground, trailing some see-through innards where my belly got sawed in two by a set of steel wheels, or else my legs would be walking around with nothing to guide them. Not that they got much guidance even back when my brains was attached, considering I spent most of my breathing life balanced in the cab, shoveling coal like I was feeding the devil.

"What do you suppose it's like out there?" she says.

She's looking out the mouth of the tunnel, down to the north fork of the Hughes River. A soft fog rises from the water, seeping into the gold-and-red forest. Beyond the trees, a collection of lights are winking on, one after another, like dead fireflies pinned against the horizon. Over time, the number of lights have doubled and tripled, and I reckon that's as good a way to mark the years as any, because the stars have pretty much stayed the same. Back in my day, Cairo was the glass marble capital of the world, and sometimes I think those marbles are not toys but eyes, looking back from the forgotten past like a mirror.

"Same as always," I say, as if I possess the wisdom granted by age. If there's one thing I've learned, but try not to dwell on, it's that foolishness never dies. Otherwise, I'd be in one piece and rotting away quiet in a pine box somewhere.

"Do you think they'll like me?" She touches her hair again.

You can see how this dance has played out over the years. She's lost her confidence, and that's an awful thing in a woman. Sure, I'm a little beyond gentlemanly judgment, and my coarser nature somehow uncoupled when the boxcars between my skull and my private parts jumped the tracks, but, Christ damn it, a man's still a man. "You'll be the belle of the ball," I say.

I reach for my pocket watch. The chain got crushed in the accident, and the watch is stuck on seven minutes before twelve, and I can never figure if that's noon or midnight. Either way, I reckon I'll never reach twelve, so it don't matter which.

"Almost time?" she asks. She asks a lot of questions. That's women for you. You can lop off their heads and still they keep yakking.

"Pretty soon now," I say, which is as safe a bet as any.

And it probably will be soon. The sun still rises and falls regular, just like it did when I was in one piece, and right now it's settling against the rounded hills, throwing a punkin-colored light across the trees. The horseshoe curve of the tunnel opening, at least on the sundown side, is outlined with light, and out beyond is all the promise of laughter, love, and life. That's probably the worst trick of this condition, knowing there's another way. Maybe there are folks like us out yonder cavorting and cutting up around graveyards and such, just drifting to hell and gone, whichever direction the wind blows. But me and her, all we got is Silver Run and time.

The people usually come from the east end, where it's darkest, but of course a tunnel runs both ways. I used to think life was just one long rail, running on and on, and all I had to worry about was raking chunks of coal from the tender, pushing the boiler gauge to the red, blinking cinders from my eyes. You don't think much about the end of the line, and when you do, you usually picture it as a nice, easy rolling stop, engine chuffing and wheels creaking as you come up on a comfortable station with lots of friends on the platform to welcome you home. You don't expect to trip over your big toe at full throttle and go ass-over-teakettle between the cars.

But a fellow gets used to the notion, bye and bye. Leastways, I have. Or so I tell myself. What choice do I got?

"Maybe I should change clothes," she says, fretting her head for no reason.

"If you was any prettier, you'd run them off faster than a pack of coyotes in a blood fever," I say. Truth is, she got no other clothes, and if she did change, well, I don't even like to think what might happen if I saw her in her undergarments. Hell, I might even blush, and I don't know what color my cheeks would be. Maybe perdition red or mortuary blue.

"I'll miss you," she says, just like always.

"Comes a time for parting," I say, though it stings a little all the same. Funny how you can just babble out any old words when you're trying to hide what you really feel.

"You've meant a lot to me. We've been through so much together."

Well, that ain't rightly true. We've pretty much been through the same thing once, over and over and over again. But try talking sense to a woman and see where it gets you.

"I never expected somebody like you to come along," I say, which is about as close as I ever brush up against honesty in my current condition.

"Well, you were here first," she says.

And now we come to it. The only real sore point between us. Now, I pretty much nipped any notion of romance in the bud, me being at least a century older than her, but maybe even us dead folk get a little territorial. I don't know how it is with others, since I only got this one example, but I figure if I'm going to be stuck in one place until the end of time, the place ought to at least belong to me. But there I go again, acting like I'd expect any different from the female gender.

The ones that come here, they call me "The Engineer," though I was always a fireman and never once laid a hand on the throttle.

I figure they forgot the way of the steam locomotive same as they forgot every other way except their own, and so it has been since back to the beginning of time. Plus I kind of like the sound of that: "The Engineer." Got more of a ring to it than "fireman" does, like a slow steam whistle on a dewy summer morn.

Trouble is, they don't call me much of anything anymore. They got this new one they come looking for. Fresh kill. "The Jilted Lady," they call her, and damned if that don't got a ring to it, too. I find myself saying it a lot, trying it out on these numb lips. Not that I ever say it aloud, especially to her.

"I have to admit, I had some adjusting to do," I say. "I never expected somebody like you to come into my life."

She doesn't laugh. She's a little humorless, but I chalk it off to the way she got here. Seems I'm always apologizing for the way she is.

"Maybe things could have been different if we'd met at a different time," she says.

Sure as shootin'. I been around long enough to know that it don't matter the reason why it don't work, just that it don't. "You never asked to be here," I say.

Indeed she didn't. She didn't ask nothing, and she couldn't even if she had wanted. That guy wrapped a rag around her mouth tight as a banjo string, and she tried and tried to scream but nary a peep came out. O' course, considering what the guy did to her, I reckon there's a blessing in that, and proof that maybe God is a merciful creature after all.

She wipes at her eyes. Maybe she's crying, or maybe she's fussing with make-up. Looks the same either way. "We were going to be married," she says.

That's plenty enough cause for waterworks, I reckon, and maybe a swift death saved her from a slower, more tortured demise. Then again, her death wasn't all that swift. The stranger who stole her heart took just a mite too much joy in her pain, and wasn't in no hurry to end the honeymoon.

Damnedest of all was having to witness it and not being able to do a thing about it. You think it's bad enough when your pecker's gone South for the winter, try failing somebody when they need you most. Try helping when you're helpless yourself. Even dead, even ground to government pork beneath the freight cars of B & O's Silver Runner Engine #52, it stings a little.

Ah, hell, at least self-pity is a feeling. At least I got that.

"Don't fret over it," I say. "What's done is done."

"I think he'll take me with him tonight," she says, and outside the punkin sky has gone all bruised and purple, rags of clouds sopping up the last daylight.

I check my watch again, wondering for the hundredth time or so why we take our watches and clothes and wounds with us when we cross over. But maybe all we are is scars, the rip we cut in the fabric of the world, and we're lucky to even do that, when you consider how big the universe must be. Like a bucket that spills over from being too full. Maybe me and her is some of the slop.

I want to tell her not to get her hopes up again, but see no reason to be mean. I've had my chances at that, but it ain't my way. She does a good enough job beating herself up the way it is. Instead, I say, "The Good Book says there's a time for every purpose under heaven."

She nods, and her head shifts just a little, and her throat gapes, then a line blacker than shadow creases her neck. Her head falls plumb off, just like it did when her gentleman caller confessed his undying love. It's laying there in the rock bed, jutting between two mossy crossties. She rolls her eyes up at me and smiles the way you do when you're making the best of a bad situation.

"Things happen for a reason," I say. "And things don't happen for the same reason. Or maybe a different reason."

I have no idea what that means. It just sounds like something a wise old coot will say when he's trying to comfort the afflicted.

She stoops down, picks up her head gentle as a kitten, fixes it back in place, then goes through the shenanigans of checking her curls. "I can't do a thing with it," she says.

I gave up praying long ago, figuring providence is best kept to them that have hope, but I'm tempted to offer up a whopper right about now. I figure maybe she's due to move on, maybe she'll catch a caboose one night and just roll on down the line. That ain't the way the legend ought to go, though, because I'm the train fellow. I'm the one they talk about when they walk through here and whisper like they're in church or something.

At least, I used to be. Until The Jilted Lady came along.

"I hear them," she says, giving her hair one more little touch with those slender, pale fingers.

Beyond the tunnel come footsteps, bunches of them, shoe leather kicking up gravel and dead leaves. They usually come in groups, especially at night. More fun that way, I figure. Most times they're giggling, the boys putting on a brave face, the girls acting like they want to be held close and protected. From cradle to grave, and even beyond, females are smart enough to act weak and dumb and vulnerable.

I can't do much about it, since for some reason I'm bound to this little stretch of abandoned rail bed, while The Jilted Lady gets to rove the tunnel from end to end. Best I can do is bite my tongue, hold in my guts, and wait. I'm a right fair hand at waiting.

"Hey," she yells, trying to get their attention.

Lights sweep the tunnel, cast out by what they call "flashlights," a kind of lantern that burns without fire. Their voices are loud enough to shake the masonry with echoes, but I can't understand a word they say. I like to think they've come looking for The Engineer, but my day is past. Time slides on down the track, spewing sparks from its smoke stack like the vomiting mouth of hell, rolling and rolling on until the conductor's lantern is little more than a wink of starlight against the deep, endless night, and then even that is gone, the rumble fading, the dust settling, and the last whisper of its passing lost in the wind.

"I love you," she says to one of them, and it could be any of them. These days, she's none too choosy. And when you get down to it, I reckon one man's as good as another for a woman's purposes. Don't matter what you're like, as long as you're willing to be owned. Hop whatever boxcar you can when the weather's bad, that's what I always say. Worry about the destination later.

But whichever man she's talking to doesn't hear, or walks

faster, or pulls one of the young ladies closer. Their breaths plume from their mouths like the ghosts of locomotive smoke, and none of them mention The Engineer. They hurry on, and by the time they're all the way through the tunnel, it's full dark. Both inside and out.

"He'll be back," she says.

"He'd be crazy not to," I say, adjusting my entrails so I don't look so shabby. "Any man would be lucky to win your charms."

Sooner or later the eastern mouth of the tunnel is filled with the light of a rising sun and the glory of birdsong.

"Almost time?" she asks.

"Pretty soon now." I check my watch and try not to grin. Things happen for a reason, and they don't happen for the same reason. Or maybe a different one.

She fusses with her hair. The Jilted Lady. I like the way that sounds. I'm only half a man, depending on which end we're speaking of, but I still got my pride. All a woman's got is vanity. There ain't no shame in letting a lady have her way. Not a lot left worth fighting over, the way I see it.

Me and her, all we got is Silver Run and time.

And each other, I reckon.

In the Family

"How could you even think of selling it?" Gaines breathed on a brass rail and polished it with his jacket sleeve.

Mother should be proud, Gaines thought. But her pride was in a new luxury sedan, twice-yearly trips to the Mediterranean, face-lifts. All fleeting, mortal things. If only she had more of the Wadell blood in her. Then she would find joy in the only things that truly last: a proper memorial, a professional embalming job, a final show of respect.

"I put up with it long enough because of your father. And now that he's gone, there's no reason to hang around this—this *mausoleum*." Mother's hair was stiff from a forty-dollar frosting job at her hairdresser's. It didn't shift as she wrung her hands and rolled her eyes in another of her classic "spells."

"We've invested so much in the Home," Gaines said. "But this isn't about money. This is about tradition."

"Tradition, my foot. Your grandfather was a drunkard and a fool. He started the business because this was the only one that couldn't possibly fail. And your father was just like him. Only he had the sense to marry somebody with a good head for business."

"And business has never been better," Gaines said. "So why sell now?"

"Why? Because I've given enough of my life to the Wadell Funeral Home. I've had it up to *here*—" she put a hand to her surgically-tucked and shiny chin,"—with death and dying. And there you go, wasting a quarter grand on remodeling."

Gaines looked around the parlor. The brooding red pine paneling was gone, the walls now covered with clear-varnished oak. Strip spotlights hung in place of the fluorescent tubes that had once vomited their weak green light. Purple velvet drapes hung from the windows, in thick folds of the regal splendor that the guests of honor so richly deserved. On a raised platform at the rear of the room, soft light bathed the bier where the guests received their final tribute.

The sinking sun pried its way through the front glass, suffusing the bleached woodwork of the dais with a red-golden light. No dust gathered on the plush cushioning he had added to the straight-backed pews. The room smelled of wax and rosewater, incense and carnations. Not the slightest aroma of decaying flesh was allowed in the parlor area.

This had been a place of peace. But lately it was a place for the same argument again and again.

"Mother, please be reasonable," Gaines said. "I know Father left you the Home in his will, but he told both of us a hundred times that he wanted me to carry on the business. It's the only thing he really felt passion for."

"That's the truth." She shook her head slowly, and in the soft light, she looked about half of her sixty-eight years. "I'm not doing this just for me. Though, Lord knows, I'm ready for a change. It's mostly for you."

"Me?"

"You think I want my only son to spend his life up to his elbows in the guts of corpses? Do you want to go home every night and take two long showers, but no matter how hard you scrub, the smell stays with you? It's in the food you eat, the air you breathe, it's in the water you drink, it's in your blood. And I want to save you from that."

In your blood. That's what Mother didn't understand. The

funeral parlor was more than a family business. It was a duty, a sacred trust. "You can't sell it," he said.

"Oh, I can't? You just watch." Mother stamped her two-inch heel onto the parquet floor and bustled from the room.

Gaines heard the side door slam as Mother left the parlor. Warmth crept up his face, a rush of emotion that no good interment man should allow to show. He couldn't lose his temper. Not with Stony Hampton's viewing a half-hour away.

He could be angry at Mother, but not at Stony's expense. Stony was a much-beloved member of the community and a top-notch mechanic. Sure, he'd had a fondness for moonshine and the cigarettes that had eventually stifled his lungs, and maybe he'd slapped his kids around a little, but all that was forgiven now, at least until the man was in the ground. For a few days, from the hour of death to service to burial, even the lowest scoundrel was a saint.

Gaines went through a curtained passage off one wing of the dais. The back room always calmed him. This, too, was a place of peace, but a peace of a different kind. This was where Gaines was alone with his art.

The sweet aroma of formaldehyde embraced him as he opened a second door. Faint decay and medicinal smells clung like a second skin to the fixtures: a stainless steel table, sloped with a drain at one end; shelves of chemicals in thick glass jars; rows of silent metal gurneys, eager to offer a final ride; garbage bins gaping in anticipation of offal and excrescence.

Here, Gaines practiced the craft of memory-polishing. Each guest had loved ones counting on Gaines' skill. The sewing shut of eyelids and lips with the thin, almost-invisible thread. The removal of uncooperative intestines, kidneys, and spleens. The draining of viscid blood, that fluid so vital in life but a sluggish, unsightly mess when settled in death. The infusing of embalming fluid, siphoned through thin hoses. Anything that suffered the sin of decay must be cut out and removed. Otherwise, it would be an affront to the solemn and still temple of flesh that the loved ones worshipped prior to burial.

After the eviscerating came the makeup. Gaines prided himself on the makeup. Of the three generations of Wadells that had worked in the business, Gaines had been most praised for his delicate touch. Just a tinge of blush here, some foundation there, a bit of powder under the eyes to blend out that depressing black. The right shade of rouge on the lips, so a loved one might imagine the wan face breaking into a smile.

Stony Hampton was handsome under his green sheet. The wrinkles caused by sixty-odd years of gravity and grimaces were now smoothed. The face, though stiff to the touch, looked relaxed. Stony might as well have been dreaming of a three-day drunk or a '57 Chevy.

Gaines pulled the sheet off the corpse and rolled the casket to the corner of the room. He pulled back the pleated vinyl curtain of the service window, then nudged the edge of the coffin onto the lip of the window. The coffin weighed nearly eight hundred pounds, but the smooth wooden rollers made the work easy. Gaines only had to give a gentle push and Stony Hampton was on the bier, under the soft lights of the viewing parlor.

Gaines checked himself in one of the mirrors that lined the wall. He adjusted his tie and joined Stony in the parlor. Stony was in the spotlight, the star of the show, buffed and polished and ready to receive tribute. The viewing was even more important than the actual funeral, because the loved ones would be examining the guest, and therefore Gaines' craft, at close proximity.

The first loved ones came in the parlor and signed the memorial book with a brass-plated pen. Gaines watched to make sure the last signer returned the pen to its holder, then went over to greet them, putting on his funeral face as he went.

More loved ones came. Stony had a lot of friends, relatives, and drinking buddies. Gaines solemnly shook hands with each. As they began filing past the guest of honor, Gaines stood against the wall with his hands clasped loosely over the lowest button on his black suit. His eyebrows furrowed in the proper mixture of sorrow and reverence, his jaw clenched so that his smirk of satisfaction wouldn't blossom like the lilies and tulips that girded the dais.

Their tears, their joy, their final respect, all their emotions were due to Gaines' handiwork. This guest, James Rothrock "Stony" Hampton, was fit for heaven. This was a man they were all proud to have known. This man was one of God's finest and most blessed creations. As the organ music fed through the speakers, not an eye remained dry.

Afterward, Stony's wife came up and gripped Gaines' elbow. Her eyes were wet and bright from too much spiritual uplifting. "He looks mighty fine, Mr. Wadell. Mighty fine."

Gaines bowed slightly, tilting his head the way his father had taught him. "Yes, ma'am. We hate to see him go, but our loss is the Lord's gain."

"You're so right," she said, dabbing at her face with a crumpled tissue. "And it won't be long till we're together again, anyway."

"That will be a joyful reunion, ma'am," Gaines said politely, "but don't you go and rush things."

"Well, this old heart can't stand up to much more. About worn down from ticking." Her skin had a slight gray pallor and was stretched tight around the bony angles of her face.

Gaines figured she would be dead within the year. Another guest, another memory to be polished for loved ones, another star born. What Father said was true: The repeat business may not be all that hot, but at least the customers never complained.

He said goodbye to the last loved ones, then locked up and returned Stony to the back room. Gaines removed his jacket and tie and hung them beside a mirror. He looked at his reflection, into the eyes that were the same color as Mother's. His face had the same oval shape as hers. But the blood, the liquid that his heart pumped behind the face and throughout his body, was all Wadell.

Heart. What was it that Alice Hampton had said? *Worn down from ticking.*

Mother had heart problems. But her doctors wanted to install a pacemaker. That would probably guarantee that she'd last another twenty years. Plenty of time to sell the funeral service and move away. Long enough to demolish everything that Gaines had trained toward since he was six years old.

Gaines looked down and saw that his fists were clenched. He

spread his fingers and willed them to stop trembling. Laura Mae Greene was waiting on a gurney in the walk-in refrigerator. She needed his skills. He would not disappoint her. Or her loved ones.

He reached for his apron and mask, then slipped rubber gloves over his eager hands.

"I'll be late tomorrow," Mother said. "I have to drive to Asheville for a checkup."

"Do you want me to drive you?"

"No. I know you have the Hampton funeral. I wouldn't want to take you away from your 'work.'"

Gaines put down his fork.

"What's the matter?" Mother said. She divided her filet mignon with delicate sawing motions.

"Just thinking, that's all," Gaines said.

"Let's not start." She sipped her wine. Sixty dollars a bottle. False pride.

"Next year I was going to buy some acreage," he said. "Carve it into burial plots. Get into monument brokering as well. Make Wadell's a one-stop shopping center for all the aftercare needs."

Mother slammed her knife onto the table. "Stop this nonsense. You're going to go out and find an honorable profession. Why, with your talents, I wouldn't even complain if you went to art school."

"I'm not going to art school."

"Why are you breaking your poor mother's heart?"

"Are you going to sell the house, too?"

The big fine house stood near the parlor. Grandpa had saved a fortune by building the parlor on property he already owned. Of course she would sell the house. So what if three generations of Wadells had walked these halls and slept in these rooms and dreamed in these beds?

"It's for your own good, don't you see that?" She pushed her plate away. "All this terrible death and funerals and corpses. How can you stand to do that to those poor people? Your father didn't have brains enough to have any choice in the matter, but you're different."

74

"Not everyone shares your convictions," Gaines said. He'd lost his appetite. Not from handling the guts of Laura Mae Greene or touching the cool smoothness of her marbled skin. No, his mother was the aberration. "I know you want to be cremated. That's your choice. But other people need the hope of eternal rest. They need a peaceful image to carry in their hearts as they say good-bye to a loved one."

"It's all so horrible. Even if the money is good."

"Poor Father. All those years, thinking you loved him."

"I did love him. But you're as hard-headed as he was. He could have sold the Home and got on with life, instead of keeping himself buried alive here."

"So now that he's dead, it's okay to betray him?"

She stood suddenly, tipping her chair over. Her face was tight from anger, almost a death-mask. "How dare you say that."

Then she gasped and clutched at her chest. She gripped the edge of the table and leaned forward. "Don't...do this...to your dear mother," she said.

Gaines rushed to her side. He found the nitroglycerin pills in her purse and put one under her tongue. "There, there," he said, giving her a glass of water. He led her to a padded chair in the living room.

She recovered after a few minutes. The color returned to her face. She asked for her wine. Gaines brought it to her, and she sipped until her lips were again pink. "Why are you breaking your poor mother's heart?" she said.

Gaines said nothing.

"Why can't you give me one thing to be proud of?"

He had given her plenty. He was an artist, well-respected in the community. He gave people their final and most important moments. He polished memories.

But Gaines was at ease with the dead. With the living, who wanted words and emotions and hugs and love, he was out of his element. He'd been born to the family work. Even with Mother's eyes, he still had a funeral face.

He left her with her wine and pills and bitterness and went upstairs to bed, to think and dream.

«« — »»

Gaines was alone in the back room.

Stony Hampton's graveside service had been beautiful. The preacher hit all of Stony's high points while overlooking the man's many sins. The loved ones were practically glowing in their melancholy. Alice Hampton had even thrown herself on the coffin.

If only she had known that Stony wasn't inside, she might have become a Wadell customer right there on the spot. The tractor lowered the coffin and pushed the red dirt over a four-thousand-dollar casket containing nothing but corrupted air. The granite marker that said "Here Lies" was itself a lie.

Stony was the proper height and build. The features were a little off, but that would be no problem. With a little polishing, Gaines had a face that would work.

He went into the walk-in refrigerator, what Father had called the "meat locker." Father was a part of the parlor, as vital to the business as the hearse and the gurneys and the casket catalog. Gaines wouldn't let his memory die. He would not allow the name "Wadell" to be removed from the big sign out front.

He took a special package from the wire shelves that lined the rear of the cooler. He clutched it to his chest. Laura Mae Greene was the only witness, and her eyes were safely sewn shut. He carried the package to where Stony lay naked and waiting on the stainless steel table.

Gaines worked into the evening, finishing just as the long fingers of night reached across the sky. The short trip home was difficult because only two of the four legs were walking.

"What did the doctor say, Mother?"

"They want to do the operation next month."

"Wonderful. I'm sure you'll be glad to get it over with."

"Yes. Then we can leave here."

Gaines nodded from discomfort of the stiff chair. Mother's living room was too severe, lacking in personality, just as the funeral parlor had been under her design. "How is your wine?"

"Very good. Crisp."

"I'm glad. Can I get you anything else?"

"You're being pleasant. What brought that on?" Mother's eyes narrowed as she studied Gaines.

"I've been thinking," he said. "Maybe you're right. If you sell the business, we can start in something else. You put up the money and I'll do the work."

Mother smiled. "What sort of business?"

"Anything. Insurance, financial services, you name it."

"I'm so glad you agree." She looked like she would have kissed him if rising weren't such an effort. "It's for the best, really."

"Yes. I want you to be proud."

"It's what your father would have wanted."

Gaines' face almost tightened then, at her pretending to know what Father wanted when the man loved the Home more than he had ever loved her. But Gaines knew not to let the rage show. He kept his features calm and somber, drawing on his years of practice.

"Are you ready for dinner? I've set the table," he said. *Try not to smile, try not to smile. Even though this is your best work ever, your highest art, your most polished memory.*

"Why, thank you, dear."

He helped her from the chair. The dining room lights spilled from the doorway. Gaines' vision blurred for a moment. His eyes were moist with joy.

As they turned the corner, they were met by the smell of meat. Not from the food piled on the plates. No. The smell came from their dinner guest.

Mother gasped, not comprehending. Then, when she finally came to accept the impossible sight before her, she tried to reel away, screaming, but Gaines held her firmly. Perhaps her heart was already giving out just from the strain of having her dead husband grinning across the table. But Gaines was taking no chances.

He pulled on the almost-invisible threads beside the doorjamb. As the threads tightened in the small eye-hooks screwed in the ceiling, Father raised his flaccid but well-preserved hand in greeting and his jellied eyes opened. And Mother's eyes closed for the final time.

In the Family

Due to her strict Southern Baptist beliefs, Alice Hampton would be terribly upset if she knew that Stony was going to be cremated. But someone's body had to be in the box that Wadell Funeral Home shipped to the crematorium in Asheville. Besides, Alice had her memories, thanks to Gaines and his craftsmanship.

And the men who rolled the body into the fires wouldn't stop to check the sex of the corpse. Why should they care whether the label said "Virginia Marie Wadell" or "James Rothrock Hampton"? To the corpse-burners, dead was dead and ashes were ashes. And a job was a job.

They had no respect. Unlike Gaines.

He had handled Mother's funeral arrangements himself, insisting that the Wadells were a family and always took care of their own. Everyone understood. Why shouldn't a son give his mother a last loving farewell? Gaines performed his magic, and the funeral was beautiful. Over two hundred attended, and all of them wiped away tears.

Except Gaines. He never cried at a service. He had kept his head bowed in perfect reverence. He solemnly shook the hands of the mourners. Though he was a firm believer in burial, he would follow mother's wishes and have her remains cremated. At least that's what he told the family friends.

But now they were gone, the last condolences bestowed, and Gaines had the parlor all to himself again.

He turned on the light in the back room. The work table gleamed with antiseptic purity, a chrome altar. His tools and blades and brushes were lined to one side, awaiting his masterful touch. A small shiver wended through his gut, a thrill of ownership, a rush of pride.

He trembled as he opened the refrigerator. A fog of condensation surrounded him as he stepped into the cool air of the vault. He went to the shelf where he kept the flesh he had peeled from Father's face. Underneath the shelf was a three-gallon container nearly full of blood. He lifted it onto the gurney and rolled it out into the light.

He lifted the sheet. Her eyes were gone, those eyes that had no Wadell in them. He had probably overlooked some tiny shred of her damaged heart when he had removed it. Perhaps some scrap of intestine had escaped his scalpel. He would open her up again to check, before he drained the embalming fluid and replaced it with Father's blood.

He would make her proud. He would make her a Wadell. He would not rest until she was fit for rest herself. If not tonight, he had tomorrow and forever.

And when she was finally perfect, then he would allow himself to weep.

THE NIGHT IS AN ALLY

I t was July 12, 1942, and the sky over Jozefow had broken with high clouds under a sun the color of a blood blister.

First Lieutenant Heinz Wolfram exited the train at Sternschanze station as the cattle doors wheeled open with a dozen rusty shrieks, allowing the reserve policemen to exit from the same stinking cars that had transported Jews to Berkinau and Belzec. The effort to make Lublin *judenfrei* had taken over a month and had sapped the energy of Reserve Police Battalion 101. His men of Third Company were haggard, tired, and their bellies probably grumbling like his. Officers might have slightly better rations, but barely two years into the war, shortages were a staple of every rank.

"*Herr Oberleutnant*," said a guard on the warped wooden platform, raising his arm with a brisk stamp of his boot heel.

Wolfram nodded to acknowledge the salute. Rear guards hadn't yet lost the crispness of their routines. "Cigarette?"

The guard smiled and Wolfram shook one from the pouch in the breast pocket of his gray tunic. He lit the guard's and then one for himself. The tobacco was Turkish, dark and sinister like the people who had cultivated it.

"Shipping *juden*?" Wolfram asked.

The guard smiled from his pale moon face. "Two thousand, maybe. Three. What's the difference? The trains are slow."

"Two trains per week. Globocnik's orders."

The guard looked around, comfortable in his post, the real war three hundred miles to the east. "Globocnik? I see no Globocnik." He leaned close, conspiratorially, as if they were two friends in a beer hall. "I don't even know if Globocnik is real, *ja*?"

Globocnik, an SS police leader, was rumored to have had personal correspondence with the Fuhrer himself. Globocnik, who had career ambitions and sought a place on Himmler's staff, had stepped up relocation efforts after a German officer had been killed during a police action against the Jews. The officer in question had died in a drunken motorcycle accident, but the German leadership had never troubled itself over accuracy when a larger purpose was served. Martyrs were cheap, Wolfram well knew.

"So it's quiet here?" Wolfram asked.

The guard shrugged. "I sleep. No one here has guns."

"Good." Wolfram drew on his cigarette as the guard sauntered to the shade of the station's long platform.

"Rest for now," Wolfram shouted at the policemen who had debarked the trains, busily wiping their brows and sipping from steel canteens. They were mostly older men, those not fit for combat but who had been pressed into some sort of duty for the Reich. Though unfit for combat, Wolfram's platoon was organized, obedient, and well-trained.

Some, like Scherr there, the fat one, were all joviality and bluster, full of the nonsense that came from believing happy lies. Kleinschmidt, a sausage maker, complained bitterly about his boots and the poor quality of the field kitchen's pork. Wassen had been a journalist and spent his evenings writing letters to his family. Few of the men in Wolfram's First Company platoon thought beyond the immediate soldier's concerns of a soft bunk and dry socks.

At age 32, Wolfram had no career ambitions himself; he thought only of his wife, Frieda, in the Hamburg apartment with their four-year-old son Karl. Wolfram had headed a small family lumber business and benefited from the initial lead-up to war. When certain high-level officers began hinting that a man like Wolfram was needed by the Fatherland, he enlisted in the Reserve Police.

During 1941, Reserve Police Battalion 101 had been largely concerned with stamping out partisan uprisings and rounding up communist Russians in Czechoslovakia. Later in the year, Jews were targeted as well. Wolfram had heard reports of entire Jewish sections of cities being burned to the ground, and truckloads of Jews occasionally disappeared. But such reports were like the wind, and Wolfram had filed enough of them to know that only a fool or a zealot dared speak the truth.

Scherr, his First Sergeant, approached Wolfram as the train engine let out a long sigh of steam. The smell of coal smoke briefly obliterated the cloying animal stench that came from the cattle cars.

"Shall I issue the orders?" Scherr said all too eagerly.

"Gather the men," Wolfram said.

Scherr obeyed, no doubt promising the men a night in the barracks and the eventual arrival of rations. As the forty reservists gathered around, Wolfram looked into their faces. He was younger than most, and a good deal healthier. Less than a third were Nazi Party members, and most were from the lower orders of society: laborers, clerks, and street merchants. Some were as old as Wolfram's father, and one, Drukker, reminded Wolfram of his own youth as he looked into the hard blue eyes.

"We have been selected for an unpleasant task," Wolfram began, attempting to mimic the words of Captain Herrmansbiel, his immediate superior. "The Jews here have been involved with the partisans. Further, their discontent has led to the *Amerikanner* boycott of Germany's goods and services. There's even talk"— Wolfram wasn't sure how to add the next part without risking damage to morale—"that the Americans will join England and Russia as allies."

"*Mein gott,*" came a voice from the rear ranks. "*Fick der juden.*"

"The Jews are confined to the ghetto, and per standing orders, any attempting to escape will be shot. We are to round up all the Jews and gather them in the marketplace for processing. Healthy males of working age are to be loaded onto trucks and transported to Lublin. Those who resist or are too frail to march will be summarily executed."

Scherr licked his lips. He'd already shown an appetite for killing Jews and was always quick to volunteer when there was the possibility of an organized firing squad. Wolfram found him distasteful, but such men made the entire operation easier to manage, and also required less of Wolfram's presence during the most brutal actions.

"This duty is necessary, and we must be strong," Wolfram said. "I don't want to see any cowards. However, any man who doesn't feel up to the task may step forward now and be reassigned."

Some of the men exchanged glances while others stared at the ground. Someone coughed. The train engine clanged. After a moment, Drukker stepped forward, shoulders sagging.

"Anyone else?" Wolfram asked. Only Drukker met his gaze.

"Very well," Wolfram said. "Drukker, you will help guard the train. The rest of you men, proceed to the marketplace in the center of town. Scherr, give them their orders there."

Scherr grinned, saluted, called the men to attention and led the platoon away. Wolfram lit another cigarette. "Drukker, you will be happy later on. You might be the only one. Before this Jewish business is over, the German nation will be shamed in the eyes of God."

"Yes, sir," Drukker said, subordinate despite being nearly twenty years older than his lieutenant.

Wolfram knew, as an officer, he shouldn't speak on equal terms with the men, especially on matters of philosophy. After all, the truth could be construed as treason. "Resettlement is a question of military efficiency, Drukker."

"Yes, sir."

Wolfram tossed his cigarette off the platform and checked his watch. He glanced at the forest that covered the rise of land above the village. "We will be efficient."

He walked into Jozefow. The village was quiet, many of the

Poles still sleeping under the thatched straw roofs. Curling pillars of sleepy smoke rose from a few chimneys. The men of Second Company had already fanned out to surround the village, as per Hermmansbiels's orders.

Already the shouts and cries could be heard inside the narrow white houses of the Jewish section. Scherr had posted four guards in the market square, where the Jews were to be collected. The other men conducted door-to-door searches, and from a small stone house came a woman carrying an infant. Hermmansbiel specifically stipulated that the infants were to be shot along with the elderly. Gunfire erupted along the next block, sending more cries into the morning sky.

Worker Jews were driven at bayonet point, most with beards and thin faces, wearing long, filthy robes. They had already suffered plenty of hardship, but nothing like what they would see today, Wolfram thought. He saw Scherr lead a small squadron of men into a long, low building that could have been a hospital or an old people's home. Automatic gunfire erupted like popcorn kernels over a fire. Minutes later, Scherr and the other reservists exited the smoky portal that led into the building. No Jews accompanied them.

Nearby, Wassen stood leaning against a stone wall. At his feet was a woman, a blossom of blood on the back of her dress. Wassen dropped his rifle and knelt, vomiting. Wolfram looked around to see if anyone noticed them. An old Jew, who might have been a rabbi, gave a grim nod. Wolfram turned away and stood over Wassen.

"We have orders," Wolfram said gently.

"I can no longer shoot," Wassen said, wiping his nose on his uniform and leaving a long, greasy smear.

"Are you out of ammunition?"

"I can no longer shoot."

Wolfram looked at the rabbi and the other Jews huddled around him on the rough, pebbled street. "Join Drukker on guard duty at the station."

"Thank you, *Herr Oberleutnant*."

"Efficiency," Wolfram said. "A man who can't shoot is more useful somewhere else."

More shots rang out. The men had been given extra ammunition before the train rolled into the station. They must have known this action was to be unusual. They must all have suspected what was coming.

Scherr jogged up, breathless, his cheeks flushed despite the heat. He appeared rejuvenated, years younger. Blood dotted his boots. "We have about three hundred workers to transfer," he said. "And the others are ready."

"March the workers to the station," Wolfram said. "Are Second and Third platoons in place?"

"Yes, sir."

"Continue the action. Captain Hermmansbiel said this should take less than a day."

It was a job, a mission. Hermmansbiel had delivered the order, probably doing the same thing Wolfram was doing, the same as Scherr. Passing a command down the ranks. No single man was responsible.

The worker Jews rose on command, flanked by guards, and moved down the street. How accepting they are, Wolfram thought. How dignified.

Then their sheepishness made him angry. He had known a German Jew in Hamburg, an engineer who built parts for milling machines. A fine craftsman who had shared some of his people's strange beliefs. Wolfram, a Lutheran, wondered if the engineer had been relocated out of Germany with all the others. He might even be among this crowd, being shuttled once again. If he were still able to walk.

More women, children, and the ambulatory older men were gathered in the square. Wolfram guessed there were maybe a thousand. A dozen reservists from the Third platoon each selected a single person from the assemblage. They urged the Jews toward the forest, one of the policemen sticking a bayonet tip into the back of his charge.

Lieutenant Von Offhen, leader of the Third platoon, flagged down Wolfram. "This is going too slowly."

"How far into the woods are they taking them?"

"A half kilometer."

A fusillade of shots sounded in the distance. Wails arose from a few of the women, causing the infants to renew their cries. The Jews' composure of the early morning was fading as the July heat settled in and realization unvelveted its claws.

"You have a guard for each Jew," Wolfram said. "But none are attempting to flee."

"It gives the men a chance to rest. The shooting is—mentally exhausting."

"They'll be more exhausted if we have to continue this into the night, working by the headlights of trucks."

"There's another problem. The forest trail is already becoming cluttered with bodies. Maneuvers are difficult."

"Try this. Use only two guards to escort each group of Jews. The others can reload and be ready when the group arrives. Start at the farthest end of the trail so that each succeeding trip is shorter."

Von Offhen's brow furrowed. "I'm not sure the men will like it. Especially those doing the shooting."

Wolfram thought of Scherr's pink, joyful face. "Let anyone who wants to be relieved come down and watch the square. I've no doubt there will be plenty who will take their places."

Though they were of equal rank, Von Offhen saluted and went to implement the suggestions. Efficiency, Wolfram thought. It all comes down to a question of efficiency.

The day wore on, in an endless parade of Jews and a cavalcade of rifle shots. Wolfram went from the square to the train station, where Drukker and Wassen shared a canteen. When Wolfram got close, he smelled the alcohol.

"Cognac," Drukker said, offering the canteen. "A gift from the Polish Catholic priest."

Wolfram declined the drink. "See if the Poles have enough for all the men on duty. A cheap price for having their dirty work done."

Drukker hurried off, a bit wobbly.

Wolfram lit a cigarette. "What will you write to your family tonight, Private Wassen?"

"I think I'll write fiction tonight."

Wolfram's laugh turned into a smoke-induced hack. "I think we all will. And I pity us for the dreams we'll suffer."

Wassen appeared uncomfortable, hearing such things from an officer. Wolfram wondered if any of the men would report him for erratic behavior. Besides Scherr, none of them had a chance of promotion if Wolfram were declared unfit for duty. He saluted the poet and said, "It's a question of efficiency."

Wolfram took a circuitous route through the forest. He came upon the first bodies several hundred feet from where the firing squads were now at work. They all lay face down, most bearing a single bullet wound to the top of the neck. Some, no doubt the victims of reluctant or inattentive shooters, had the tops of their skulls blown off, and bits of blood, bone, and brain pocked the carpet of leaves.

It was evening, and he knew he should make an appearance for the benefit of morale. He followed the trail, bodies girding its length on both sides where the Jews had willingly and tacitly participated in their own deaths. In some ways, the Jews were even more efficient than their killers, as if they were in a hurry to help.

The nearest group of shooters was comprised of members of Wolfram's platoon. Kleinschmidt recognized him and lifted a tired arm in greeting. He appeared drunk. The priest must have had a good supply of cognac.

"*Herr Oberleutnant*," the corporal shouted, nearly as jolly as Scherr had been earlier. "We are doing good work now."

"There are only eight in your squad," Wolfram said.

"Some of the men became sick after only a couple of rounds. Scherr relieved them."

As Wolfram watched, another group of Jews was led along the trail. Von Offhen had bettered Wolfram's suggestion and now used only one guard to march each group to the woods. "Down," Kleinschmidt bellowed. "Filthy Jew pigs."

The ten Jews, all but two of them women, fell onto their hands and knees, then prone onto their stomachs. Some of them held hands with the persons beside them. Wolfram noticed that when the echo of the shots died away, the forest was eerily quiet.

"Aim," Kleinschmidt ordered, and the squad placed the tips of their bayonets at the bases of the skulls of the Jews in front of them. "Fire."

The two Jews on the end, one a boy of about four, the other a gray-haired woman wearing a cowl, had to wait for two policemen to reload. The boy wore a small Dutch cap similar to the one Wolfram had given his son Karl for Christmas. The boy whimpered while the old woman tried to calm him with what Wolfram believed must be some kind of prayer. Whether her words asked God for mercy or for a swift death, he couldn't tell. Hebrew was a crude, inferior language and any god worth knowing wouldn't abide such a tongue.

The nearest two shooters touched the tips of their bayonets to the assigned victims. The boy's cap was blown off as the bullet demolished his skull. The old woman's shot wasn't immediately fatal, and she flopped on the ground for a moment as if suffering a severe electrical shock.

"Inefficient," Wolfram said, though he kept his own Luger holstered. A stream of guttural Hebrew spilled from her throat, a demonic, animal howl. Finally she lay still.

Scherr came along with the next group of Jews. He had apparently assigned himself to guard duty rather than participate in further shooting. His hands shook and his eyes were wide and bloodshot.

"How many more in the village square?" Wolfram asked

"Fewer than fifty," Scherr said.

"We'll be done before dark. Hermannsbiel will be pleased."

"Good," Scherr said. "I don't want to be here at night."

"The night is an ally," Wolfram said. "In the darkness, all things are hidden."

Scherr gave an uneasy glance into the growing gloom, then trotted back to the village. Wolfram paced the trail, encouraging the men, reminding them of the rations waiting back at the barracks after their duty was finished. The priest had plenty more to drink, he told them.

By now, nearly the full length of the trail was lined with dead

Jews. The bodies were no longer bodies; they were merely dark shapes on the shadowy forest floor. Occasionally one of the shapes would moan and lift a limb, but among the trees, who could tell flesh from wood?

Once the marketplace was empty and the Jewish quarters were quiet, a few Poles ventured into the streets. Wolfram appointed a detail to stand guard in case any stray Jews had been hiding and attempted to flee in the night, then ordered the rest of the platoon back to the station. He took a final walk along the twilit forest trail. He needed to own this memory, though he knew the reservists would speak little of it. A day's work well done.

He came upon a figure standing on the trail, a darker silhouette against the sunset-dappled forest. It was a boy wearing a small Dutch cap.

"*Juden?*" Wolfram asked.

"*Ja,*" the boy said, and for a moment, the voice sounded like his son Karl's, who was probably now asleep, nestled against his mother's nightgown in a soft bed back in Hamburg.

Wolfram fumbled for his Luger, swallowing, the air thick with the wet-fur smell of blood and loam. Hermannsbiel had been quite clear. No survivors.

He drew the pistol, though it was heavy in his hand. A leader should never ask his men to do what he was unwilling to do himself.

He pointed the Luger at the boy, who still hadn't moved.

If only the boy would run, Wolfram could finish it.

But the boy didn't run. Instead, he moved toward Wolfram, feet making no sound in the leaves. Wolfram stood aside as the boy passed, accompanied by a cool breeze from the wind that rattled dead leaves. A last stray beam of sunlight pierced the canopy and shone on the boy's cap, revealing a single bullet hole in the wool.

Wolfram holstered his weapon as the boy merged with the gathering darkness.

Later, at the barracks, he availed himself of the priest's cognac. He sat down at a small table and in the midnight glow of a candle, he filed his full report for the day:

July 12, 1942. Jozefow, Poland

Third Company, Reserve Police Battalion
101, was given cold rations of sausage,
bread, marmalade, and butter. In the future,
please note that cold rations do not hold up
well in the summer heat. Jewish resettlement
actions continued. No special incidents
occurred.

Wolfram lit a Turkish cigarette and watched the smoke rise
from the glowing red tip toward the flickering ceiling of the barracks, then out into the deepest and blackest places of the world.

WORK IN PROGRESS

The cutting was the most demanding.

During his career as an artist, John Manning had sliced glass, trimmed paper, chipped granite, chiseled wood, shaved ice, and torched steel. Those materials were nothing compared to flesh. Flesh didn't always behave beneath the tool.

And bone might has well have been marble, for all its delicacy and stubbornness. Bone refused shaping. Bone wanted to splinter and curl, no matter how light John's touch on the hammer.

How did you build yourself alive?

Bit by bit.

Karen on the wall was a testament to that. Because Karen never lied.

And was never finished, an endless work in progress.

So building himself had become a mission from God. John knew from his time at college that art required suffering. He'd suffered plenty, from no job to canceled grants to broken fingers to Karen's last letter. His art had not improved, though he'd faithfully moved among the various media until his studio was as cluttered as a crow's nest.

He crushed out his cigarette and studied the portrait. Much of it had been done from memory. The painting had grown so large and oppressive in his mind that it assumed capital letters and became The Painting.

When he'd started it three years ago, the memory had flesh and was in the same room with him. Now he had to stagger through the caves of his brain to find her and demand she undress and model. And she had been so elusive lately.

Karen.

Her letter lay in a slot of his sorting shelf, just above a cluster of glass grapes. The paper had gone yellow, and rock dust was thick across its surface. If he opened the letter and read it, maybe she would come out of the smoky caves inside his skull. Except then he'd have to finish The Painting.

Looking out the window was easier, and had a shorter clean-up period. Painting had been foolish anyway. Every stroke was wrong. When he needed a light touch, he cut a fat swath. When he needed bold colors, he bled to mud.

He was born to sculpt, anyway. And now that he had the perfect subject, his frustrations could fall away. The anger and passion and sickness and hatred could go into the new work in progress and not poison his brain any longer. No more dallying with oil and charcoal, no more dancing with acrylics. That was a dilettante's daydream, and the dream was over.

Because this was real.

This was the most important moment in the history of art.

This was The Living Painting.

Except the materials didn't cooperate. Not Cynthia nor Anna and not Sharon in the trunk of his Toyota.

Life was a work in progress. Nothing was sacred. Art was a work in progress. Nothing was sacred.

If you rearranged the letters of "sacred," you got "scared."

John had not been scared when he asked Cynthia to be his material. Cynthia was a work in progress. Cynthia was an artist. Cynthia was art.

The body beneath the canvas in the corner of John's studio dripped.

John wondered if the blood would seep between the cracks in the floor and then through the ceiling of the used bookstore below. Even if it did, no one would notice for months. His studio was above the Classics, a section almost as long-dead as the authors themselves. Proof that even when you created something for the ages, the ages could care less.

So all that was left was pleasing himself. Envisioning perfection, and striving for it. Pushing his hands and heart to match his mind's strange hope.

He lifted the razor and was about to absolve himself of failure forever when the knock came at the door.

The studio was a shared space. John loathed other human beings, and other artists in particular, but his lack of steady income had forced him to join five others in renting the makeshift gallery. They were drawn together by the same fatalistic certainty of all other dying breeds.

Knock, knock.

And the knock came again. Some people didn't take "no answer" for an answer.

One of the five must have knocked. Probably wanted to chat about art. Not like they had anything better to do. John threw a spattered sheet of canvas over the corner of the room and went to the door.

Karen.

Karen in the hallway, glorious, almost perfect.

The last person he expected to see, yet the right person at this stage of the work in progress.

Karen as a statue, as a painting, as the person who shaped John's life. John tried to breathe but his lungs were basalt. Karen had not aged a bit. If anything, she had grown younger, more heavenly. More perfect.

John could read her eyes as if they were mirrors. She tried not to show it, but truth and beauty couldn't lie. Truth and beauty showed disapproval. That was one look she hadn't forgotten.

John weighed every ounce of the gray that touched his temples, measured the bags under his eyes, counted the scars on his hands.

"Hello, John," Karen said.

Just the way she'd started the letter.

"Hi." His tongue felt like mahogany.

"You're surprised." Karen talked too fast. "My old roommate from college still lives here. I had her look you up."

"And you came all this way to see me?" John wanted a cigarette. His hands needed something to do.

"I was passing through anyway. Mountain vacation. You know, fresh air and scenic beauty and all that."

John glanced out the window. A plume of diesel exhaust drifted through his brick scenery. College buildings sprawled against the hillsides in the background. The mountains were lost to pollution.

John had been silent too long and was about to say something, but his words disappeared in the smoky caves inside his head.

"I'm not interrupting anything, am I?" Karen asked.

"You're not interrupting. I was just thinking about my next piece."

That meant his next sculpture rather than his next sexual encounter. Karen knew him well enough to understand.

She could never interrupt, anyway. John was an artist, and artists never had anything to interrupt. Artists had years of free time, and artists would rather give their free time to other people. Art was sacrifice.

His time was her time. Always had been. At least, it had been years ago. Now she lived two thousand miles away with no forwarding address and John had endless buckets of time to devote to his art.

Except now she stood at the door of his studio, eyes like nickels.

"Can I come in, then?"

Come.

In.

To John's studio.

With Cynthia lying in the corner, weeping blood and becoming. Becoming what, John wasn't sure.

Himself, maybe. His soul. The shape of things. A work in progress.

John tried on a smile that felt fixed in plaster. "Come in."

Karen walked past him and lifted objects from his workbench. "A metal dolphin. I like that."

She touched the stone sailboat and the driftwood duck and the rattlesnake walking stick and John watched her until she finally saw the portrait.

Or rather, The Painting.

"Damn, John."

"I haven't finished it yet."

"I think you just liked making me get naked. You painted me slow."

Not as slow as he should have. He wanted the painting to take a lifetime. She had other plans, though she hadn't known it at the time.

"It's a work in progress," he said.

"What smells so funny?"

Oh, God. She had flared her wondrous nostrils. John did not like where this was headed.

"Probably the kerosene," John said. "Cheaper than paint thinner, and works just as well, if you overlook the stink."

"I remember."

She remembered. She hadn't changed.

Had John changed?

No, not "Had John changed?" The real question was how much John had changed. A soft foam pillow in the corner was studded with steak knives.

"Did you ever make enough money to buy an acetylene torch?" She ran a finger over the rusted edge of some unnamed and unfinished piece. "I know that was a goal of yours. To sell enough stuff to—"

John knew this part by heart. "To buy an acetylene torch and make twelve in a series and put an outrageous price on them, hell, add an extra zero on the end and see what happens, and then the critics eat it up and another commission and, bam, I'm buying food and I have a ticket to the top and we have a future."

Karen ignored that word "future." She was the big future girl, the one with concrete plans instead of sandstone dreams. John's future was a dark search for something that could never exist. Perfection.

Karen walked to the corner, hovered over the spattered canvas. No one could see it until he was finished.

John looked at the shelf, saw a semi-carved wooden turtle. He grabbed it and clutched it like a talisman. "Hey. I'll bet you can't guess what this is."

Her attention left the mound beneath the canvas. "How could I ever guess? You've only made five thousand things that could fit in the palms of your hands."

"Summer. That creek down by the meadow. The red clover was fat and sweet and the mountains were like pieces of carved rock on the horizon. The sky was two-dimensional."

"I remember." She turned her face away. Something about her eyes. Were they moist? Moister than when he'd opened the door?

She went to the little closet. John looked at her feet. She wore loafers, smart, comfortable shoes. Not much heel.

Beneath the loafers rested Anna. The experiment.

The smell had become pretty strong, so John had sealed the area with polyurethane. The floor glowed beneath Karen's shoes. John let his eyes travel up as far as her calves, then he forced his gaze to The Painting.

"Aren't you going to ask me about Hank?" she said.

As if there were any possible reason to ask about Hank. Hank had been Henry, a rich boy who shortened his name so the whiz kids could relate. Hank who had a ladder to climb, with only one possible direction. To the top where the money was.

Hank who could only get his head in the clouds by climbing. Hank who didn't dream. Hank who was practical. Hank who offered security and a tomorrow that wasn't tied to a series of twelve metal works with an abstract price tag.

"What about Hank?" he heard himself saying.

"Ran off." She touched a dangerous stack of picture frames. "With an airline attendant. He decided to swing both ways, a double member in the Mile High club."

"Not Hank?" John had always wondered about Hank, could picture him reverting to Henry and going to strange bars. Hank had been plenty man enough for Karen, though. Much more man than John.

At least the old John. The new John, the one he was building, was a different story.

A work in progress.

"What are you doing here?" he asked.

She turned and tried on that old look, the one that worked magic four years ago. Four years was a long time. A small crease marred one of her perfect cheeks.

"I came to see you," she said. "Why else?"

"Oh. I thought you might have wanted to see my art."

"Same difference, silly."

Same difference. A Karenism. One of those he had loathed. And calling him "silly" when he was probably the least silly man in the history of the human race. As far as serious artists went, anyway.

"No, really. What are you doing here?"

"I told you, Hank's gone."

"What does that have to do with me?"

She picked up a chisel. It was chipped, like his front tooth. She tapped it against a cinder block. Never any respect for tools.

"It has everything to do with you," she said.

A pause filled the studio like mustard gas, then she added, "With us."

Us. Us had lasted seven months, four days, three hours, and twenty-three minutes, give or take a few seconds. But who was counting?

"I don't understand," he said. He had never been able to lie to her.

"You said if it weren't for Hank—"

"Henry. Let's call him 'Henry.'"

Her eyes became slits, then they flicked to the Andy Warhol poster. "Okay. If it weren't for Henry, I'd probably still be with you."

Still. Yes, she knew all about still. She could recline practically motionless for hours on end, a rare talent. She could do it in the nude, too. A perfect model. A perfect love, for an artist.

No.

Artists didn't need love, and perfection was an ideal to be pursued but never captured.

The work in progress was all that mattered. Anna under the floorboards. Cynthia beneath the canvas. Sharon in the trunk of his Toyota.

And Karen here before him.

His fingers itched, and the reflections of blades gleamed on the work bench.

"I thought you said you could never be happy with an artist," he said. "Because artists are so self-absorbed."

"I never said that, exactly."

Except for three times. Once after making love, when the sheets were sweaty and the breeze so wonderful against the heat of their slick skin, when the city pulsed like a live thing in time to their racing heartbeats, when cars and shouts and bricks and broken glass all paved a trail that led inside each other.

"You said that," he said.

She moved away, turned her back, and pretended to care the least little bit about the Magritte print. "I was younger then."

Karen didn't make mistakes, and if she did, she never admitted them. John didn't know what to make of this new Karen. How did she fit with this new John he was building? Where did she belong in the making?

Art, on a few rare occasions, was born of accident. Or was even accident by design? Karen had entered his life, his studio, his work, right in the midst of his greatest creation. This making of himself.

She walked past the collection of mirror shards he had cemented to the wall. Suddenly there were a dozen Karens, sharp-edged and silvery. All of them with that same fixed smile, one that welcomed itself back to a place it had never truly belonged. John's jagged world.

"What are you working on?" she asked. She'd wondered such things in the beginning, when showing interest in his art was the best way into his head. Then she'd slowly sucked him away, drained his attention until all he could think about was her. She became the centerpiece of his gallery, the showcase, the *magnum opus*. And when at last she'd succeeded in walling him off from his art, when she herself had become the art, along came Henry who called himself Hank.

"Oh, something in soapstone."

The piece was on his bench. She hadn't even noticed. Her eyes were blinded ice.

"Oh, that," she said. "That's pretty neat."

Soapstone had a little give, some flexibility. You could miss your hammer stroke and create an interesting side effect instead of complete and utter rubble. Soapstone could be shaped. Unlike Karen, who was already shaped to near perfection.

The soapstone piece was called "Madonna And Grapefruit." Madonna was a long graceful curve, skin splotched by the grain of the stone. Grapefruit was the part he hadn't figured out yet.

He hadn't touched it in four months.

"I'm calling it 'Untitled,'" he said. That statement was a lie for the piece called "Madonna and Grapefruit," but was true for the work in progress for which three women had given their lives.

"Neat. You always were better at sculpting than painting." She looked again at her unfinished portrait on the wall. She added, "But you're a good painter, too."

"So, what's new with you?" As if he had to ask. What was new was that Henry was gone, otherwise she was exactly the same as she'd always been.

"Visiting. My old roommate."

"The sky was two-dimensional," he said.

"What?"

"That day. That day we were talking about a minute ago."

"Don't talk about the past."

"Why not?" he said. "It's all I have."

Her face did a good job of hiding what she was thinking. Marble, or porcelain maybe.

"Where are you staying now?" she asked.

He didn't want to admit that he was sleeping on the couch in the gallery. "I have a walk-up efficiency. Not enough elbow room to get any work done, though. That's why I rent this place."

"So, have you done any shows lately?"

He considered lying, then decided to go for it. "I won second place in a community art show. A hundred bucks and a bag of art supplies."

"Really? Which piece?"

John pointed toward a gnarled wooden monstrosity that sulked in one corner. It had once been a dignified dead oak, but had been debased with hatchet blows and shellac.

"What do you call it?" Karen asked.

"I call it . . ." John hoped his hesitation played as a dramatic pause while he searched his index of future titles. "I call it 'Moment of Indecision.'"

"Heavy."

"I'll say 'heavy.' Weighs over two hundred pounds. I'm surprised it hasn't fallen through the floor."

"And you made a hundred dollars?"

"Well, 'make' isn't the right word, if you're calculating profit and loss. I spent forty dollars on materials and put in thirty hours of labor. Comes in at less than half of minimum wage."

He was surprised how fast he was talking now. And it was all due to Karen walking toward the rumpled canvas in the corner, leaning over it, examining the lumps and folds and probably wondering what great treasure lay underneath.

The artist formerly known as Cynthia.

"Say, Karen, how's your old roommate?" The same roommate who wouldn't leave the room so they could make love in Karen's tiny bed. The roommate who thought John was stuck up. The roommate who was so desperately and hideously blonde that John wished for a moment she could become part of the work in progress.

The distraction worked, because Karen turned from the canvas and stroked a nest of wires that was trying to become a postmodern statement.

"She's the same as ever," Karen said.

"Aren't we all?" John looked at the handles of the steak knives. They almost formed the outline of a letter of the alphabet.

"I don't know why I'm here. I really shouldn't be here."

"Don't say that. It's really good to see you."

John pictured her as a metal dolphin, leaping from the water, drops falling like golden rust against the sunset. Frozen in a moment of decision. A single framed image that he could never paint.

He looked at the oil of Karen. The endless work in progress. Maybe if he ran a streak of silver along that left breast, the angle of the moonlight would trick the viewer.

If Karen weren't here, such a moment of inspiration would have brought a mad rush for brushes and paints. Now, he felt foolish.

Because Karen was here after all. This was life, not art. This was life, not art. This was life, not art.

He clenched one fist behind his back.

Ah.

Untitled.

Sharon in the trunk of his Toyota.

"The sky was two-dimensional," John said.

"What?"

"That day."

"John." She picked up his fluter, a wedged piece of metal. Nobody touched his fluter.

"What?"

She nodded toward The Painting, the one that showed most of her nude body. "Did you like painting me just because you could get me naked that way?"

A question that had two possible answers. Yes or no.

The artist always chose the third possible answer.

"Both," he said. "How's Henry?"

"I think he goes by 'Hank' now. At least that's what his boyfriend calls him." Karen wiggled her hands into the pockets of her blue jeans. Tightening the fabric.

John's fingers itched.

"So, how's the job?" he asked.

As if he had to ask. Accounting. The same as always.

"The same as always," she said. "I got another raise last year."

The ladder and how to climb it. Karen knew the book by heart, learned by rote at the feet of Henry who called himself Hank. Or was it Hank who changed his name to Henry?

Such confusion.

So many sharp edges and reflections.

"Why are you here?" John asked.

"I already told you."

"No. I mean, really."

She picked up a piece of colored glass, a remnant from a miniature church John had built and then smashed. She held the glass to her eye and looked through. Blue behind blue.

"I got to wondering about you," she said. "How you were getting along and all that. And I wanted to see how famous artists lived."

Famous artists didn't live. All the most famous artists were long dead, and the ones who swayed the critics during their own lifetimes made John suspicious.

"I'm the most famous artist nobody's ever heard of," he said.

She rubbed her thumb along the edge of the glass. "That's one thing I don't miss about you. Your insecurity."

"Artists have to go to dangerous places. You can't get too comfortable if you want to make a statement."

Karen put the piece of blue glass on the desk beside his mallet. She went to the portrait again. She pointed to the curve of her painted hip. "Maybe if you put a little more red here."

"Maybe."

She turned. "This is really sad, John. You promised you were going to throw yourself into your work and make me regret ever breaking up with you."

He hated her for knowing him so well. Knowing him, but not understanding. That was something he'd never been able to forgive her for.

But then, she wasn't perfect. She was a work in progress, too.

"You can't even finish one lousy painting," she said.

"I've been working on my crow collection."

"Crow collection? What the hell is that?"

"Shiny stuff. Spiritual stuff."

"I thought you were going to make that series of twelve that was going to be your ticket to the top."

He looked out the window. The room smelled of kerosene and decay.

She waved her hands at the mess on the workbench. "You gave up me for this."

No. She left him for Hank or Henry. John never made the choice. She wanted him to give up art. That was never an option.

"I guess I'd better get going," she said.

He thought about grabbing her, hugging her, whispering to her the way he had in the old days. He wanted her naked, posing. Then, perhaps, he could finish the portrait.

"It was really good to see you," he said.

"Yeah." Her face was pale, a mixture of peach and titanium white.

She paused by the studio door and took a last look at The Painting. "Frozen in time," she said.

"No, it's not frozen at all. It's a work in progress.

"See you around."

Not likely, since she lived two thousand miles away. The door closed with a soft squeak, a sigh of surrender.

John looked at the portrait again.

Karen here before him.

Not the one who walked and breathed, the one he could never shape. This was the Karen he could possess. The real Karen. The Painting.

He possessed them all. Anna under the floorboards. Cynthia beneath the canvas. Sharon in the trunk of his Toyota.

John hurried to the bench and grabbed up his tools.

The Muse had spoken. He realized he'd never wanted to build himself, or dream himself alive. Art wasn't about sacrificing for the good of the artist. Art was about sacrificing for others.

105

For Karen.

She was the real work in progress, the one that could be improved. The canvas awaited his touch.

John uncovered Cynthia and went to work. By midnight, The Painting was finished.

It was perfection.

THE ENDLESS BIVOUAC

The day that James Wilkie killed his first man dawned hell-hot and humid, and didn't get any better as the hours dragged on.

He'd just gotten over a touch of the bilous fever, and sweat clung to his collar and soaked through the brim of his cap. Wilkie had seen what happened to men who took the fever, and a few days in the sentry box was better than some extra bed rest. In the makeshift field hospital, bed rest often turned out to be permanent.

Wilkie was a private in the Third Regiment Georgia Volunteers. Back home, all his friends had talked about was glory, honor, and the freedom to keep working the coloreds. Wilkie was from a family too poor to have slaves. But he'd joined up just the same, even though he was only fifteen. By the fourth year of the war, recruiters were enlisting men and boys alike with no questions asked.

Wilkie wasn't sure how he would react to battle. He'd heard tales of the blue-bellies who would cut you down and then stir in your guts while looking you dead in the eyes. They were devils, rapists, the worst kind of trash. So he had been relieved when he was assigned as a guard at the prison camp near Andersonville. Except he didn't see how this duty could be worse than that of the front lines.

Sometimes he felt that both sides were prisoners here. Rations were often short and the Confederate camp up the hill wasn't a whole lot better than the pieces of torn blankets and old coats that the prisoners rigged up for shebangs. Dysentery didn't respect stockade walls or uniform color. The heat stifled everybody the same whether they were twenty feet up in a lookout or huddled by the swamp relieving themselves.

At least Wilkie could leave the endlessly sick and dying at the end of his watch. The Yankees were trapped inside with it, the groans of the starving, the septic stench of gangrenous flesh, the thick odor of human waste, the constant stirring of bottle-flies, the shouts and fights, the songs that the prisoners sang in the evenings that always seemed to find a minor key. They didn't look so high-and-mighty down there, unwashed and scruffy, thin as locust posts. Not like devils at all, though the prison was closer to hell than any place Wilkie had ever heard described in a sermon.

But all Wilkie could do was his duty. Ten hours in the box, trying to breathe, fanning his cap to keep the fever down. He kept the musket in the shade so he could occasionally press the cool metal barrel to his forehead. It wasn't even his musket; the guards had to trade off at the end of the day since supplies were short.

He was drowsing, so close to full sleep that he could see the dream image of the little garden back home, Susan sitting in the big oak tree, him with flowers in his hand. He was just about to say something kind to her, to lure her down from the tree and into his arms, when he heard the shouts. At first he thought it was part of his dream, just some raiders hooting drunk in town, but the shouts grew louder, a strident chorus. Wilkie's eyes snapped open and he looked down on the compound.

The prisoner was running straight for him. Even from thirty yards away, Wilkie could see the wide, haunted eyes, the mouth torn open in a silent scream. Other prisoners were shouting at him, telling the crazed Yankee to stop. One man gave chase, but the prisoner was driven by some strange energy that belied his knobby bones and stringy muscles.

The prisoner was making for the dead line.

Captain Wirtz's orders were clear: shoot any sorry Yankee dog that crossed the line. The single-rail fence ran about fifteen feet from the stockade walls. Not that any of the prisoners could scale the timbers before one of the boys put him down. But Wirtz said rules were rules and a civilized camp was in the best interest of both sides.

Wilkie lifted his musket and stood on legs still trembling from sleep. "Hold it there, Yankee," he said, but his throat was so dry that the words barely reached his own ears. Still the prisoner ran, his ragged tunic flapping.

"Stop or I'll shoot," Wilkie shouted, louder this time. The prisoner reached the dead line, vaulted the fence, and made for the wall. The man who had given chase stopped and backed away from the dead line. Wilkie felt a hundred eyes on him, and the shouts died away. Only then did Wilkie realize that half the Yankees had been urging the prisoner on, the other half yelling at him to stop.

As Wilkie raised the musket and sighted along the barrel, he took a deep gulp of August air. He closed his eyes and opened them again. If he paused long enough, maybe one of the other sentries would pull the trigger first. But duty was duty, and the prisoner was halfway to the wall.

It was no worse than shooting a rabbit or wild turkey, at least as far as aiming went. As the powder exploded, Wilkie thought he heard some other shots. The stricken man fell to one knee, jerking like a toppled stack of kindling, then reached a hand toward the wall. An additional shot rang out and the man's skull shattered.

Wilkie was sweating from more than just the fever. Prisoners crowded near the dead line like a harvest of gray scarecrows. One of the guards let out a whoop of triumph. A lieutenant ran from the officer's quarters and hurried up the ladder to Wilkie's sentry box.

"What happened here, private?" The officer was a bearded man of about forty. He stood with his arms folded, tapping one of his knee-high leather boots. Union boots, taken from the last round of new prisoners.

Wilkie could barely speak. "He crossed the dead line, sir."

Wilkie's eyes crawled from the officer's face to the corpse on the ground below. Flies had already settled on the wounds, their wings bright blue in the sun. Eggs would soon be laid, and maggots would be born in the man's rotting meat. Some of the larvae would crawl through the shallow grave dirt and make their way back here to continue the endless cycle.

"Good man," said the lieutenant, though his expression was of sorrowful weariness. "The war's over for one poor fool, at least."

Some of the prisoners below were mumbling. The lieutenant leaned over the sentry box. "Any man crossing the dead line will be shot," he said in a commanding voice.

The rumbles of discontent continued, but no Yankees approached the fence. Wilkie stared at the corpse until his vision blurred. He felt the officer's hand on his shoulder.

"Reload, private, then come with me." The lieutenant ignored Wilkie's tears.

Wilkie knelt in the sentry box and rubbed at his eyes. He opened them and let the heat dry them. Even staring at the clouds, he could still see the corpse, as if the vision had been burned into his retinas. Wilkie tried to tell himself that it wasn't his shot that killed the prisoner, but he knew he had aimed true for the chest. Then he grew angry at himself and rapped the gun with his knuckles, letting the pain distract him from such thoughts.

He climbed down the ladder, the musket cradled across one forearm. Guards opened the front gate, and a second private joined Wilkie and the lieutenant. They walked the no-man's-land between the wall and the dead line, eyes straight ahead, not acknowledging the watching Union soldiers.

"If I had a gun," said some brave anonymous soul.

"You'll get yours, Reb," said another. The lilting opening notes of "Amazing Grace" issued from the lips of a third.

When the detail reached the corpse, Wilkie and the other private rolled it over, so that the dead man was staring sightlessly at the sky. The lieutenant stood some distance away, talking to a Union officer.

"He just up and ran," Wilkie said to the private. "I had to shoot him."

"Hell, you're lucky you found a good reason. I seen 'em killed for less." The private spat a stream of tobacco juice to the ground. "Chamberlain, over in Second, tossed some bread scraps over the wall just down the foot of the dead line, then sat waiting for some Yankee to reach for it."

The private folded the dead man's arms over his chest and grabbed the shoulders of the bloodstained tunic. Wilkie balanced his musket over his arm again and grabbed the man's ankles. Pale, wrinkled toes poked from the boots.

"Boots ain't worth stealing," said the private. "Lately the dead have been just about worthless."

Wilkie said nothing, surprised by the dead man's lightness as they lifted him. He must be hollow, Wilkie thought.

"Except I hear the prisoners are selling rights on the corpses," said the other soldier. "First out on burial detail get the best trading, you know."

Wilkie nodded, grunted, hoping to hurry the private along. The lieutenant finished with the Union officer and joined them.

"Tibbets," said the lieutenant. "Eighty-Second New York."

Tibbets. Wilkie tried the name on his tongue, pushed it against his teeth. Tibbets, a man with family somewhere, a man who may have enlisted under the same sense of duty that had brought Wilkie to their shared destination. A man. A name.

A corpse.

Flies buzzed about them. They reached the front gate and laid the corpse out in the line of the twenty other fresh dead just inside the wall. Tibbets would rest there until the morning, feeding flies in the company of his cold comrades. Wilkie and the other Confederates left the compound as the Union soldiers dispersed. A single death was not the subject of much rumination, not when thousands had already made their final exit through those gates.

Wilkie had grave detail the next morning. He had slept fitfully, his dreams haunted by Tibbets's rigid face. He waited by the wagon while Union soldiers tossed the corpses as casually as if stacking cordwood. Another fifty had died during the night, and the air was ripe with disease. When the first wagon was full, it began its trip to the dead-house, where the corpses were counted.

The Union volunteers marched in the wagon's wake, Wilkie bringing up the rear. When they reached the dead-house, the corpses were unloaded and brought inside for identification. This gave the prisoners a little free time. Some sat against trees, smoking, but a few slipped into the bushes surrounding the dead-house. They were the hucksters, ones who smuggled goods inside and profited from the hardship and deprivation of their fellow soldiers.

Guards were scattered around the grounds, and escape was rare. The Confederates turned a half-blind eye to the trading. An unwritten rule was that a huckster had to share a portion of his trade goods, slipping some eggs, tobacco, or the occasional greenback to the captors. It was a system that worked well, the kind of thing befitting a civilized camp. Except for those on the inside who had no money or barter.

Wilkie went into the shade of the woods and rested his musket against an oak. To the left of him was the mass cemetery, a long shallow ditch waiting for the day's dead. The thin layer of loose clay over the bodies did little to quell the stench of decay. Five thousand were already buried here, according to the corpse counters.

Wilkie lit his corncob pipe. The tobacco was stale, but at least it burned the smell of death from his nostrils.

He heard a rustle in a nearby laurel thicket. "Is that you, Yankee?" he said, to warn the prisoner not to attempt escape.

The bushes shimmied and the waxen leaves parted. A man in a shabby Union uniform stepped out. Wilkie first saw the toes protruding from the boots, then his gaze traveled slowly past the bloodied rips in the tunic to the man's face. The top of his skull was peeled away, but Wilkie knew that face, those eyes.

Tibbets.

Wilkie grabbed for his musket, accidentally knocking it to the ground. As he fell to his knees and scrabbled for it among the leaves, the boots approached, crackling in the dead loam and forest detritus. Wilkie gripped the musket and brought it to bear. What good was a musket ball against a dead man?

Tibbets stopped several feet away. His hands were spread wide, palms up. The dark eyes were solemn, the lips pressed tight. He was waiting.

"I...I didn't mean to kill you," Wilkie sputtered.

Tibbets said nothing.

A single sentence flew out from the chaos of Wilkie's thoughts: You can't talk when you're dead.

But neither could you walk. Neither could you stand there before the man who had shot you and make some silent pleading demand.

Tibbets raised his arms higher, then looked briefly heavenward. Wilkie followed the dead man's gaze. Nothing up there but a rag-barrel's worth of clouds and the screaming orange eye of the sun.

When Wilkie looked again at Tibbets, the corpse's hands were full of goods. Eggs, squash, a small rasher of bacon. And soap. Wilkie hadn't seen soap in six months.

Tibbets held his hands out to Wilkie. The meaning was clear. The goods were a gift to Wilkie. He set down his musket, trembling, and reached out to the corpse.

The eggs were cool to the touch, cooler than the dead fingers. The bacon had oozed some grease in the heat, but hadn't yet spoiled. The squash was shriveled but whole. And the soap . . .

Wilkie put the soap to his nose. The scent made him think of Susan, her clean hair, the meadow behind her father's cornfield.

Wilkie gazed gratefully into the dead man's eyes. "Why?" he asked.

The pale lips parted, and Tibbets's words came like a lost creek breeze. "You cried."

Tibbets turned and headed back toward the stand of jack pine.

Wilkie bit into the neck of one of the summer squashes. It was real. The impossible had become probable, and all that was left was for Wilkie to accept the evidence of his eyes, ears, hands, and mouth. "Wait," Wilkie called after Tibbets.

The dead Yankee paused, tilted his head as if heeding some distant command, then slowly waved for Wilkie to follow. Wilkie looked back toward the stockade, where nothing waited but the duty of another day's death watch. He peered through the branches to the dead-house, where maggots roiled. When he looked back, Tibbets was gone, the pine limbs shaking from his passage.

Wilkie stuffed the food and soap into his pockets. Leaving the musket, he slipped into the pines and wandered until he saw Tibbets far ahead. Wilkie walked, occasionally breaking into a run, never gaining on Tibbets. His limbs were heavy with fatigue, his uniform soaked with sweat. A blister rose on his big toe. Surely he had followed for hours, yet the sun still hung high in the sky.

At last he heard the soft twanging of a mouth harp, the duet of a banjo and guitar. Laughter came from behind the next stand of trees, and wood smoke filled the air. Someone was broiling meat over a fire. The clank of flatware and tin was accompanied by the rich aroma of brewed coffee. An unseen horse whinnied.

Wilkie burst into a run, using the last of his strength. He fought through a tangle of briars and scrub locust, kicking at the vines that kept him from those delightful sounds and smells. Finally he fell from the grip of the forest into an expanse of twilight. The air had gone crisp with chill. Campfires dotted the horizon as far as he could see. Around them huddled groups of men, joking, eating, drinking, writing letters or playing music.

Rows of tents stood lined in uniform rank, not a rip among them. This had to be a Union camp. If so, he would gladly surrender for just one good meal and a chance to hear that peaceful laughter and camaraderie. Wilkie approached the nearest campfire.

Two men rose from the log they were sitting on. One was dressed in a Union cavalry uniform, bright with polished leather and buttons. The other was Tibbets, in his prisoner's rags. Tibbets made a motion with his hand for Wilkie to sit. Wilkie nodded to the cavalry officer and sat rubbing his hands before the flames.

"This is Wilkie," Tibbets said.

Wilkie glanced up, about to ask the dead prisoner how he knew Wilkie's name. But in the land of the impossible, why shouldn't he?

The officer gave the open-handed Rebel salute. "Welcome."

Wilkie wondered why no one brought weapons to bear on him. Then he noticed that none of the men were armed. He studied the men sitting across the fire from him. They wore gray Confederate jackets. One of the men had cornbread crumbs in his beard. The soldiers nodded in greeting, then turned their attention back to the warm pork that filled their hands.

"Where do I go to surrender?" Wilkie asked the officer.

The officer's mouth fell open, then, after a moment, a laugh rolled from deep inside his chest. The other men around the fire joined in, along with several groups from nearby campfires. When the officer regained his composure, he said, "You don't have to surrender, son. Why, the war's over."

"Over?" Wilkie knew the South was getting beat, after Chattanooga and Gettysburg everybody recognized it was just a matter of time, but there was still plenty of Confederate pride and bodies yet to be used up. He couldn't imagine Lee handing over his sword without playing a last trump card or two.

"It's over for all of us," Tibbets said, waving his arm to indicate the entire camp that seemed to stretch on toward the stars.

"But you're dead."

The laughter fell away. Wilkie looked around, expectant, a sheen of fear on his cool skin.

"How many did you see die?" the officer asked quietly and not unkindly, like a wise uncle explaining something to a wayward nephew. "How many did you help kill?"

Wilkie looked at Tibbets.

"The bullet bites both ways," said Tibbets. "Doesn't matter whether you're breathing or not. You're still dead."

"This is a war," Wilkie said.

"War's over now," the cavalry officer said. "A civilized camp is in the best interest of both sides."

The officer sat and pulled a stick from the fire. It bent with the weight of a hunk of cooked ham. He passed the stick to Wilkie.

Someone strummed the guitar chords to "The Battle Hymn Of The Republic." The officer began singing in a rich bass voice. The Confederates wiped their lips with their sleeves and added their voices to the chorus that rose across the camp. Wilkie didn't know the words, so he listened as he ate, listened, listened, as the night fell on, forever.

SHE CLIMBS A WINDING STAIR

Outside the window, a flat sweep of sea. The ocean's tongue licks the shore as if probing an old scar. Clouds hang gray and heavy, crushed together by nature's looming anger. In the distance is a tiny white sail, or it might be a forlorn whitecap, breaking too far out to make land.

I hope it is a whitecap.

Because she may come that way, from the lavender east. She may rise from the stubborn sandy fields behind the house, or seep from the silver trees beyond. She could arrive a thousand times, in a thousand different colors, from all directions above or below.

I can almost her hear now, her soft footsteps on the stairs, the whisper of her ragged lace, the mouse-quick clatter of her finger-bones on the railing.

Almost.

It's not fear that binds my limbs to this chair, for I know she's not bent on mortal vengeance. If only I could so easily repay my sins.

Rather, I dread that moment when she appears before me, when her imploring eyes stare blankly into mine, when her lost lips part in question.

She will ask me why, and, God help me, I will have no answer.

I came to Portsmouth in my position as a travel writer on assignment for a national magazine. In my career, I had learned to love no place and like them all, for it's enthusiasm that any editor likes to see in a piece. So neither the vast stone and ice beauty of the Rockies, the wet redwood cliffs of Oregon, the fiery pastels of the Southwestern deserts, the worn and welcoming curves of the Appalachians, nor the great golden plains of the central states tugged at my heart any more or less than the rest of this fair country. Indeed, much of my impression of this land and its people came from brief conversations and framed glances on planes, trains, and the occasional cab or boat.

So the Outer Banks held no particular place in my heart as I ferried across Pamlico Sound to Ocracoke. To the north was the historic Hatteras Lighthouse, the tallest in the country, which was currently being moved from its eroding base at a cost of millions. I thought at the time that perhaps I could swing up to Hatteras and cover the work for a separate article. But assignments always came before freelance articles, because a bankable check feeds a person much better than a possibility does.

So on to bleak Portsmouth for me. At Ocracoke, I met the man who was chartered to take me to Portsmouth. As I boarded his tiny boat with my backpack and two bags, my laptop and camera wrapped against the salt air, he gave me several looks askance.

"How long you going to stay?" he asked, his wrinkled face as weathered as the hull of his boat.

"Three days, though I'm getting paid for seven," I said. "Why?"

"You don't look like the type that roughs it much, you don't mind me saying." His eyes were quick under the bill of his cap, darting from me to the open inlet to the sky and then to the cluttered dock.

"I'll manage," I said, not at all pleased with this old salt's assessment of me. True, I was more at home in a three-star hotel than under a tent, but I did hike a little and tried to be only typically overweight for a middle-aged American.

The man nodded at the sea, in the distance toward where I

imagined Portsmouth lay waiting. "She can be harsh, if she's of a mind," he said. Then he pushed up the throttle and steered the boat from the dock in a gurgle and haze of oily smoke.

We went without speaking for some minutes, me hanging on the bow as the waves buffeted us and Ocracoke diminished to our rear. Then he shouted over the noise of the engine, "Hope you brought your bug repellent."

"Why?" I said, the small droplets of ocean spray making a sticky film on my face.

"Bugs'll eat you alive," he said.

"Maybe I can borrow some at the ranger station," I said.

The man laughed, his head ducking like a sea turtle's. "Ain't no rangers there. Not this time of year."

"What do you mean?"

"Hurricane season. That, and federal cuts. Government got no business on that island no way. Places like that ought to be left alone."

My information must have been wrong. Portsmouth was now administered by the National Parks Service, since the last residents had left thirty years before. An editorial assistant had assured me that at least two rangers would be on duty throughout the course of my stay. They had offices with battery-operated short-wave radio and emergency supplies. That was the only reason I had agreed to take an assignment to such a desolate place.

Not for the first time, I silently cursed the carelessness of editorial assistants. "The forecasts are for clear weather," I said, not letting the boatman know that I cared one way or another.

"You should be all right," he said. "Least as far as the weather's concerned. Still, they blow up quick sometimes."

I looked around at the great blue sea. The horizon was empty on all sides, a far cry from the past glories of this area's navigational history. In my research, I had learned that this inlet was one of the first great shipping routes in the south. Decades before the Revolutionary War, ships would come to the shallow neck and offload their goods to smaller boats. Those boats then distributed the cargo to towns across the mainland shore. Spurred by this industry, Portsmouth had grown up from the bleak gray-white sands.

"A lot of shipwrecks below?" I asked, more to keep the old man talking than to fill any gaps in my background knowledge.

"Hells of them," he said. "Got everything from old three-mast schooners to a few iron freighters. Some of them hippie divers from Wood's Hole said they saw a German U-boat down there, but they was probably just smoking something funny."

"So the bottom's not too deep here?"

"Depends. The way the sand shifts here from one year to the next, could be fifteen feet, could be a hundred. That's why the big boys don't come through here no more."

And that's why Portsmouth had died. As the inlet became shallower, ships no longer wanted to risk getting stranded or else breaking up on the barrier reefs. The town had tried to adapt to its misfortune, and was once an outpost for ship rescue teams near the end of the 19th century. More than a few of the town's oarsmen were lost in futile rescue or salvage attempts.

Then ships began avoiding the area entirely, and the town residents left, family by family. The population dwindled from its height of 700 to a few dozen in the 1950s. The stubborn Portsmouth natives continued to cling to their home soil despite the lack of electricity, no steady food supply, irregular mail service, and a dearth of doctors and teachers. But even the hardiest finally relented and moved across the sound to a safer and less harsh existence, leaving behind a ghost town, the buildings virtually intact.

"There she is," the boatman said, and I squinted against the sparkling water. The thin strand came slowly into view. The beach was beautiful but bleak, a scattering of gulls the only movement besides the softly swaying seagrass. Low dunes rolled away from the flat white sands.

"Used to be a lot of wrecks right along this stretch," the boatman said.

"I read that they'd go out in hurricanes to rescue shipwrecked crews," I said.

"Brave folks, they was," he said, nodding. "'Course, you'd

have to be brave to set down roots in that soil, or else crazy. My people came from here, but they left around the First World War, when the getting was good. They's still lots of them on the island, though."

I was confused. "I thought the town was abandoned, except for the rangers."

He gave his dolphin-squeak of laughter. "Them that's under the sand, I mean. In the cemeteries. Got left where they was buried."

He guided the boat toward a crippled dock that was barely more than black posts jutting from the shallow water. The engine dropped to a groaning whine as he eased back the throttle. When we came broadside to the dock, he tied off with his crablike hands. I climbed out onto the slick, rotted planks.

"You ever go back?" I asked. "To have a look around, to walk through the houses that your folks used to live in?"

He studied the swirling foam and shook his head. "Nope. The past is best left dead and buried. You'd be wise to remember that."

I took my baggage from him, and I thought he might at least help me carry it to dry land. But he didn't move from the helm.

"You'll meet me here at four o'clock on Friday?" I asked.

He nodded, avoiding my eyes. "Unless a hurricane blows up, I'll be here."

"I trust the check came through okay?" I knew that publishers' checks could sometimes be excruciatingly slow in arriving, and I didn't want my ticket back to the mainland to be voided. This man was my only link with civilization, unless I somehow gained access to the short-wave radios.

"The money's good," he said. "I reckon that's the only reason you're doing this."

"That, plus I'm curious," I said. "There's not many places where a person can get lost in time anymore."

"Just make sure you don't get too lost," he said. "See you on Friday. Be sure and stay out of the houses, and for the Good Lord's sake, don't go in the graveyards."

He untied and shoved away, then turned the rudder until his back was to me. I waved, but he didn't turn around. The boat was out of sight by the time I had wrestled my bags up to the sandy hills that protected the island from the worst of the wind.

As I crested the dunes, the dead homes of Portsmouth lay sprawled before me. They were as gray-white as the ground, the paint flaked from the Colonial-style houses by decades of natural sand-blasting. The houses were hundreds of feet apart, all perched several feet off the ground by concrete or brick piers. A few water oaks and scrubby jack pines filled the expansive gaps between the structures. I set down my bags on the first porch I came to, at a three-story home that was the tallest on the island.

I didn't believe the boatman that the island was completely lifeless. Even if the ranger stations were abandoned, surely a few campers or day-tripping sailors were on the island. I didn't think my equipment would be stolen, but my laptop was worth several thousand dollars. And if my food supplies were stolen, I couldn't walk around the corner to a convenience store and replenish them.

Despite the boatman's warning, I entered the house, the old dark pine boards groaning under my feet. The shade was a relief from the August sun, and the narrow windows broke the breeze until it was comforting instead of brutal. The several rooms on the bottom floor were empty. I found the stairs to the left of the parlor and climbed the well-dried treads. On the second floor, I found a couple of old chairs, one a rocker. I then explored the third floor, which was barely more than a gabled attic. The view was spectacular from the lone window, and I could see most of the town as well as both the lee and Atlantic shores, since the island was scarcely a mile wide. The window also had a small ledge suitable for typing. I determined to make the room my headquarters for the brief duration of my visit.

Under park rules, visitors could tour the homes but were forbidden to stay in them. I was usually scrupulous about such matters, but if even the rangers had left this place to the elements, then I rationalized my squatter's rights by the fact that I myself was a natural force. Besides, after my article came out, perhaps renewed interest in the place could generate some users' fees for the National Park Service. Good publicity never hurt come budget time.

The sun was sliding rapidly behind the sea to the west. I stuck my supplies in a dark doorless closet, carried the rocker up to the room, and sat before the window to rest. Looking down, I imagined the town as it must have been a hundred-and-fifty years ago, with a bustling trade down by the shore, children running through the rutted sandy streets, women in long dresses going about their business. Perhaps a horse or two, certainly no more, had plodded along pulling carts laden with shipping goods, kegs of water, thick coils of rope, and sacks of meal or flour. I could almost hear the sailors' cries and shanties as they loaded and unloaded their longboats.

Behind an old drooping oak to the north lay a gated cemetery. Some of the markers had fallen over, and the few angels and crosses that still stood against the wind were pitted and worn. I thought of the boatman's words, how the cemeteries should be avoided. But nothing wrote out the history of a place better than the names and dates of its dead, and I knew I could not resist visiting them.

I may have dozed, though I rarely slept before the sun did. The next thing I knew, I was walking in the cemetery, feet bare against the wiry grass. The sky was a deep azure, moving toward a nearly starless twilight. The sea breeze moaned between the marble markers, the air tasting of salt and seaweed and driftwood.

She arose from nowhere, as pale as the sand. Dark hair spilled across her pretty face, and her eyes were in black contrast to her skin. Her dress was Victorian-era, long-sleeved and elegantly white, the waistband high, the shoulders and hems sewn with lace. She came forward from the shadows and held out her hands.

She was young, probably eighteen, though her hair was not at all of modern fashion. For a moment, I thought she and some of her friends might be having a costume party on the shore, gathered round the bonfire with guitars and wine and laughter before coupling off for sandy sex. But her expression was far too serious for a beach party refugee's.

"Please, sir, there's a wreck in the bay," she said, her voice tremulous but strong. "Can you help?"

"Pardon me?" I said.

"They're out there," she said, waving a wild hand to the east. "The *Walker Montgomery* ran aground, forty hands on her, sir. Our men shoved off in the boats, but now I fear they, too, have found trouble. They have been gone so long, sir, so very long."

Her eyes brimmed moistly in the glimmer of the sallow moon. I shook my head, sure someone was playing a prank on me. They must have seen me and taken advantage of the isolation at my expense. I fully expected her companions to emerge from the darkness, laughing boisterously, then inviting me for drinks.

But her eyes stared, beautifully haunted eyes, eyes that bore into me like harpoons. No mirth was hidden in them. She touched my arm, and her fingers were cool. "Help them," she said. "Help *him*."

"Him?" I said stupidly.

"My Benjamin," she said. "At helm of the lead rescue boat."

I held my hands apart. "I…I don't understand."

She pulled on my sleeve, her hair shielding her eyes. "There's another boat by the bay," she said. "Perhaps you and I, working the oars together, can reach them in time. Please hurry, before the storm takes them all."

There was no storm. The waves broke on the shore in their eternal, soft wash of sound. The wind was hardly strong enough to raise a kite. But something in her voice made my heart beat faster at the same time that my blood chilled. The moon was suddenly swallowed by the high clouds.

"Follow me," she said, turning and heading between the gravestones into darkness.

I stood where I was, then glanced back at the three-story house where I was staying. A dim light shone there, perhaps the candle I had used for reading. When I looked back, she was gone, and though I ran some distance through the sand, I couldn't find her.

Just then the wind gained speed, the clouds divided, and the quarter-moon's glare bathed the beach. The bay was barren and calm. There was no sign of the lady in white, not even a footprint in the wet sand.

Somewhat disconcerted, I finally made my way back to the

house. I went upstairs to the room where I had spread my sleeping bag and laid out my books and laptop. The candle had burned down to half its length. I must have been out on the beach for hours. Numb, I crawled into the bag and sought refuge in sleep, images of her beautiful face dominating my restless thoughts.

In the morning, I laughed at my strange dreams and laid out a few more of my supplies. I opened a tin of fish and ate an apple, then spent an hour at the keyboard, typing my impressions of yesterday's debarkment. Satisfied that I had given my editor a good start for her money, I changed into shorts and a light shirt and headed into the heart of the ghost town.

As I walked past the vacant homes and blank windows, I felt as if eyes were upon me. I even shouted once, a great questioning "Hello," still not convinced that the island was completely uninhabited. Nothing answered me but a keening gull's cry.

I found the ranger station, but it was securely locked, the doors and windows barred with steel. Next to it was a building that must have been a general store, for it had benches and a watering trough out front, and assorted rusty hooks and hangers covered its front wall. The interior was desolate, though. I walked past the long, collapsed counter to where the rear of the building opened onto a pier.

I pushed the door aside from where it dangled on warped hinges, then went to the end of the pier. The Atlantic was laid out before me, bejeweled and glorious, a million diamonds on its surface. I looked out across the bay to the protective cup of dunes four hundred yards away. Then I recalled the previous night, and for the briefest of moments, I saw a clipper, its bulkheads shattered, the prow tilted toward the sun, the sails like tattered ghosts. I blinked and the illusion passed. I laughed to myself, though sweat pooled under my arms.

The day grew rapidly warm, and since the tide was calm, I removed my shirt and shoes and jumped into the water. After a swim, I returned to my makeshift studio, regretting the lack of a shower. I ate a ready-made lunch, then gathered my camera to make the four-mile journey to the island's southern tip.

As I walked that narrow barrier island, I discovered why all the settlement was on the upper end. The land was little more than a grim cluster of dunes, with swampy pockets of trapped water scattered here and there along the interior. They weren't the vibrant, teeming swamps such as those in Florida. These were bleak, lifeless pools where only mosquitoes seemed to thrive. The parasitic insects set upon me in clouds, and I spent more time beating them away than I did finding suitable photography subjects.

I gave up barely halfway to my destination because the scenery was so hopelessly unvarying. I decided I'd capture some sunsets and sunrises instead, to focus more on the grandly archaic buildings and the Portsmouth beaches. I slogged back to the abandoned town, hoping to write a little more before dark. But I couldn't concentrate on my work. Instead, I stared out the window as the fingers of night reached across the town, thinking of my dream woman and comparing her beauty to that of all the other women I'd known.

Restless, I walked the beach at gray dusk. I kept to the Atlantic side, along the bay. I was nearing the old store when she came from the darkness beneath the pier. She wore the same dress that had graced her gentle curves on the previous night. Her fine hair fluttered in the wind, and rarely had I seen such a fine creature. Her pallid skin was the only flaw, the only thing that separated her from perfection.

Once again her dark eyes searched me, silently begging. "Can we go now?" she said. "They must surely be near drowning."

I had decided that perhaps she had lived on the island for some time. And though I had convinced myself that the night before had been a dream, a part of me had been hoping it was real, that I might have a chance to gaze upon her lovely likeness again. And there she was before me. "Where are they?" I asked, nearly breathless.

She raised her hand and pointed across the bay to where a streak of moonlight rippled across the water. "See them, oh, what a terrible storm."

And for an instant, I saw, waves rearing fully fifteen feet high, the rain falling in solid silver sheets, the longboats tossed on the angry ocean like bits of cork in a storm grate. I felt the blood drain from my face.

"Please hurry, sir," she said. "My poor Benjamin is out there."

She brushed past me, grabbing my hand. She was solid, not a mere captivating vision. My senses swirled, sound, touch, and sight all confused. I was as enthralled by her beauty and nearness as I was mortified by the vision of the storm. I let her pull me along, her hurried entreaties competing with the roar of the vicious wind. In those moments when I could take my eyes from here, I glanced at the shoreline ahead of us.

A boat lay beached on the sand, the tide frothing around the stern. The waves grew in force, slapping angrily and reaching farther and farther up the beach. The first drops of rain needled my skin, but the sky was nearly cloudless. I didn't question any of the impossible events. I thought of nothing but the delicate yet strong hand that gripped mine, and how I hoped it would never let go.

We reached the boat, and she made to shove off. The rain's intensity had increased, and her wet dress clung closely to her corseted body, her hair draped in wild tangles about her shoulders and back. I must have watched transfixed for some moments, because she turned to me and shouted, "Come, help me. We've not much time."

I ran to her side, bent my energies against the bow, and felt the boat slide into the water. A tremendous wave lapped up and pulled it free of the sand. She clambered over the side, motioning for me to follow. The storm raged about us, the wind now so strong that I could scarcely stand against it. In the darkness, I could no longer see the broken, tilted ship or the would-be rescuers.

She reached her hand to me. "Come, I can't work the oars alone. Benjamin is out there."

I lifted my hand to take hers, then dropped it suddenly. I shook my head, more to myself than to her. This was madness. All madness.

A great wave crashed and rolled back into the sea, the current pulling her away in the boat. The last I saw was her open mouth and startled eyes, stark against the whiteness of her exquisite features. Then she disappeared into the howling storm. I backed away from the rising waters, my arms thrown over my face to block the blinding rain. I came to the dunes and scrambled onto and over them, and found myself among the houses of Portsmouth. I collapsed in exhaustion.

The storm abated as suddenly as it had arisen. When I finally opened my eyes again, the moon was out and the wind softly blew the tickling seagrass against me. I stood, disoriented, and looked over the bay. The water was as smooth as dark glass.

I walked between those silent houses, back to my room. Surely I was dreaming, I would wake up and find my article half-written, a litter of empty cans and dirty clothes around me, my face stubbled and in need of a shave. Surely I was dreaming.

Yet I awoke in clothes soaked with saltwater.

I spent the next day wandering around the town. I forgot all about my assignment, and left my camera sealed in its bag. I told myself over and over that I only had to get through one more night, and then a boat would arrive to ferry me back to the sane, ordinary world. I wouldn't let myself go mad there in that isolated and grim ghost town of Portsmouth.

I came upon the cemetery and impulsively passed through its fallen corroded gates. I went to that place where I had first seen the young woman. In that brilliant light of day, the sun reflecting off sea and sand, I saw the details on the markers I had not observed on my first night on the island. The two tombstones were identical in both shape and the amount of erosion.

The first read "Benjamin Elijah Johnson, 1826-1846." Under that, in smaller script: "Taken By The Sea." The one beside it, etched in alabaster, read "Mary Claire Dixon, 1828-1846." Hers bore a subscript identical to the neighboring marker's.

What was most striking about the stones were the engraved hands. The hand on Benjamin Johnson's marker, though well-worn by a century-and-a-half of exposure, was clearly reaching to the left, toward Mary Dixon's marker. Mary's hand, slimmer and more graceful in bas-relief, reached to the right, as if yearning for a final touch. The poignancy was plainly writ in that eternal arrangement.

Mary's hand. I bent forward and placed my fingers on it, lightly explored it. I knew those curves and hollows, those slender fingers, the sculptor's skill too finely honed. I had held that hand before.

I don't know how long I stood in the graveyard. The shadows eventually grew long, the breeze changed direction, and I knew that if I didn't move soon I might be forever rooted in that spot. I tore myself away from the twin graves and raced back to my room. I would not leave it, I decided. I would remain there, in the sleeping bag or rocking chair, until my boat arrived.

That night the clouds massed from the southeast and the wind rattled the few remaining shutters of the ancient house. I hoped with all my might that the weather would hold clear, lest my boatman lose his nerve. But as I watched from my high window, the storm raged toward the island, the wind screaming as the rain began. Suddenly a bolt of lightning ripped across the charred sky, and I saw her in the yard below the house.

My Mary.

She looked up at me with those familiar, ravishing eyes, that long hair darkened by rain, her comely form encased in that grand dress. My heart beat faster and my pulse throbbed with equal parts dread and desire. On a second lightning strike that followed closely on the heels of the first, I saw that she was motioning for me. I tried to pull my eyes away, but I could not.

Though I commanded my flesh to remain by the window, my legs found a will of their own and carried me to the stairs. I went down, a step at a time, my heart racing with dreadful anticipation. When I reached the first floor, the rain had increased, and the whole house shook on its flimsy pilings. She was waiting on the porch for me.

"Will you come?" she asked.

"Mary," I said.

She nodded, then, without a word, she turned and ran into the brunt of the storm.

I jumped after her, dashing madly through the dead town of Portsmouth, shouting at the sky, my curses lost against the fury. The wind among the hollow houses sounded like the laughter of a great crowd. I ran on, toward the beach where I knew the longboat would be.

She had already worked the boat into the water, and beckoned me with an oar. I fought through the turbulent sea, finally gaining the stern and climbing aboard. She had locked two of the oars and arched her back, dipping the oars into the churning sea. I found two more oars in the bottom and locked them into place, clumsily trying to match my strokes with hers.

It was useless, I knew. We were two against the ocean's might, two against nature, two alone. But I didn't care. All that mattered was Mary, pleasing Mary, being with Mary.

Lightning lashed again, and I saw the now-familiar tableau of sinking clipper and endangered rowboats. It may have been my imagination, but I thought I saw a man standing in the fore of one of the rowboats, waving his arms in our direction. Certainly I imagined it.

"Benjamin!" she shouted, looking over her straining shoulders. A wave crested nearby and the salt stung my eyes and nose and throat.

"Row faster," Mary yelled to me. "We have to save Benjamin."

And if we did? If somehow we managed to beat the brutal sea and pull alongside his boat, if we then were blessed with the miracle of returning to shore, what then?

Mary would have her Benjamin, and I would have nothing. I would lose Mary.

I stopped rowing, and the longboat careened against the waves. Mary saw that I had stopped.

"Help me," she said, those beautiful eyes confused, her precious mouth moving in silent question.

I shook my head. "No," I said. "Benjamin's dead. You're mine, now."

I reversed direction with the oars, working one side until I turned the boat around. I expected her to fight, to thrash her own oars opposite mine. But she released them, and they slid into the waves.

She stood in the rocking boat, all grace and glory and the deepest beauty ever crafted. Without a word, she dove into the sea.

I shouted, "I love you," but I don't know if she heard me.

I waited several minutes that seemed hours, fighting the currents, watching for her to surface. The lightning struck again, and in its luminance, I saw that the clipper and rescue boats were gone, victims of the callous ocean. I imagined that each flash of foam, each breaking wave, was the lace of Mary's dress.

But she didn't appear. I battled the oars and clawed my way toward shore, though I lost my sense of direction. All that remained was to row and row, to drag the foundering boat through the sea that desperately wanted to swallow it.

The storm soon dwindled and died, and I found myself on the sand. As I coughed the salt water from my lungs, the east glowed with the pink of dawn. I struggled to my hands and knees and looked across the bay. No boat, no wreck, no Mary.

I hauled myself back to the house where I was staying. It took me many minutes to navigate the stairs, then I finally made it to my room and my chair and my high window. I took up my post, a watcher, a lighthouse keeper for the dead.

Three days, and still I keep my post.

I hope the boatman has given up on me. As much fear as filled his eyes when he hinted at the island's secrets, I don't think he even came ashore. I wonder if he will report my absence, or if he has his own orders, his own obsessions. It may take a week or more before anyone finds me.

Plenty of time for her to find me first, if she so desires.

Desire is an odd thing, a destructive thing, a strangely beautiful thing. Perhaps that is the lesson of this tale, the one that has replaced the travel article on my laptop. Whoever finds this account can make of it what they will. For the story was written many decades before, the ending the only thing left in the balance.

The ending.

I hear her now, below me, her footsteps as graceful as the rhythm of the sea. She climbs a winding stair, closer now.

Or perhaps it's only the wind creaking ancient wood.

I don't know which I dread the most.

Her arrival in lace and deceived rage?

Or her never arriving, never again granting me a glimpse of her everlasting and non-existent beauty?

I can almost hear her now.

Almost.

WATERMELON

icky bought the watermelon on a warm Saturday afternoon in
September.

The early crop had arrived at the local grocer's in late June,
fresh from California, but the available specimens were hard and
heartless. Ricky had decided to wait for a Deep South watermelon,
and those traditionally arrived many weeks after the annual Fourth
of July slaughter. Besides, that was early summer. He had yet to
read about the murder and his home life with Maybelle was in a
state of uneasy truce.

But now it was the last day of summer, a definite end of something and the beginning of something else. The watermelon was
beautiful. It was perfectly symmetrical, robust, its green stripes running in tigerlike rhythms along the curving sides. A little bit of vine
curled from one end like the cute tail of a pig. He tapped it and
elicited a meaty, liquid thump.

It was heavy, maybe ten pounds, and Ricky brought it from the
bin as carefully as if it were an infant. His wife had given him a
neatly penned list of thirteen items, most of them for her personal
use. But his arms were full, and he didn't care to trudge through the

health-and-beauty section, and he had no appetite for Hostess cupcakes and frozen waffles. Sheryl Crowe was singing a bright ditty of sun and optimism over the loudspeakers, music designed to lobotomize potential consumers. Ricky made a straight path to the checkout counter and placed the watermelon gently on the conveyor belt.

Now that his hands were free, he could pick up one of the regional dailies. The front page confined the woman's picture to a small square on the left. Her killer, the man who had sworn to love and honor until death did them part, merited a feature photograph three columns wide, obviously the star of the show and the most interesting part of the story.

"That's sickening, isn't it?" came a voice behind him.

Ricky laid the newspaper on the belt so the cashier could ring it up. He turned to the person who had spoken, a short man with sad eyes and a sparse mustache, a man who had never considered violence of any kind toward his own wife.

"They say he was perfectly normal," Ricky said. He wasn't the kind for small talk with strangers, but the topic interested him. "The kind of man who coached Little League and attended church regularly. The kind the neighbors said they never would have suspected."

"A creep is what he is. I hope they fry him and send him to hell to fry some more."

"North Carolina uses lethal injection."

"Fry him anyway."

"I wonder what she was like." Since the murder last week, Ricky had been studying the woman's photograph, trying to divine the character traits that had driven a man to murder. Had she been unfailingly kind and considerate, and had thus driven her husband into a blinding red madness?

"A saint," the short man said. "She volunteered at the animal shelter."

"That's what I heard," Ricky said. The cashier told him the total and he thumbed a credit card from his wallet. People always took kindness toward animals as a sign of divine benevolence. Let children starve in Africa but don't kick a dog in the ribs. For all this man knew, she volunteered because she liked to help with the euthanizing.

"At least they caught the bastard," the man said.

"He turned himself in." Obviously the man had been settling for the six-o'clock-news sound bites instead of digging into the real story. Murder was rare here, and a sordid case drew a lot of attention. But most of the people Ricky talked with about the murder had only a passing knowledge of the facts and seemed quite content in their ignorance and casual condemnation.

Ricky took the watermelon to the car, rolled it into the passenger seat, and sat behind the wheel reading the paper. The first days of coverage had focused on quotes from neighbors and relatives and terse statements by the detectives, but now the shock had worn off. In true small-town fashion, the police had not allowed any crime scene photos, and the early art had consisted of somber police officers standing around strips of yellow tape. A mug shot of the husband had been taken from public record files, showing mussed hair, stubble, and the eyes of a trapped animal. The District Attorney had no doubt kept him up all night for a long round of questioning, to ensure that the arrest photo would show the perpetrator in the worst possible light. No matter how carefully the jurors were selected, that first impression often lingered in the minds of those who would pass judgment.

A week later, the coverage had made the easy shift into back story, digging into the couple's history, finding cracks in the marriage. The only way to keep the story on the front page was for reporters to turn up personal tidbits, make suggestions about affairs and insurance, and build a psychological profile for a man who was so perfectly average that only hindsight revealed the slightest flaw.

Ricky drove home with the images playing in his mind, a reel of fantasy film he'd painted from the police reports. The husband comes home, finds dinner on the table as always, green peas and potatoes, thinly sliced roast beef with gravy, a cheesecake that the wife must have spent hours making. They eat, watch an episode of "Law & Order," then she takes a shower and goes to bed.

Somewhere between the hours on either side of midnight, the husband makes his nightly trek to share the warmth and comfort of the marital bed. Only, this time, he carries with him a seven-inch companion of sharp, stainless steel.

Seventeen times, according to the medical examiner. One of the rookie reporters had tried to develop a numerology angle and assign a mystical significance to the number of stab wounds, but police suspected the man had simply lost count during the frenzy of blood lust. The first blow must have done the trick, and if the man had only meant to solve a problem, that surely would have sufficed. But he was in search of something, an experience that could only be found amid the silver thrusts, the squeaking of bedsprings, the soft moans, and the wet dripping of a final passion.

By the time Ricky pulled into his driveway, he was moist with sweat. He found himself comparing his and Maybelle's house with that of the murderer's, as shown in the Day Two coverage. The murderer's house was in the next county, but it would have been right at home in Ricky's neighborhood. Two stories, white Colonial style, a stable line of shrubbery surrounding the porch. Shutters framing windows framing curtains that hid the lives inside. Both houses were ordinary, upper middle class, with no discernible differences except that one had harbored an extraordinary secret that festered and then exploded.

Ricky fanned his face dry with the newspaper, then slipped it under the seat. He wrestled the watermelon out and carried it up the front steps. He could have driven into the garage, but his car had leaked a few drops of oil and Maybelle had complained. He nearly dropped the watermelon as he reached to open the door. He pictured it lying burst open on the porch, its shattered skin and pink meat glistening in the afternoon sun.

But he managed to prop it against his knee and turn the handle, then push his way inside.

Her voice came from the living room. "Ricky?"

"Who else?" he said in a whisper. As if a random attacker would walk through the door, as if her ordered life was capable of attracting an invader. As if she deserved any type of victimhood.

"What's that, honey?"

He raised his voice. "Yes, dear. It's me."

"Did you get everything? You know how forgetful you are."

Which is why she gave him the lists. But even with a list, he had a habit of always forgetting at least one item. She said it was a deliberate act of passive aggression, that nobody could be that forgetful. But he was convinced it was an unconscious lapse, because he did it even when he wrote out the list himself.

"I had to—" He didn't know what to tell her. A lie came to mind, some elaborate story of helping someone change a flat tire beside the road, and how the person had given him a watermelon in gratitude, and Ricky wanted to put the watermelon in the refrigerator before shopping. But Maybelle would see through the story. He wondered if the murdering husband had told such white lies.

"I had to come back and take my medicine," he said, heading down the hall to the kitchen. "You know how I get."

Maybelle must have been sitting in her chair, the one that dominated the living room and was within reach of the bookcase, the telephone, and the remote control. Her perfect world. White walls. Knickknacks neatly dusted, potted plants that never dared shed so much as a leaf. Photographs of her relatives lining the walls, but not a single member of Ricky's family.

"You and your medicine," she said. "You were gone an hour."

He pretended he hadn't heard her. He put the watermelon on the counter and opened the refrigerator. He thought of hiding it in one of the large bottom bins but he wasn't sure it would fit. Besides, this was his refrigerator, too. He'd paid for it, even though Maybelle's snack foods took up the top two shelves. In a moment of rebellion, he shoved some of his odd condiments aside, the horseradish, brown mustard, and marinade sauces that occupied the bottom shelf. He slid the watermelon into place, though its girth caused the wire rack above it to tilt slightly and tumble a few Tupperware containers. He slammed the refrigerator closed with an air of satisfaction.

He turned and there was Maybelle, filling the entryway that divided the kitchen and dining room. Her arms were folded across her chest, wearing the serene smile of one who held an even temper in the face of endless trials. Ricky found himself wondering if the murdered wife had possessed such stolid and insufferable equanimity.

"What was that?" Maybelle asked.

Ricky backed against the refrigerator. There was really no reason to lie, and, besides, it's not like she wouldn't notice the first time she went rummaging for a yogurt. But, for one hot and blind moment, he resented her ownership of the refrigerator. Why couldn't he have a watermelon if he wanted?

"A watermelon," he said.

"A watermelon? Why didn't you get one back in the middle of summer, like everybody else?"

He couldn't explain. If she had been in the grocery store with him, she'd have been impressed by the watermelon's vibrancy and vitality. Even though the melon was no longer connected to its roots, it was earthy and ripe, a perfectly natural symbol for the last day of summer. But he was afraid if he opened the door, it would just be an ovate mass of dying fruit.

"I liked this one," he said.

"Where are my things?"

"I—" He looked at the floor, at the beige ceramic tiles whose seams of grout were spotless.

"You forgot. On purpose. Just like always."

"I'm sorry," he said, and suddenly his throat was dry and tight, and he thought of the husband and how he must have slid open the cutlery drawer and selected something that could speak for him when words were worthless.

"Of course, you're sorry. You've always been sorry. But that never changes anything, does it?"

"My medicine—"

"Have a seat in the living room, and I'll bring it to you."

He went and sat on the sofa, afraid to muss the throw pillows. The early local news came on the television. A fire on the other side of the county had left a family homeless. Then came the obligatory follow-up on the murder.

"Investigators say they may have uncovered a motive in last week's brutal slaying—"

Click. He looked away from the screen and Maybelle stood there, the remote raised. "Evil, evil, evil," she said. "That nasty man. I just don't know what goes through people's minds, do you?"

Ricky wondered. Maybe the husband had a wife who controlled the television, the radio, the refrigerator, the garage, and wrote large charity checks to the animal shelter. Maybelle gave him his pills and a glass of water. He swallowed, grateful.

"I read that he was an accountant," Ricky said. "Just like me."

"Takes all kinds. The poor woman, you've got to feel sorry for her. Closes her eyes to go to sleep and the next thing you know, the man she trusted and loved with all her heart—"

"—is standing over her, the lights are off but the knife flashes just the same, he's holding the handle so tight that his hand is aching, except he can't feel it, it's like he's got electricity running through his body, he's on fire and he's never felt so powerful, and—"

Maybelle's laughter interrupted him. "It's not a movie, Ricky. A wife-killing slasher isn't any more special than a thief who shoots a stranger for ten bucks. When it comes down to it, they're all low-down dirty dogs who ought to be locked up before they hurt some-body else."

"Everybody feels sorry for her," Ricky said. "But what about the husband? Don't you think he probably feels sick inside? She's gone, but he's left to live with the knowledge of what he's done."

"Not for long. I hear the D.A. is going after the death penalty. She's up for re-election next year and has been real strong on domestic violence."

"He'll probably plead temporary insanity."

"Big surprise," Maybelle said. "Only a crazy man would kill his wife."

"I don't know. With a good lawyer—"

"They're always making excuses. He'll say his wife made him wear a dress when no one was looking. That he had to lick her high heels. That she was carrying on with the pet store supplier. It's always the woman's fault. It makes me sick."

Ricky looked at the carpet. The stains must have been tremendous, geysers of blood spraying in different directions, painting the walls, seeping into the sheets and shag, soiling the delicate undergarments that the wife no doubt wore to entice her husband into chronic frustration.

"Ricky?"

Her voice brought him back from the last reel of his fantasy film and into the living room.

"How are you feeling?"

"Better," he said, lying only a little.

"Ready to go back to the grocery store?"

"Yes."

"And not forget anything this time?"

He nodded.

After shopping, getting all the items on the list, he sat in the grocery store parking lot and re-read all the newspapers hidden beneath the seat. He looked at the mug shot and visualized his own face against the grayish background with the black lines. He pored over the details he already knew by heart, then imagined the parts not fleshed out in the news accounts: the trip up the stairs in the silent house, a man with a mission, no thought of the act itself or the aftermath. One step, one stroke at a time. The man had chosen a knife from the kitchen drawer instead of buying one especially for the job. It had clearly been a crime of passion, and passion had been missing from Ricky's life for many years.

He looked at the paper that held the wife's picture. He tried to juxtapose the picture with Maybelle's. He failed. He realized he couldn't summon his own wife's face.

He drove home and was in the kitchen putting the things away when Maybelle entered the room.

"You've stacked my cottage cheese three high," she said. "You know I only like it with two. I can't check the date otherwise."

"There's no room," he said.

"Take out that stupid watermelon."

"But I like them when they're cold."

"Put it in the bathtub or something."

He squeezed the can of mushroom soup he was holding, wishing he were strong enough to make the metal seams rip and the cream spurt across the room.

"I put dinner on the table," she said. "Roast beef and potatoes."

"Green peas?"

"No, broccoli."

"I wanted green peas."

"How was I to know? You'll eat what I served or you can cook your own food."

"I guess you didn't make a cheesecake."

"There's ice cream in the freezer." She laughed. "Or you can eat your watermelon."

He went to the dinner table. Maybelle had already eaten, put away her place mat, and polished her end of the table. Ricky sat and worked the potatoes, then held the steak knife and studied its serrated edge. He sawed it across the beef and watched the gray grains writhe beneath the metal.

Maybelle entered the dining room. "How's your food?"

"Yummy."

"Am I not a good wife?"

He made an appreciative mumble around a mouthful of food.

"I'm going upstairs," she said. "I'm going to have a nice, long bath and then put on something silly and slinky."

Ricky nodded.

"I'll be in bed, waiting. And, who knows, you might get lucky." She smiled. She'd already brushed her teeth. Her face was perfectly symmetrical, pleasing, her eyes soft and gentle. He felt a stirring inside him. How could he ever forget her face? Ricky compared her to the murdered wife and wondered which of them was prettiest. Which of them would the press anoint as having suffered a greater tragedy?

"I'll be up in a bit," he said. "I want to do a little reading."

"Just don't wait too long. I'm sleepy."

"Yes, dear."

When he was alone, he spat the half-chewed mouthful of food onto his plate. He carried the plate to the kitchen and scraped the remains into the garbage disposal. He wondered if the husband had thought of trying to hide the body, or if he had been as surprised by his actions as she must have been.

The watermelon was on the counter. Maybelle had taken it from the refrigerator.

He went to the utensil drawer and slid it open. He and Maybelle had no children, and safety wasn't a concern. The knives lay in a bright row, arranged according to length. How had the husband made his decision? Size? Sharpness? Or the balance of the handle?

If he had initially intended to make only one thrust, he probably would have gone for depth. If he had aspired to make art, then a number of factors came into play. Ricky's head hurt, his throat a wooden knot. He grabbed the knife that most resembled the murder weapon shown in the press photographs.

Ricky turned the lights low, then carried the knife to the counter. He pressed the blade to the watermelon and found that the blade trembled in his hand. The watermelon grew soft and blurred in his vision, and he realized he was weeping. How could anyone ever destroy a thing of such beauty?

He forced himself to press the knife against the cool green rind. The flesh parted but Ricky eased up as a single drop of clear dew swelled from the wound. The husband hadn't hesitated, he'd raised the knife and plunged, but once hadn't been enough, neither had twice, three times, but over and over, a rhythm, passion, passion, passion.

He dropped the knife and the tip broke as it clattered across the tiles. The watermelon sat whole and smooth on the counter. Tears tickled his cheeks. Maybelle was upstairs in the dark bed, his pillows were stacked so he wouldn't snore, the familiar cupped and rounded area of the mattress was waiting for him.

The husband had been a crazy fool, that was all. He'd cut his wife to bits, no rhyme or reason. She hadn't asked for any of it. She was a victim of another person's unvoiced and unfulfilled desires, just like Maybelle.

Ricky spun and thrust his fist down into the melon, squeezed the red wetness of its heart. He ripped the rind open and the air grew sweet. He pulled at the pink insides, clawed as if digging for some deeply buried secret. He was sobbing, and the pulp spattered onto his face as he plunged his hands into the melon again and again.

A voice pulled him from the red sea of rage in which he was drowning.

Maybelle. Calling from upstairs.

"Ricky?"

He held his breath, his pulse throbbing so hard he could feel it in his neck. He looked down at the counter, at the mess in the kitchen, at the pink juice trickling to the floor.

"Ricky?" she called again. He looked toward the hall, but she was still upstairs. So she hadn't heard.

He looked at his sticky hands.

"Are you coming to bed?"

He looked at the knife on the floor. His stomach was as tight as a melon. He gulped for some air, tasted the mist of sugar. "Yes, dear."

She said no more, and must have returned to bed in her silly and slinky things. The room would be dark and she would be waiting.

Ricky collected the larger scraps of the watermelon and fed them into the garbage disposal. He swept the floor and scooped up the remaining shreds, then wiped the counter. He wrung out a dish cloth and got on his hands and knees, scrubbing the tiles and then the grout.

The husband had harbored no secrets. A pathetic man who made another person pay for his shortcomings. He was a sick, stupid animal. Ricky would think no more of him, and tomorrow he would throw the newspapers away.

He washed his hands in the sink, put the knife away, and gave the kitchen a cursory examination. No sign of the watermelon remained, and his eyes were dry, and his hands no longer trembled.

Tomorrow, summer would be over. It was the end of something, and the beginning of something else. Maybelle was waiting, and he might get lucky. Ricky went to the stairs and took them one step at a time, up into darkness.

THE MEEK

The ram hit Lucas low, twisting its head so that its curled horns knocked him off his feet. The varmint was good at this. It had killed before. But the dead eyes showed no joy of the hunt, only the black gleam of a hunger that ran wider than the Gibson.

Lucas winced as he sprawled on the ground, tasting desert dust and blood, his hunger forgotten. As the Merino tossed its head, the horns caught the strange sunlight and flashed like knives. Lucas had only a moment to react. He rolled to his left, reaching for his revolver.

The ram lunged forward, its lips parted and slobbering. The mouth closed around the ankle of Lucas' left boot. He kicked and the spur raked across the ram's nose. Gray pus leaked from the torn nostrils, but the steer didn't even slow down in its feeding frenzy.

The massive head dipped again, going higher, looking for Lucas' flank. But Lucas wasn't ready to kark, not out here in the open with nothing but stone and scrub acacia to keep him company. Lucas filled his hand, ready to blow the animal back to hell or wherever else it was these four-legged devils came from.

But he was slow, tired from four days in the saddle and weak from hunger. The tip of one horn knocked the gun from his hand, and he watched it spin silver in the sky before dropping to the sand ten feet away. Eagles circled overhead, waiting to clean what little bit of meat the steer would leave on his bones. He fell back, hoping his leather chaps would stop the teeth from gnawing into his leg.

Just when he was ready to shut his eyes against the coming horror, sharp thunder ripped the sky open. At first he thought it was Gabriel's trumpet, harking and heralding and all that. Then Lucas was covered in the explosion of brain, bits of skull, and goo as the ram's head disappeared. The animal's back legs folded, and then it collapsed slowly upon itself. It fell on its side and twitched once, then lay still, thick fluid dribbling from the stump of its neck.

Gunsmoke filled the air, and the next breath was the sweetest Lucas had ever taken. He sat up and brushed the corrupted mutton from his face, then checked to make sure the animal's teeth hadn't broken his skin. The chaps were intact, with a few new scrapes in the leather.

" 'Bout got you," came a raspy voice. Lucas cupped his hand over his eyes and squinted as a shadow fell over him. The man was bow-legged, his rifle angled with the stock against his hip, the white avalanche beard descending from a Grampian mountain range of a face.

"Thank you, mate," Lucas said, wiping his mouth. "And thank the Lord for His mercy."

The old man kicked at the carcass, and it didn't move. He spat a generous rope of tobacco juice onto the oozing neck wound. Flies had already gathered on the corpse. Lucas hoped that flies didn't turn into flesh-eating critters, too. Having dead-and-back-again sheep coming after you was plenty bad enough.

"A stray. Third one today," the old man said, working the Remington's action so that the spent shell kicked free. He stooped to read the brand on the ram's hip. "Come from Kulgera. They never could keep 'em rounded up down those parts."

Lucas struggled to his feet, sore from the sheep-wrestling. He found his hat and secured it on his head, then returned his revolver to its holster. "If you hadn't come along when you did—"

The man cut in, his eyes bright with held laughter. "Hell, son, I been watching you for five minutes. Wasn't sure which of you was going to walk away. I'd have put two-to-one on the Merino, but nobody much left around to take the bet."

Lucas thought about punching the stranger in the face, but Lucas was afraid his hand would shatter against that stone-slick surface. The man must have seen the anger in Lucas' eyes, because the laugh busted free of the thin lips, rolling across the plateau like the scream of a dying wombat.

"Never you mind," the man said, slapping the barrel of his Remington. "I'd sooner sleep with a brown snake than watch a man get ate up."

He held his hand out. It was wrapped in a glove the color of a chalky mesa, stained a rusty red. Lucas took it and shook quickly, feeling a strength in the grip that didn't match the man's stringy muscles.

"Name's Camp," he said.

"Lucas," Lucas said. "Is 'Camp' short for something?"

"Not that I know of. Just Camp, is all."

"You're not Aussie."

"Hell, no. Come from Texas, U.S. of A. Had to leave 'cause the damned place was perk near run over by Mexicans and Injuns. You know how it is, when the furriners come in and take over, don't you?"

Lucas nodded, and said, "Things are crook in Musclebrook, no doubt." He walked toward his horse twenty yards away, to where it had fallen in a shallow gulley. Camp followed, solemn now. Nobody laughed at the loss of a good horse.

The horse whinnied softly, froth bubbling from its nose. A hank of flesh had been ripped from its side. The saddle strap had broken, tossing Lucas' canteen and lasso into a patch of saltbrush. The horse's tail whisked at the air, swatting invisible flies.

"Never thought I'd see the day a sheep could outrun a horse," Camp said.

"Never thought I'd see a lot of things," Lucas answered.

Camp spat again, and a strand of the brown juice clung to his beard. He was the first person Lucas had ever met who chewed tobacco. "Want to borrow my Remington?" he asked, holding out the rifle.

"Mate's got to do it his own way."

"Reckon so," Camp said, then turned so as not to see the tears in Lucas' eyes.

Lucas drew the revolver and put two bullets in the horse's head. Vickie, he'd called her. Had her for six years, had roped and broken her himself. Now she was nothing but eagle food. But at least she wouldn't rise up tonight, bucking and kicking and hungry for a long mouthful of the hand that had once fed her.

"Where you headed?" Camp asked when they'd reached the top of the gulley.

Lucas scanned the expanse of plateau ahead of them. Finally he shrugged. "I was mostly headed away from something, not toward something."

"Sheep's everywhere now, is the word. Perth, Adelaide, Melbourne, all your big transport cities. They roam the streets scrounging for ever scrap of human cud they can find."

"Even back Queensland?"

"Queensland got it bad. 'Course, them damned banana benders deserve everything they get, and then some." Camp took a plug of tobacco from his shirt pocket that looked like a dry dingo turd. He bit into it with his four best teeth, then worked it until he could spit again. He held out the plug to Lucas.

"No. You're a gent, though." Lucas was thirsty. He took a swig from his canteen, thought about offering a drink to Camp, then shuddered at the thought of the man's backwash polluting the water.

"I'm headed for Wadanetta Pass. Hear word there's a bunch holed up there."

"I didn't know some were trying to fight," Lucas said. "I figured it was every mate for himself."

He hadn't seen another person for three days, at least not one that was alive. He'd passed a lump of slimy dress this morning, a bonnet on the ground beside it. Might have been one of them pub girls, or some schoolmarm fallen from a wagon. The sight had about made him launch a liquid laugh.

"You hungry?" Camp asked.

"Nobody not? What the blooming hell is there to eat out here except weeds and poisoned meat? It was a fair go I'd have ended up eating my horse, and I liked my horse."

"Wadanetta is thataway," Camp said, pointing into the shimmering layers of heat that hung in the west. "Might reach it before night."

"Damn well better. I don't want to be out here in the dark with that bunch playing sillybuggers."

"Amen to that." Camp led the way, moving as if he had a gun trained on his back. It was all Lucas could do to keep up.

They walked in silence for about half an hour. Lucas' feet were burning in his boots. He was about convinced that hell lay only a few feet beneath the plains and that the devil was working up to the biggest jimbuck roundup of all time. First killer sheep, then a sun that glowed like a bloody eye.

"Suppose it's like this all about?" Lucas asked.

"You mean, out Kimberly and all that?"

"New Zealand. Guinea."

"Don't see why not. Sheep are sheep all over the world."

"Even over in England?"

"Bloody hope so."

"Beaut," said Lucas. "That bugger, God, ought to be half sporting, you'd think."

"Hell, them Merino probably would stoop to eating Aborigines. I heared of a country run all by darkies, hardly a white man there. These darkies, they worship cows. I mean, treat them like Jesus Christ come again."

Lucas almost smiled at that one. "Cows likely went over with the sheep. Bet the darkies changed their tune a little by now."

"Them what's left," Camp said, punctuating the sentence with tobacco spit.

They walked on as the sun sank lower and the landscape became a little rougher. A few hills rolled in the distance, dotted with scrub. They came to a creek, and Lucas pointed out the hoof-prints in the muddy banks.

They stopped for a drink and to rest a few minutes, then continued. The sun was an hour from dark when they reached the base of a steep mesa. The cliffs were eroded from centuries of wind and weather. A small group of wooden humpies huddled in the shadow of the mesa.

"Wadanetta, dead ahead," Camp said. They broke into a jog. When they were a hundred yards away from the town, they shouted. Their voices echoed off the stone slopes. Nobody came from the gray buildings to greet them.

"Anybody here?" Lucas yelled as they reached a two-story building that looked like a knock shop. Camp pushed open the door. The parlor was empty, a table knocked over, playing cards spread across the floor. A piano sat in one corner, with a cracked mug on top.

They went inside, and Lucas yelled again. The only answer was the creaking of wood as a sunset wind arose. "Thought you said blokes was here," Lucas said.

"Said I heared it. Hearing and knowing is different things."

Camp walked around the bar and knocked on one of the wooden kegs that lined the shelf. "They left some grog."

He grabbed a mug and drew it full. In the fading light, the lager looked like piss, flat and cloudy. Camp wrinkled his nose and took a drink without bothering to remove his chaw. He swished the ale around and swallowed.

"Any good?" Lucas asked, eyeing the stairs, expecting some grazed-over jackaroo to come stumbling down the stairs with his pants around his ankles.

"Nope," said Camp, but he quickly drained the rest of his glass and refilled it.

Lucas pulled a stool out from the bar and sat down. He thought about trying the ale, but decided against it. Night was nearly here, and he didn't want to be slowed down by drunkenness. "What do we do for a bite?"

"Well, we can't eat no mutton, that's for damned sure."

"I've been eating kangaroo. Hasn't karked me yet, but I used up the last of it a couple of days ago. Thought about killing a rabbit, but it's hard to bang one with a pistol."

"How do you know rabbits don't got it, same as the sheep?"

"Rabbits haven't been eating people."

"Least as far as you know."

Lucas had to nod in agreement.

Camp gulped down another mugful and wiped his mouth on his sleeve. "Nearly time."

Lucas nodded again. "Saw a general store up the street. Might have some rifles and ammo."

Camp pulled another ale, the yeasty stench filling the room. Or maybe it was Camp himself that stank. "You go ahead. I'm aiming to knock back one or two more, to get my nerve up."

Lucas got off the stool and went outside, pausing on the porch to make sure no sheep had strayed from the herd. The sun was almost gone now, the west streaked with purple and pink rags. It had been three weeks since Lucas had last watched a sunset without dread crawling through his bones. Three weeks since a sheep was just a sheep. Things go full-on berko real fast.

He went up the street, his hand on the butt of his revolver. Something rustled in an alley to his left. He spun and drew, his hand trembling. A crumpled hat blew out into the street. He sagged in relief.

He shook like a blue-assed fly in a windstorm. He pulled the brim of his hat low over his eyes, glad no one was around to see him like this. Word got around fast when a fellow broke down.

A small rise of land to the left was bathed in the dying sunlight. A few wooden crosses still stood askew, but the picket fence marking off the cemetery had been trampled into ruin. Wadanetta's boneyard had been plowed up by gut-hungry sheep. Lucas pictured a whole herd of them, pawing and snorting to bust into those pine boxes and get at the goods inside.

He hurried to the general store. It was just as desolate as the knock shop had been. Cobwebs hung on the shelves, but he found a few blankets and a box of bullets for the revolver. All the rifles were gone. Some money was left in the register. Lucas didn't take it.

Camp staggered into the store, his Remington over his shoulder. "Could have told you they'd be no rifles," he said, his words slurred. "I took the last one."

"Bloody hell? You been here before?"

"We'd best get over to the jail. Sheep smell us, they'll be going crazy. They might be able to climb stairs, I don't know. But they sure as hell can't bust through steel bars."

They went into the street again, Camp leading the way. A soft bleating swept in from across the plateau. It was followed by another, then more of the man-eating sheep raised their voices.

"Ever wonder who's riding herd on them things?" Camp asked, not slowing.

Lucas looked behind them and saw a dust cloud roiling on the horizon. Appeared to be several hundred of them. The drum of hoofbeats filled the air. He hoped the jail was well-built.

"I mean, you figure it's the devil or something?" Camp said, belching. "A sister from Lady of the Faith Church told me them which don't repent would have the devil to pay someday. Figure maybe someday's finally here?"

"I don't deadcert know," Lucas said, his voice thin from fright. Darkness was settling like molasses, clogging Lucas' lungs and tightening his throat. He saw the jail and almost wept in relief. It was brick, squat, and solid, with iron bars across the windows.

Camp pulled a key from his pocket and opened the thick wooden door. A pungent odor struck Lucas like a fist. The stink reminded him of something, but the hoofbeats were so much louder now that they filled his senses, bounced around in his skull, drove every thought from his brain but the thought of sanctuary.

He stumbled into the dark room and Camp closed the door behind them. Camp dropped a crossbar into place, then shook it in its hasps. "Safe as milk," he said. "Let's see them woolly-eyed buggers bust into here."

Lucas bumped into a table. He ran his hands over its surface. Something fell to the floor and glass shattered. Flies buzzed around his head.

"Damn," Camp said. "You busted my lamp."

The stench was stronger, so thick that Lucas could barely breathe. The herd was closer now, stampeding into Wadanetta, a hundred haunted bahs bleating from bottomless mouths.

Camp's voice came from somewhere near the wall. "I like to watch them come in," he said. "They's something lovely about it. 'Specially when the moon's up, and all them eyes are sparkling."

Lucas put his hands over his ears, squeezing tight to drive out the noises of the stampede. He thought of all the people who had filled those bellies, who had been stomped and ground into haggis, who had served as leg of lamb for this devil's herd. The first of the horns rattled off the brick. The building shook, but Camp laughed.

"They can't get us in here," the old man shouted over the din. "You'd figure the dumb bastards would quit trying. But night after night they come back. Guess I ought to quit encouraging them."

A match flared. Camp's face showed in the orange circle of light. He was beside the window, grinning, his rotted teeth like mossy tombstones. The Remington was pointed at Lucas' heart.

Lucas forgot about the sheep. He'd had guns pointed at him a time or two before. But never like this, with his guard so far down. He was in no shape for a quick draw.

"Don't try it," Camp said. "You might be fast, maybe not, but you're not likely faster than a bullet."

Horn and snout hammered against the window bars. Camp put the bobbing matchlight to the end of a candle. The room grew a little brighter, and Lucas saw what stank so badly.

Naked bodies, three of them, hanging upside down inside one of the cells. Chains were wrapped around their ankles. One of them might have been a woman, judging from the swells in the red rags of flesh, but Lucas couldn't be sure. His heartbeat matched the rumble of the herd outside.

"Remember out there, when I rescued you, and I said I don't like to see a man get ate up?" Camp said, his voice as low and sinister as that of the sheep. "Don't like to let good meat go to waste, seeing as how it's getting so scarce and all. This free-range hunting is hell on an old man like me."

Camp sat on a chair, the rifle barrel steady. Lucas held his hands apart. He could see the tabletop, scarred and pitted, a dark and thick liquid on it. A nun's habit was folded over the back of a chair.

"Our Sister of the Lady of the Faith," Camp said, picking at his teeth with a thumbnail. "Mighty good eating. Figure it's the pureness of the flesh what makes it so sweet."

Lucas wouldn't have minded going down from a bullet. In fact, he'd always suspected that's the way he'd meet the Lord. Beat getting eaten by a Merino any day. But to know that this greasy bugger would be carving him into dinner portions was more than he could stomach.

"Hell, it's the way of things," Camp said, tilting back in his chair. "People eat sheep, then sheep eat people. What's so wrong about people eating people?"

Something slammed against the door, and two horn tips poked from the wood beneath the crossbar. Camp turned to look, and Lucas knew it was time. He rolled to his left, filling his hand with his oldest friend the revolver, and squeezed off three rounds without thinking. Camp gave a gasp of pain and the Remington clattered to the floor.

Lucas lifted himself up and blew the smoke from the revolver's barrel. Camp slumped in the chair, holes in his chest. The scent of fresh blood aroused the herd, and heads butted frantically against the brick walls. Camp's eyes flickered, the light in them dying like the last stars of morning.

Lucas wondered how long the herd would mill around. Daylight usually made them get scarce, but one or two of the orneriest would probably hang around. Maybe they'd get rewarded for their trouble, if they just happened to find some fresh meat out on the porch. One thing for sure, Camp would be nothing but gristle and rawhide. Hardly worth fooling with.

Lucas sat at the table. He'd heard that other people had turned to it, but the thought had sickened him. Until he'd run out of kangaroo. Hardly seemed unreasonable anymore, even for a man who followed the Lord. Camp's logic of the food chain fit right in with these balls-up times. And his stomach was squealing with all the intensity of a fresh-branded sheep.

Camp had been a fine butcher. The meat was thin and tender. Lucas stuck Camp's butcher knife into a slice and held it under his nose, checking its scent. Hell, not much different from mutton, when you got right down to it. His belly ached from need, and he wondered if that's how the sheep felt.

He chewed thoughtfully. The taste wasn't worth savoring, but it wasn't so terrible that he spat it out. He speared a second piece and held it up to the candlelight.

"You know, Sister," he addressed the meat. "Maybe you were right. Someday might just be here after all."

Maybe the Good Book was right, too, that the meek were busy inheriting the earth at this very moment. Lucas figured it would be humble and proper to offer up a word of prayerful thanks. He bowed his head in silence, then continued with the meal that the Holy Father had provided.

Outside, in the dark ghost town of Wadanetta, the chorus of sheep voiced its eternal hunger.

THE ROCKING CHAIR

he rocking chair was out of place in the nursery.

Darla had spent two weeks painting the walls a warm sky blue, complete with clouds and bordered with rainbow wallpaper. The nursery was nearly free of all the toys, clothes, and blankets that Darla had accumulated during her first pregnancy. The patchwork quilt with "Veronica" stitched in a crooked cursive, given to them by Allen's grandmother, was packed away with the other things. The crib had been trundled off to the Salvation Army, and a varnished cradle had been bought in its place. Even the carpet was new, of an off-peach color that Darla hoped would disguise stains better.

Allen had supported her in her wanton act of forgetting, had been right beside her during the funeral, had patiently waited for her to recover enough to try again. They opened a credit account at the hardware store so she could fill her days with window treatments, shelves, and picture hangers instead of memories. He had been a nearly perfect husband. Except for insisting on the damned rocking chair.

"It's a family heirloom," he said.

"It's old," Darla said. With her hands on her hips, she had to lean backwards so that her swollen tummy didn't cause her to slouch.

Allen let his tape measure slide into its sheath. He was wearing one of his weekend, beer-drinking T-shirts and the armpits were damp. The room was warm, the heat from their bodies stronger than the draft from the window.

"I know you want everything to be new," Allen said. "But this means so much to Grandma."

"It's nice that your family is involved, but shouldn't I matter more than she?"

"Honey, she's not going to live much longer. Why can't you make an old woman happy in her last days?"

"Seems like you'd rather make your wife happy. I'm the one who has to sleep with you."

"This is a valuable antique," Allen said. "Six generations of Benson babies have been rocked in this chair."

The scarred chair sat under the window like a stubborn old relative. The cherry arms and seat were worn smooth. The wooden pegs, used in place of nails, made dark circles where the pieces joined. The back slats didn't quite match, each one carved by some forgotten Benson's hands. Benson, Benson, Benson. Six generations, how many babies?

Darla said, "But the chair was here when—"

Silence fought the heat for domination of the room. Allen stared out the window.

"...when she slept here," Darla finished.

She didn't say "died." Funny how you could play tricks with words, especially tricks on yourself.

"That's over and done with," Allen said. "We promised we were starting over, like nothing ever happened."

"Which is exactly why we need to get rid of the chair."

Allen sighed.

"I don't mean junk it," Darla said. "I mean just put it away for a few years. Or we can give it back to your grandmother."

"Yeah, she'll really love that." Allen's upper lip curled in sarcasm. "After all she's done for us."

"I don't care that she paid your way through law school. In fact, I'm tired of hearing about it." Darla caught her voice rising, wondered what the angry adrenaline was doing to the fetus.

She took a deep breath to calm herself. "We don't have to tell her, Allen."

"She'll know."

"No, she won't. We can hide it in the attic, bring it out when she comes over, if that will make you happy." There. An olive branch. Darla didn't want to fight with Allen when the delivery date was so near. She needed him.

Allen moved over to the rocker, put his hand on the back support, and gave it a small push. The chair eased back and forth on its runners, tilting slightly to the right on its forward swings. The soft squeak of its movement almost seemed to whisper, "Ben-son, Ben-son, Ben-son."

"Don't try to push my family out of it," Allen said. "I know you don't like Grandma, but she's all I've got left since Momma died."

"Except me. You still have *me*, remember?" She hated herself for sounding whiny, knowing Allen was faithful, that his loyalty was part of what made him a good mate, but her emotions were screwed up by the flood of hormones coursing through her system. She'd never wanted to be the clingy, harping wife, but here she was, bitching about a stupid chair.

"Don't forget, this baby is half Benson," Allen said.

Darla looked at the teeth marks on the back of the chair, perhaps put there a hundred years ago by a small, dark-eyed Benson. She closed her eyes. If only she could tell Allen the real truth.

Because the real truth sounded even stupider than in-law jealousy.

The real truth was that the chair *scared* her, made her skin crawl every time she saw it. The one time she'd sat in it, right before going to the hospital the last time, she'd felt as if long fingers had snaked inside her, had caressed her belly, had gently squeezed the seven-pound creature that would soon be born.

She hadn't said anything, of course not, such delusions would lock a person into years of therapy. And any decent therapist could get inside your head and find enough wrong to turn you into a career customer.

She hadn't told Allen about the day Veronica died, how Darla had come into the nursery and found the little baby burning up with fever, a pool of vomit by its mouth, everything happening so fast that even now she could almost convince herself she'd imagined it.

The chair. Rocking by itself.

But surely that hadn't happened, she'd been panicked by her baby's faint, flushed features and shallow breathing, no way could she have heard the soft whisper of the chair moving back and forth, whispering "Ben-son, Ben-son, Ben-son."

"Half Benson," Darla said. "But half mine, too."

"Look, honey, let's not fight. This is no good for you. The baby's both of ours."

Both of ours. Darla had hidden her true feelings about the chair. But she'd kept other secrets from Allen as well.

She nodded, guilt making her blush. "Okay," she said. "The chair can stay for now."

Allen grinned, looking as boyish as he had in college when they'd first met. He came over and hugged her, exaggerating the effort required to wrap his arms around her belly. "A growing family," he said, kissing her on the lips.

On Monday, when Allen headed out on his morning commute, Darla went to the adjoining townhouse and tapped on the back door. A curtain parted, a bearded face frowned, and the door swung open. Even though they'd swapped keys, Wallace was peculiar about his privacy. Darla glanced at the neighboring balconies before entering.

The morning sun shone through the kitchen windows, the sink gleaming and spotless, the tiled floor an anchor of domesticity. She poured herself a cup of coffee.

"That's bad for the baby," Wallace said.

"I thought you didn't care."

"I never said that." He poured himself a cup of coffee, added two teaspoons of sugar. They sat at the kitchen table. From her seat,

Darla could see the computer screen in the living room bright with the phosphor of Wallace's work.

She would never have married a writer. The income was too unreliable, they were too insufferably moody and self-absorbed. But they made perfect lovers. Home during the day, only too happy to have an excuse to escape the keyboard, clever with the pleasing phrases during lovemaking.

Or was it love? What exactly had they been making these past two years? Besides babies, that was?

"You just want everybody to be happy," she said. "Happy ever after. Damned Hollywood endings."

Wallace's dark eyes flashed briefly, and a small thrill of triumph surged through Darla. Wallace was usually so cold, so distant, rarely showing emotion outside of the bedroom. "You wanted it this way," he said. "And I promised to let this thing go the way you wanted."

"But it's your child. Doesn't that mean a damned thing to you?"

He took a sip of coffee. "Not as long as my name's not on the birth certificate."

"You bastard." She raised her coffee cup, about to dash the hot liquid into his face, but his smile stopped her.

He reached out and took her wrist, lowered her cup to the table. He squeezed so hard that she was afraid he'd leave bruises. She didn't need more mysterious marks to explain away.

"Look," he said. "You want children. Your loving hubby does, too. I don't."

"He works hard, he's good to me. Tender, gentle, and—"

"And boring as hell. What does an estate lawyer make these days? Two hundred grand? Three? Listen to yourself, sitting here selling your lover on your husband's good qualities."

His teeth were crooked, giving him a feral look. That aura about him, his wildness, that hint of danger, had attracted her, lured her into becoming chatty neighbors during her slow, quiet days as a childless housewife. Without her really being able to pinpoint a change, the chats had led to the bedroom, and the bedroom led to Veronica. And now this new one.

Oh, she could have insisted on birth control, but she wanted a baby. She and Allen had been trying for three years. And the joy on Allen's face when she told him she was pregnant that first time...

"I didn't come over here to fight."

"Sure. That's the other thing you don't get enough of at home." Wallace let go of her wrist, his eyes daring her to splash the coffee.

She looked away. "I came to tell you about the rocking chair."

"Rocking chair?"

"In the nursery. You know how I wanted it to be all new, so we could forgot about what happened to Veronica?"

"Don't ever say that name again."

"But she was yours."

"No, dear. Possession is a voluntary state. Things belong to those that own them, and those that own them belong to the things."

Damned writer. Always coming up with those deep, meaningless sayings. "The rocking chair was given to us by Allen's grandmother. When Veronica—when *she*—died, the chair was rocking by itself. I saw it."

Wallace leaned so far back in his chair that Darla thought he was going to tip over. Instead, he laughed. "A haunted chair?"

"It knew," she said. "I swear, it knew that the baby wasn't Allen's, and it's been in his family forever, and—"

Wallace laughed harder, even as tears gathered in the corners of her eyes. "A chair that came back from somebody else's grave," he said. "Sounds like something those hack assholes King or Koontz would write."

Darla wiped her eyes, finally seeing an opening, an oozing wound where she could dig, the only weakness in the steel that encased Wallace. "If you could write half as well as those 'hacks,' I wouldn't have to slip you Allen's money to keep your rent paid."

Wallace stood and knocked over his chair. He stormed into the living room, hunched over the computer, and clicked a couple of keys. "Fifty-seven pages," he said. "Who gives a damn if I delete them?"

She hurried to him, put a hand on his shoulder, pulled him around to face her. "I'm sorry, hon. You're as good as those guys. You'll make it someday, and Wallace Hatcher will take up three shelves in every bookstore."

He patted her stomach. "Looks like I'm not the only Hatcher. That's a pun, in case you didn't get it, my dim-witted sex slave."

"Bastard," she said, kissing him. The odor of his Kenyan coffee-and-cigarette breath inspired simultaneous queasiness and desire. The smell was all Wallace.

In his bed, after the second time, she stared at the ceiling as he rubbed her belly. "How does it really make you feel?" she asked.

"I don't know."

"I thought you writers always had a line handy."

"I want you to be happy."

"Cheap."

"Okay, how about 'I want you both to be happy.' Is that noble enough?"

"Boy, you're creepy."

"As creepy as a haunted chair?" He took his hand away. "You know this will be the end, don't you?"

"The end?"

"Of us. You're going to feel guilty, then decide the only way you can redeem yourself is to dedicate your life to your family. No more sneaking over to play Boff-the-Bard."

"No. I love you. I never asked you to love me back, but I can't lie to myself."

"Sure you can. You're a born liar and you're getting better with practice."

Darla pushed him away, turned and faced the wall, staring at his Hemingway poster. "Bastard."

"A baby will definitely come between us. Just like after the first. You never came over. Until she…went away."

"I thought you never wanted to talk about it again."

"Oh, it's a survival mechanism. Family planning, you might say. Because when sweetie goes away, starts devoting herself to changing diapers and visiting the pediatrician and having hubby's supper on the table when he walks through the door, well, the money will go away soon after. You won't need a kept man because you'll be busy keeping the one you married."

"Wallace Hatcher, you're a real son of a bitch."

"Because I know you far too well."

"Oh, God." Darla froze, tensed. She took his hand from her breast and put it on her stomach. "Do you feel that?"

"No."

The twitch came again, harder this time. The real thing, not Braxton-Hicks. She rolled out of bed, then bent with effort to retrieve her clothes from the floor. "I'd better call Allen."

Susannah Hart Benson came home that Friday. Everybody at the hospital said she had her father's eyes. Allen's grandma said the child was Benson through and through, and then she embarked on a recitation of Benson genealogy, from her own mother Veronica, back through the twins Hannah and Susannah, then to Luke, Mark, and a host of other Biblical names.

Of course, Darla had let Allen pick the child's name. It was only natural he'd choose one of the family favorites. Rocking chairs, names, money, everything had to be Benson in his family.

"Oh, Susannah, don't you cry for me," Allen sang in off-key giddiness, as Darla leaned over the changing table and checked her daughter's diaper.

Wallace had come over for the occasion, "to help the new member of the family get settled," he'd said when Allen answered the door. Grandma Benson was there, too, just as she'd been on hand to help when Veronica came home. Grandma stood by the rocking chair.

"Been a long time," Grandma said. "But, finally, it's seven generations of Bensons for this old rocking chair."

"No, it's not," Wallace said. "Not officially. Darla hasn't sat in it with her yet."

Darla shot him as harsh a look as she dared. Allen was also staring at Wallace. Allen rarely mentioned their neighbor, considering him a deadbeat who could use a trip to the barber. But now he seemed pleased to have an ally.

"Why not?" Allen said. "Come on, honey."

Allen rolled his eyes toward Grandma as if to say to Darla, *This will make her happy, and then we can put away the chair like you wanted.*

Darla backed away, clutching the baby to her chest. She could feel the milk leaking from her nipples and wondered if the stains showed. "Not right now, I'm feeling a little…a little dizzy."

Allen came to her and took her elbow to give support. Grandma said, "All the more reason to sit down for a spell."

Then, to Allen, Grandma said, "I can remember the hours and hours I spent rocking your dear Momma, God rest her soul. Got troubles, rock them away, I say."

"Rock them away, Darla," Wallace said gleefully. "Welcome that child into the Benson family."

They were blocking Darla's path to the door, all of them smiling, and Darla hugged the baby tighter. What could she do? Tell them all that the chair was going to get her, was going to take the baby away, was Benson through and through? That the chair was going to chew her up with its wooden teeth, then swallow her and the child, and spit only one of them back into the land of the living?

Allen's eyebrows arched in concern. "Honey, you really do look flushed. Just sit down for a minute. *Please*."

He tried to take the baby but she turned away. Their eyes, their smiles, they all *knew*. They were closing in, backing her toward the rocking chair, into the ancient cherry that had mingled with and absorbed so much of that Benson flesh over the years.

Now she really did feel faint. Just before her legs collapsed, she sat.

She tried to scream, but the wind died in her lungs. The baby squirmed between her breasts, sensing mother's panic. Grandma stood over them, breath smelling of denture paste. Wallace folded his arms, victorious in this latest cruel game.

Allen knelt beside Darla, feeling her forehead. "Maybe we should get you back to the doctor."

"No, I'm fine," she said.

And she was. Because nothing had happened. The chair was only wood, old cherry, nicked, pocked, rubbed smooth by a hundred Bensons. Not a monster. Only a chair.

She looked up at the "family" gathered around her, then kissed

Susannah's forehead. She leaned slowly forward, then rested back, pushed again, gathered momentum. Grandma clasped her shriveled hands together, eyes misted by tears and cataracts.

The chair's runners squeaked the Benson name as Darla laughed at her foolish delusions. Allen beamed like a proud papa, seeing her evident relief. Everything would be okay. Wallace was still a jerk, but this would work out. Susannah would be a Benson, Darla would have her family and her lover, Grandma would have her descendant, and Allen could keep his goddamned chair that was nothing but wood and scars.

Allen was in the middle of an estate war and couldn't take time off from work. Grandma stayed on for a few days. Grandma had stayed with Veronica, too. Up until the end.

Darla wanted the baby to sleep in the bed with she and Allen, but Allen said that was too dangerous. A baby could get smothered, a sleeping parent could crush her little lungs, a pillow could fall over her face. Too many things could go wrong. Better to let her sleep in her own bed. That's why they'd bought the cradle, after all.

They kept the cradle in the bedroom the first four nights, but Darla had awakened every twenty minutes to check on Susannah. Allen made her move the cradle into the nursery because Darla was so exhausted she could hardly feed the baby. As helpful as Grandma was, she couldn't provide breast milk. So Susannah ended up in the nursery, where the rocking chair waited under the window.

The day Allen started back to work, Darla settled down for a nap on the sofa. She'd left Grandma in the nursery with the baby, the old woman rocking in the Benson chair and singing "Bye Baby Bunting." Darla felt as if she'd hardly closed her eyes when a hand tugged her shoulder.

She looked up into Wallace's face.

"You're not supposed to let yourself into the house," Darla said, bleary. "What if Allen were home?"

"I saw Hubby Dearest drive away."

"How long have you been here?"

"Long enough. I'm getting lonely. And horny."

"Be patient. The doctor told me four weeks. You don't won't to tear my episiotomy stitches, do you? How would I explain that to Allen?"

"Tell him you cut yourself shaving."

"You're still a bastard, aren't you?"

"Just the way you like me. Is the old bat still here, the Underworld's answer to Mother Theresa?"

Darla smiled. "She can't keep her hands off the baby. Her first great-grandchild."

"Not her first."

"The other one didn't count."

"If she only knew—"

"—she'd probably claw your eyeballs out. Now get out of here before she sees you." Darla gave Wallace a peck on the cheek. He grabbed her chin and kissed her hard, sliding his tongue in her mouth as she tried to wriggle away.

"Hey, I'm a happily married woman," she whispered when the kiss ended.

They heard a noise behind them. Darla turned. "Guh-Grandma?"

Darla waved Wallace away. He sauntered through the kitchen toward the back door. She pulled her nightgown closed and hurried down the hall. She heard a door close.

Oh, God, Allen hadn't come home, had he?

She took the stairs, out of breath by the time she reached the top. She glanced out the window. The drive was empty. She gasped in relief and headed for the nursery.

"Grandma?"

Darla could tell something was wrong before she even entered the room.

She didn't even have to look in the cradle to know. It was too perfectly still to hold any life. The cradle was dead silent, hushed, quiet as a coffin.

The air in the room was heavy as grave dirt. The world shrank, condensed to a series of broken senses: sunlight streaming through the window, Grandma answering in a concerned voice from down the hall, shivers drawing her skin tight, Wallace's kiss drying on her lips.

The empty rocking chair wobbled back and forth. Its runners whispered a family name, a name that owned the chair, a name that the chair possessed.

Except this time the rockers whispered "Hat-cher, Hat-cher, Hat-cher."

THE WEIGHT OF SILENCE

ilence wasn't golden, Katie thought. *If silence were any metal, it would be lead: gray, heavy, toxic after prolonged exposure.* Silence weighed upon her in the house, even with the television in the living room blasting a Dakota-Madison-Dirk love triangle, even with the radio upstairs tuned to New York's big-block classic rock, even with the windows open to invite the hum and roar from the street outside. Even with all that noise, Katie heard only the silence. Especially in the one room.

The room she had painted sky blue and world green. The one where tiny clothes, blankets, and oversized books lined the shelves. Wooden blocks had stood stacked in the corner, bought because Katie herself had wooden blocks as a child. She'd placed a special order for them. Most of the toys were plastic these days. Cheaper, more disposable.

Safer.

For the third time that morning, she switched on the monitor system that Peter had installed. A little bit of static leaked from the speaker. She turned her head so that her ear would be closer. Too much silence.

Stop it, Katie. You know you shouldn't be doing this to yourself.

Of course she should know it. That's all she heard lately. The only voices that broke through the silence were those saying, "You shouldn't be doing this to yourself." Or else the flip side of that particular little greatest hit, a remake of an old standard, "Just put it behind you and move on."

Peter said those things. Katie's mom chimed in as well. So did the doctors, the first one with a droopy mustache who looked as if he were into self-medication, the next an anorexic analyst who was much too desperate to find a crack in Katie's armor.

But the loudest voice of all was her own. That unspoken voice that led the Shouldn't-Be chorus. The voice that could never scream away the silence. The voice that bled and cried and sang sad, tuneless songs.

She clicked the monitor off. She hadn't really expected to hear anything. She knew better. She was only testing herself, making sure that it was true, that she was utterly and forever destroyed.

I feel FAIRLY destroyed. Perhaps I'm as far as QUITE. But UTTERLY, hmm, I think I have miles to go before I reach an adverb of such extremity and finality.

No. "Utterly" wasn't an adverb. It was a noun, a state of existence, a land of bleak cliffs and dark waters. And she knew how to enter that land.

She headed for the stairs. One step up at a time. Slowly. Her legs knew the routine. How many trips over the past three weeks? A hundred? More?

She reached the hall, then the first door on the left. Peter had closed it tightly this morning on his way to work. Peter kept telling her to stop leaving the door open at night. But Katie had never left the door open, not since—

Leaving the door open would fall under the category of *utterly.* And Katie wasn't *utterly.* At least not yet. She touched the door handle.

It was cold. Ice cold, grave cold, as cold as a cheek when—
You shouldn't be doing this to yourself.

But she already was. She turned the knob, the sound of the latch like an avalanche in the hush of a snowstorm. The door swung inward. Peter had oiled the hinges, because he said nothing woke a sleeping baby faster than squeaky hinges.

The room was still too blue, still far too verdant. Maybe she should slap on another coat, something suitably dismal and drab. This wasn't a room of air and life. This was a room of silence.

Because silence crowded this room like death crowded a coffin. Even though Led Zeppelin's "Stairway To Heaven" jittered forth from the bedroom radio across the hall, even though the soap opera's music director was sustaining a tense organ chord, even though Katie's heart was rivaling John Bonham's bass beat, this room was owned by silence. The absence of sound hit Katie like a tidal wave, slapped her about the face, crushed the wind from her lungs. It smothered her.

It accused her.

She could still see the impressions that the four crib legs had made in the carpet. Peter had taken apart the crib while she was still in the hospital, trundled it off to some charity. He'd wanted to remove as many reminders as possible, so she could more quickly forget. But the one thing he couldn't remove was the memory that was burned into her eyes.

And any time, like now, that she cared to try for *utterly*, all she had to do was pull the vision from somewhere behind her eyelids, rummage in that dark mental closet with its too-flimsy lock. All those nights of coming in this room, bending over, smiling in anticipation of that sinless face with its red cheeks, sniffing to see if the diaper were a one or a two, reaching to feel the small warmth.

And then the rest of it.

Amanda pale. Amanda's skin far too cool. Amanda not waking, ever.

Katie blinked away the memory and left the room, so blinded by tears that she nearly ran into the doorjamb. She closed the door behind her, softly, because silence was golden and sleeping babies didn't cry. Her tears hadn't dried by the time Peter came home.

He took one look at her, then set his briefcase by the door as if it were fireman's gear and he might have to douse the flames of a stock run. "You were in there again, weren't you?"

She stared ahead, thanking God for television. The greatest invention ever for avoiding people's eyes. Now if only the couch would swallow her.

"I'm going to buy a damned deadbolt for that room," he said, going straight to the kitchen for the martini waiting in the freezer. Mixed in the morning to brace himself for the effort of balancing vermouth and gin all evening. He made his usual trek from the refrigerator to the computer, sat down, and was booted up before he spoke again.

"You shouldn't be doing this to yourself," he said.

Julia debated thumbing up the volume on the television remote. No. That would only make him yell louder. Let him lose himself in his online trading.

"How was your day?" she asked.

"Somewhere between suicide and murder," he said. "The tech stocks fell off this afternoon. Had clients reaming out my ear over the phone."

"They can't blame you for things that are out of your control," she said. She didn't understand how the whole system worked, people trading bits of paper and hope, all of it seeming remote from the real world and money.

"Yeah, but they pay me to know," Peter said, the martini already two-thirds vanished, his fingers going from keyboard to mouse and back again. "Any idiot can guess or play a hunch. But I'm supposed to outperform the market."

"I'm going to paint the nursery."

"Damn. SofTech dropped another three points."

Peter used to bring Amanda down in the mornings, have her at his feet while he caught up on the overnight trading in Japan. He would let Katie have an extra half-hour's sleep. But the moment Amanda started crying, Peter would hustle her up the stairs, drop her between Katie's breasts, and head back to the computer. "Can't concentrate with her making that racket," was one of his favorite sayings.

Katie suddenly pictured one of those "dial-and-say" toys, where you pulled the string and the little arrow spun around. If Peter had made the toy, it would stop on a square and give one of his half-dozen patented lines: "You shouldn't be doing this to yourself" or "Just put it behind you and move on" or "We can always try again later, when you're over it."

"I was reading an article today," she said. "It said SIDS could be caused by—"

"I told you to stop with those damned parenting magazines."

SIDS could be caused by several things. Linked to smoking, bottle feeding, stomach-sleeping, overheating. Or nothing at all. There were reports of mothers whose babies had simply stopped breathing while being held.

Sometimes babies died for no apparent reason, through nobody's fault. The doctors had told her so a dozen times.

Then why couldn't she put it behind her?

Because Amanda had Katie's eyes. Even dead, even swaddled under six feet of dirt, even with eyelids butterfly-stitched in eternal slumber, those eyes stared through the earth and sky and walls to pierce Katie. They peeked in dreams and they blinked in those long black stretches of insomnia and they peered in from the windows of the house.

Those begging, silent eyes.

The eyes that, on dark nights when Peter was sound asleep, watched from the nursery.

No, Katie, that's no way to think. Babies don't come back, not when they're gone. Just think of her as SLEEPING.

Katie changed channels. Wheel of Fortune. Suitably vapid. Peter's fingers clicked over some keys, another fast-breaking deal.

She glanced at him, his face bright from the glow of the computer screen. He didn't look like a millionaire. Neither did she. But they were, or soon would be. As soon as the insurance money came in.

She almost hated Peter for that. Always insuring everything to the max. House, cars, people. They each had million-dollar life policies, and he'd insisted on taking one out for Amanda.

"It's not morbid," he'd said. "Think of it as life's little lottery tickets."

And even with the million due any day now, since the medical examiner had determined that the death was natural, Peter still had to toy with those stocks. As addicted as any slot-machine junkie. He'd scarcely had time for sorrow. He hadn't even cried since the funeral.

But then, Peter knew how to get over it, how to put it behind him.

"I'm going up," she said. "I'm tired."

"Good, honey. You should get some rest." Not looking away from the screen.

Katie went past him, not stooping for a kiss. He'd hardly even mentioned the million.

She went up the stairs, looked at the door to the nursery. She shuddered, went into the bedroom, and turned off the radio. A faint hissing filled the sonic void, like air leaking from a tire. The monitor.

She could have sworn she'd turned it off. Peter would be angry if he knew she'd been listening in on the nursery again. But Peter was downstairs. The silence from the empty room couldn't bother him.

Only her. She sat on the bed and listened for the cries that didn't come, for the tiny coos that melted a mother's heart, for the squeals that could mean either delight or hunger. Amanda. A month old. So innocent.

And Katie, so guilty. The doctors said it wasn't her fault, but what did they know? All they saw were blood tests, autopsy reports, charts, the evidence after the fact. They'd never held the living, breathing Amanda in their arms.

The medical examiner had admitted that crib death was a "diagnosis of exclusion." A label they stuck on the corpse of a baby when no other cause was found. She tried not to think of the ME in the autopsy room, running his scalpel down the line of Amanda's tiny chest.

Katie stood, her heart pounding. Had that been a cry? She strained to hear, but the monitor only vomited its soft static. Its accusing silence.

She switched off the monitor, fingers trembling.

If she started hearing sounds now, little baby squeaks, the rustle of small blankets, then she might start screaming and never stop. She might go *utterly*, beyond the reach of those brightly colored pills the doctors had prescribed. She got under the blankets and buried her head beneath the pillows.

Peter came up after an hour or so. He undressed without speaking, slid in next to her, his body cold. He put an arm around her.

"Honey?" he whispered. "You awake?"

She nodded in the darkness.

"SofTech closed with a gain." His breath reeked of alcohol, though his speech wasn't slurred.

"Good for you, honey," she whispered.

"I know you've been putting off talking about it, but we really need to."

Could she? Could she finally describe the dead hollow in her heart, the horror of a blue-skinned baby, the monstrous memory of watching emergency responders trying to resuscitate Amanda?

"Do we have to?" she asked. She choked on tears that wouldn't seep from her eyes.

"Nothing will bring her back." He paused, the wait made larger by the silence. "But we still need to do something about the money."

Money. A million dollars against the life of her child.

He hurried on before she could get mad or break down. "We really should invest it, you know. Tech stocks are a little uneven right now, but I think they're going to skyrocket in the next six months. We might be able to afford to move out of the city."

She stiffened and turned away from him.

"Christ, Katie. You really should put it behind you."

"That article on SIDS," she said. "There's a link between smog levels and sudden infant death."

"You're going to make yourself crazy if you keep reading that stuff," he said. "Sometimes, things just happen." He caressed her shoulder. "We can always try again later, you know."

She responded with silence, a ten-ton nothingness that could crush even the strongest flutters of hope. Peter eventually gave up, his hand sliding from her shoulder, and was soon snoring.

Katie awoke at three, in the dead stillness of night. A mother couldn't sleep through the crying of her baby. As she had so many nights after the birth, she dragged herself out of bed and went to the nursery. They should have put the crib in their bedroom, but Peter said they'd be okay with the monitor on.

Katie's breasts had quit leaking over a week ago, but now they ached with longing. She closed her robe over them and went into the hall, quietly so that Peter could get his sleep. She opened the door and saw the eyes. The small eyes burned bright with hunger, need, love, loss. Questions.

Katie went to them in the dark, and leaned over the crib. The small mouth opened, wanting air. The light flared on, stealing her own breath.

"What are you doing in here?" Peter said.

"I...couldn't sleep." She looked down at the empty carpet, at the small marks where the crib legs had rested.

Maybe if she cried.

"We should paint this room," Peter said.

She went to him, sagged against his chest as he hugged her. After she was through sobbing, he led her to the bedroom. He fell asleep again, but she couldn't. Behind her eyelids lived that small, gasping mouth and those two silent, begging eyes.

As she listened to the rhythm of Peter's breathing, she recalled the line from that movie, the cop thriller that they'd gone to see when she was seven months' pregnant. The tough plainclothes detective, who looked like a budget Gene Hackman, had said, "There's only two ways to get away with murder: kill yourself, or put a plastic bag over a baby's head."

What a horrible thing to say, she'd thought at the time. Only a jerk Hollywood writer would come up with something like that, so callous and thoughtless. Peter had later apologized for suggesting the movie.

"Is it really true?" she'd asked. "About the plastic bag?"

"Who knows?" he'd said. "I guess they do research when they write those things. Just forget about it."

Sure. She'd put that behind her, too. She wondered if Peter had been able to forget it.

He had taken out the insurance policy for Amanda a week after her birth. Peter had always wanted to be a millionaire. That's why he played the market. He wanted to hit one jackpot in his life.

She turned on the lamp and studied Peter's face.

Amanda had some of his features. The arch of the eyebrows, the fleshy earlobes, the small chin. But Amanda's eyes had been all Katie. When those silent eyes looked imploringly out from Katie's memory, it was like looking into a mirror.

Katie shuddered and blinked away the vision of that small stare. She pressed her face against the pillow, mimicking a suffocation. No. She wouldn't be able to smother herself.

She wrestled with the sheets. Peter was sweating, even though he wore only pajama bottoms. She pulled the blanket from him. He sleepily tugged back, oblivious.

She must have fallen asleep, dreamed. Amanda at the window, brushing softly against the screen. Katie rising from the bed, pressing her face against the cold glass. Amanda floating in the night, eyes wide, flesh blue, lips moving in senseless baby talk. The sounds muffled by the plastic bag over her head.

When Katie awoke, Peter was in the bathroom, getting ready for work. He was humming. He was an ace at putting things behind him. You'd scarcely have known that he'd lost a daughter.

Why couldn't she show an equally brave face?

She made her morning trek into the nursery. No crib, no Amanda. The books were dead on the shelves, words for nobody. The toys were dusty.

"I'm going to stop by on my way home and pick up a couple of gallons of paint," Peter said from the doorway. He put his tooth-brush back in his mouth.

"Was she ever real?" Katie asked.

"Shhh," Peter mumbled around the toothbrush. "It's okay, honey. It wasn't your fault."

Even Peter believed it. She looked at his hands. No. They would never have been able to slip a bag over a baby's head, hold it loosely until the squirming stopped.

She was surprised she still had tears left to cry. Maybe she would run out of them in a week or two, when she was beyond *utterly*. When she had put it behind her.

"Peach," she said. "I think peach walls would look good."

"It's only for a little while. Until we have enough money to move. The sooner we get you away from this house, the better."

The million wouldn't buy Amanda back. But at least it would help bury her, confine her to a distant place in Katie's memory. Maybe one day, Katie really would be able to forget. One morning, she would awaken without guilt.

She made coffee, some eggs for Peter. He rushed through breakfast, checking over the NASDAQ in the newspaper. She kissed him at the door.

"I promise to try harder," she said to him.

He put a hand to the back of her neck, rubbed her cheek with his thumb. "She had eyes just like yours," he said, then he looked away. "Sorry. I'm not supposed to talk about it."

"We'll be away from here soon."

"It wasn't your fault."

She couldn't answer. She had a lump in her throat. So she nodded, watched him walk to his car, then closed the door. After he'd driven away, headed for the Battery in Manhattan, she went up the stairs.

She reached under the bed and pulled out the keepsake box. She untied the pink ribbon and opened it. Amanda Lee Forrester, born 7-12-00. Seven pounds, nine ounces. Tiny footprints on the birth certificate.

Katie shuffled through the photographs, the birth announcement clipped from the newspaper, the hospital bracelet, the two white booties, the small silver spoon Peter's mom had given them. Soon Katie would be able to put these things behind her and move on. But not too soon.

She could cry at will. She could pretend to be *utterly* if she needed to, if Peter ever suspected. She could hide her guilt in that perfect hiding place, her disguise of perpetual self-blame.

Katie put all the items of Amanda's life into the plastic bag, then tied the box closed with the ribbon. She returned the box to its place under the bed. Peter would never understand, not a trade such as the one she'd made.

A million dollars to forever carry the weight of silence.

She clicked on the nursery monitor, sat on the bed, and listened.

THE HOUNDS OF LOVE

exter licked his lips. His stomach was shivery. October was
brown and yellow and crackly and tasted like candy corn. He
knelt by the hutch that Dad had built back before the
restraining order was filed.

He touched the welt under his eye. The wound felt like a busted
plum and stung where the flesh had split open. Mom had accidentally
left her thumb sticking out of her fist when she hit him. She hadn't
meant to do it. Usually, she was careful when she punched him.

But one good thing about Mom, she didn't hold a grudge for
long. She'd turned on the television and opened a beer, and after the
next commercial break had forgotten all about him. It was easy to
sneak out the back door.

Dexter poked some fresh blades of grass through the silver
squares of wire. The rabbit flashed its buck teeth and wrinkled its
nose before clamping down on the grass and hopping to the back of
the hutch. It crouched in the shadows and chewed with a sideways
gnashing of its jaws. The black eyes stared straight ahead. They
looked like doll's eyes, dead and cold and stupid.

Dexter's stomach was still puke-shivery. He opened the cage

and snaked his hand inside. The rabbit hopped away and kept chewing. Dexter stroked the soft fur between the rabbit's eyes.

Gotta tell 'em that you love 'em.

He snatched the leathery ears and pulled the rabbit forward into the light. He held it that way for a moment, like a magician dangling a trick above a hat, as it spasmed and kicked its four white legs. This was October, after all, the month when anything could happen. Even stupid old magic, if you dressed like a dork in a wizard's cape for Halloween.

Dexter looked over his shoulder at the house. Mom was most likely passed out by now. After all, it was four o'clock in the afternoon. But Dexter had learned from his dad that it never hurt to be paranoid.

He tucked the rabbit under his windbreaker and crossed the backyard into the woods. When he reached the safety of the trees, he took the leash from his pocket. This was the tricky part. With his tongue hanging out from concentration, he squeezed the rabbit between his knees.

He pressed harder until he heard something snap and the rabbit's back legs hung limp. He almost puked then, almost wept, but his first tear rolled across the split skin beneath his eye and he got angry again. "I'll teach you better than to love me," he whispered, his breath ragged.

It was the rabbit's fault. The dumb creature shouldn't have tried to love him. The rabbit was trying to get him, to play the trick on him, to make him care. Well, he wasn't going to belong to nothing or nobody.

Dexter used both hands to attach the leather collar. The collar had belonged to his little redbone hound. Uncle Clem let Dexter have the pick of the litter. Dexter had chosen the one with the belly taut from milk that wagged its thin rope of a tail whenever Dexter patted its head. Dexter had named it Turd Factory. Well, stupid old Turd Factory didn't need the collar anymore.

Dexter fastened the collar and let the rabbit drop to the ground. It rolled on its side and twitched its front legs. Sometimes they died too fast, sometimes before he even started. Dexter headed deeper into the woods, dragging the rabbit behind him by the leash. It was a hundred feet to the clearing where he liked to play. There, the sun broke through the tree-limbs and a shallow creek spilled over the rocks. Dexter squinted at the scraps of the sky, his eye almost swollen shut now. The clearing smelled like autumn mud and rot, the magic odors of buried secrets.

Dexter tightened the leash around the rabbit's neck until its veins bulged. He put one hand under the soft white chest and felt the trip-hammering heart that was trying to pump blood through the tourniquet. The rabbit began kicking its front legs again, throwing leaves and dark forest dirt into the air.

This was the part Dexter hated. The fear that came to the animals sooner or later as he tortured them, that little frantic spark in the eyes. The desperation and submission as they gave all that they had. Stupid things, they made him sick, they made him want to throw up. It was all their fault.

Dexter opened the pocketknife and went to work. This one was a relief. The rabbit had started out scared and stayed scared, paid for loving him without a whimper. Dexter was blind from tears by the time he finished.

He buried the carcass between the roots of a big oak tree. Right next to old Turd Factory. Dexter washed his hands in the creek. It was almost dinnertime. He turned and walked back through the clearing, past the depressions of soil where he had buried the other animals.

His own little pet cemetery. He had seen that movie. It had given him the creeps, but not badly enough to make him give up his hobby. Plus, by the time he was finished with them, no chunk was big enough to stand up by itself, much less walk.

Three cats were underground here, two of them compliments of dear old Grandma. She'd given him the rabbit as an Easter present. He'd swiped a rooster from a caved-in coop up the road, but he didn't think he'd be pulling any more of those jobs. The rooster had spurred him, plus the dumb bird had squawked and clucked loud enough to wake the dead. There was a box turtle buried somewhere around. But that had mostly been a mercy killing. Mom kept pouring beer into its water.

Same with the goldfish. He told her he'd flushed them down the toilet. Goldfish were boring, though. They didn't scream or whimper. They didn't make him want to throw up while they bled. They were too dumb to love.

Dexter giggled at the thought of a goldfish coming back from the dead and haunting him. He'd like to see that in a movie someday. *The Revenge of the Zombie Fish.* He wiped his eyes dry and headed down the trail to the house.

Mom was boiling some macaroni when he came in the back door. She wiped at her nose as she opened a can of cheese sauce. The sight of her moist fingers on the can opener killed Dexter's appetite. He sat down at the table and toyed with an empty milk carton.

She must have passed out in her clothes again. They were wrinkled and smelled like rancid lard. "Where you been, honey?" she asked.

"Out playing."

"Where?"

"Out," he said. "You know."

She slid a plate of steaming macaroni in front of him. Dexter could see dried egg yolk clinging to the edge of the plate. "How was school?"

"The usual."

"Hmm. What you going to be for Halloween?"

"I don't know. I'm getting too old for dress-up and make-believe."

"Whatever." She opened the refrigerator. It was empty except for a dozen cans of beer, a wilted stalk of celery, and something in a Tupperware dish that had a carpet of green stuff across the top.

Dexter watched as she cracked a beer. She was red. Her hands were red, her face was red, her eyes were red.

"You not hungry?" she asked.

"No. Maybe later."

"Well, you need to eat. You'll get me in trouble with Social Services again."

"To hell with them."

"Dexter! If your Grandma heard that kind of language—"

—the old bag would probably slap me upside the head, he thought.

But the good thing about Grandma, she always felt guilty afterwards. She would go out and buy something nice to make up for it. Like the pocketknife or the BB gun. Or a new pet.

He didn't mind if Grandma made his ears ring. At least with her, there was profit in it. With Mom or Dad, all he got was a scar to show for it. Maybe Grandma loved him most. He picked up his fork and scooted some noodles around.

"That's a good boy," Mom said. She bent and kissed him on top of the head. Her breath smelled like a casket full of molded grain. "Your eye's looking better. Swelling ought to be down by tomorrow. At least enough for you to go to school."

Dexter smiled weakly and shoved some macaroni in his mouth. He chewed until she left the room. The telephone rang. Mom must have finally had it reconnected.

"Hello?" he heard her say.

Dexter looked at her. He could tell by her crinkled forehead that Dad was on the other end, trying to worm his way back into the bed he'd paid for with the sweat of his goddamned brow, under the roof he'd laid with his own two motherfucking hands. And no snotty-eyed bitch had a right to keep him out of his own goddamned house and away from his only son. Now that it was getting toward winter—

"You know you're not supposed to be calling me," she said into the phone. She bit her lip as Dad responded with what was most likely a stream of cusswords.

That was the problem with Dad. No subtlety. If only he'd play it smooth and easy, pretending to care about her, he'd be back in no time. And after a few months of acting, family life could go back to the way it was before. Back to normal.

But the bastard couldn't control himself. Why couldn't he just shut up and pretend to love her? It was easy. Everybody else was doing it.

Riley Baldwin down the road said that was the secret. The word "love."

"Gotta tell 'em that you love 'em," he always said, with all the wisdom of an extra year and two more inches of height. "Works like magic."

Said love had gotten him a hand up under Tammy Lynn Goolsby's dress. Inside her panties, even. And Grandma said she loved Dexter. Of course, that was different, that kind of love gave you presents. Love got you what you wanted, if you used it right, even if it hurt sometimes.

"Don't you dare set foot near this place or I'll call the cops," Mom screeched into the phone. Her face turned from red to a bruised shade of purple.

She stuttered into the phone a couple of times and slammed the handset down, then drained the last half of her beer. As she went past him to get to the refrigerator, she didn't notice that Dexter hadn't eaten his dinner. He slipped away to his tiny cluttered bedroom and closed the door. He stayed there until Mom had time to pass out again. He fell asleep listening to her snores and the racket of the television.

Nobody said a word about his black eye at school the next day. Riley was waiting for him when he got off the bus. Riley had skipped. Dexter wished he could, too, but he didn't want Mom to get another visit from the Social Services people, showing up in their squeaky shoes and perfume and acting like they knew how to run a family they didn't belong to.

"Got my .22 hid in the woods," Riley said, showing the gaps in his teeth as he grinned. His eyes gleamed under the shade of his Caterpillar ball cap.

"Cool, dude. Let me get my BB gun."

Riley waited by the back door. Dexter dropped his books in a pool of gray grease on the dining room table, then got his gun out of his room. Mom wasn't around. Maybe she'd gotten one of her boyfriends to make a liquor run to the county line. A note was stuck to the refrigerator, in Mom's wobbly handwriting: "Stay out of trouble. Love you."

Dexter joined Riley and they went into the woods. Riley retrieved his gun from where he had buried it under some leaves. He tapped his pocket and something rattled. "Got a half box of bullets."

"Killed anything with that yet?"

"Nope. But maybe I can get one of those stripedy-assed chip-munks."

"Them things are quick."

"Hey, a little blood sacrifice is all it takes."

"What do you mean?"

"Breaking it in right." Riley patted the barrel of the gun. "Making them pay for messing with me."

Riley led the way down the trail, through Dexter's pet cemetery and over the creek. Dexter followed in his buddy's footsteps, watching the tips of his own brown boots. October hung in scraps of yellow and red on the trees. The shadows of the trees grew longer and thicker as the sun slipped down the sky.

Riley stopped after a few minutes of silent stalking. "What's up with your dad?" he asked.

"Not much. Same old."

"That must be a pain in the ass, seeing him every other weekend or so."

"Yeah. He ain't figured out the game."

"What game?"

"You know. Love. Like you said."

"Oh, yeah. Gotta tell 'em that you love 'em."

"If he played the game, we wouldn't have Social Services messing around all the time."

"Them sons of bitches are all alike. The cops, the truant offi-cers, the principal. It don't matter what the fuck you do. They always get you anyway."

"I reckon so." Dexter's stomach was starting to hurt. He changed the subject. "What was it like, with Tammy Lynn?"

Riley's face stretched into a jack-o'-lantern leer and he thrust out his bony chest. "Hey, she'll let me do anything. All you got to do is love 'em. I know how to reach 'em down deep."

"Did she let you....?"

Riley twiddled his fingers in the air, then held them to his nose and sniffed.

"What about the other stuff?" Dexter asked.

"That's next, buddy-row. As soon as I want it."

"Why don't you want to? I thought you said she'd do anything."

Riley's thick eyebrows lowered, shading the rage that glinted in his eyes. He turned and started back down the trail toward the creek. "Ain't no damned birds left to shoot. Your loud-assed yakking has scared them all away."

Dexter hurried after him. The edge of the sky was red and golden. The forest was darker now, and the moist evening air had softened the leaves under their feet. Mom would be waking up soon to start on her second drunk of the day.

They walked in silence, Riley hunched over with his rifle tilted toward the ground, Dexter trailing like a puppy that had been kicked by its master. It was nearly dark when they reached the clearing. Riley jumped over the creek and looked back. His eyes flashed, but his face was nothing but sharp shadows.

Dexter hurdled the creek, caving in a section of muddy bank and nearly sliding into the water. He grabbed a root with one hand and scrambled up on his elbows and knees, his belly on the rim of the bank. When he looked up, Riley was pointing the rifle at him. Dad had taught Dexter about gun safety, and the first rule, the main rule, was to never point a loaded gun at somebody. Even a dickwit like Riley ought to know that.

"You ever kill anybody?" Riley was wearing his jack-o'-lantern expression again, but this time the grin was full of jagged darkness.

"Kill anybody?" Dexter tried not to whimper. He didn't want Riley to know how scared he was.

"Blood sacrifice."

Riley was just crazy enough to kill him, to leave him out here leaking in the night, on the same ground where Dexter had carved up a dozen animals. Dexter tried to think of how Dad would handle this situation. "Quit screwing around, Riley."

"If I want to screw around, I'll do it with Tammy Lynn."

"I didn't mean nothing when I said that."

"I can get it any time I want it."

"Sure, sure," Dexter was talking too fast, but he couldn't stop the words. He focused on the tip of Riley's boot, the scuffed leather and the smear of grease. "You know how to tell 'em. You're the magic man."

Riley lowered the gun a little. "Damn straight."

It was almost as if Dexter were talking to the boot, he was close enough to kiss it. "Just gotta tell 'em that you love 'em, right?"

Riley laughed then, and cool sweat trickled down the back of Dexter's neck. Maybe Dexter wasn't going to die after all, here among the bones and rotten meat of his victims. The boot moved away and Dexter dared to look up. Riley was among the thicket of holly and laurel now, the gun pointed away, and Dexter scrambled to his feet.

He saw for the first time how creepy the clearing was, with the trees spreading knotty arms all around and the laurels crouched like big animals. The place was *alive*, hungry, holding its breath and waiting for the next kill.

"Tell you what," Riley said, growing taller in the twilight, a looming force. "Come here tomorrow after school. Be real quiet and watch from behind the bushes. I'll get her all the way."

Dexter nodded in the dark. Then he remembered. "But tomorrow's Halloween."

"What the hell else you got to do? Go around begging for candy with the babies?"

He couldn't let Riley know he was scared. "No, it's just—"

"Better fucking be here," Riley said.

Dexter ran down the trail toward home, his stomach fluttering. He was half scared and half excited about what he was going to witness, what he dared not miss.

Mom was slumped over the kitchen table, a pile of empty beer cans around her chair. An overturned bottle leaked brown liquid into her lap. Dexter hurried to the bed before she woke up and asked for a goodnight hug or else decided he needed a beating for something-or-other.

The next day after school, he went straight from the bus to the clearing. The sky was cloudy and heavy with dampness. He heard voices as he crawled on his hands and knees through the undergrowth. He looked through a gap in the branches. Riley sat on the ground, talking to Tammy Lynn, who was leaning against the big oak tree.

Tammy Lynn's blonde hair was streaked with red dye. She already looked fourteen. Her chest stretched the fabric of her white sweater. Freckles littered her face. She had cheeks like a chipmunk's, puffed and sad.

Riley rubbed her knee beneath the hem of her dress. He glanced to his left at the bushes where Dexter was hiding. Dexter gulped. His stomach was puke-shivery.

"I love you," Riley said to Tammy Lynn.

She giggled. She wore lipstick, and her mouth was a thin red scar across her pale face. Riley leaned forward and kissed her.

He pulled his face away. She touched her lower lip where her lipstick had smeared. Riley's hand snaked farther under her dress. She clamped her legs closed.

"Don't, Riley," she whispered.

"Aw, come on, baby."

"I don't want to."

"Hey, I said I loved you. It's okay to do it if I love you."

"I'm scared."

Riley stopped rubbing her. He spoke so low that Dexter barely heard. "Pretend you're a princess and I'm a prince, and we're in a fairy tale. Don't you love me?"

Tammy Lynn lowered her eyes. Riley cupped her chin and tilted her face up. Her cheeks were pink from shame or fear.

"Don't you love me?" Riley repeated, and this time he was wearing his jack-o'-lantern face. Tammy Lynn nodded slowly. Dexter's stomach felt as if he'd swallowed a handful of hot worms.

"If you love me, then you owe me," Riley said. She shook her head from side to side, her hair swaying against her shoulders.

Riley suddenly drove his hand deeper under her dress. Tammy Lynn gave a squeal of surprise and tried to twist away. Riley grabbed her sweater and pulled her towards the ground. Bits of bark clung to her back.

"No," she moaned, flailing at his hands as he wrestled her to the ground. One of her silver-polished nails raked across Riley's nose. He drew back his arm and slapped her. She cried out in pain.

Dexter hadn't counted on it being like this. He almost ran out from under the bushes to help her. But he thought of Riley and the gun. Dexter could barely breathe, his gut clenching like he was going to throw up, but he couldn't look away.

Riley pinned her down with one arm and unzipped his blue jeans, then covered her mouth as he pulled her dress up. Riley moved between her legs and Tammy Lynn screamed into his palm. They struggled for a few seconds more before Riley shoved away from her. He stood and fastened his pants. Tammy Lynn was crying.

"I told you I loved you," Riley said, as if he were disgusted at some cheap toy that had broken. Then he looked at the laurels and winked, but Dexter saw that his hands were shaking. Dexter hoped they couldn't see him. The shiver in his stomach turned into a drumroll of tiny ice punches.

Tammy Lynn was wailing now. Her dress was bunched around her waist, her panties twisted against her white thighs. Scraps of leaves stuck to her ankle socks. One of her shoes had fallen off.

"Works like magic," Riley said, too loudly, his voice a hoarse blend of triumph and fear. "I told you I loved you, didn't I?"

He kicked some loose leaves toward her and walked down the trail. He would want Dexter to follow so he could crow about the conquest. But Dexter's muscles were jelly. He couldn't take his eyes away from Tammy Lynn.

She sat up, her sobs less forceful now. She slowly pulled up her panties and pushed her dress hem down to her knees, moving like one of those movie zombies. She stared at her fingers as if some tiny treasure had been ripped out of her hands. Tears streamed down her face, and a strand of blood creased one side of her chin. Her lower lip was swollen.

She stood on her skinny legs, wobbling like a foal. Her dress hung unevenly. She looked around the clearing with eyes that were too wide. Dexter shrank back under the laurels, afraid to be seen, afraid that he was supposed to help her and couldn't.

Blood ran down her legs, the bright red streaks of it vivid

against her skin. Drops spattered onto the leaves between her feet. She looked down and saw the blood and made a choking sound in her throat. She waved her hands in the air for a moment, then ran into the woods, not down the trail but in the direction of the road that bordered one side of the forest. She'd forgotten her shoe.

Dexter lifted himself from the ground and stared at the dark drops of blood. Rain began to fall, slightly thicker than the mist. He parted the waxy laurel leaves and stepped into the clearing.

Blood. Blood sacrifice. On Halloween, when anything could happen. The clearing was alive again, the sky waiting and the trees watching, the ground hungry.

Dexter felt dizzy, as if his head was packed with soggy cotton. He knelt suddenly and vomited. When his stomach was empty, he leaned back and let the rain run down his face. That way, Riley wouldn't be able to tell that he had been crying.

He looked down at the shoe for a moment, then stumbled down the trail toward home. He expected Riley to be waiting by the porch, the sleeves rolled up on his denim jacket, arms folded. But Riley was gone. Dexter went in the house.

"Hey, honey," Mom said, not looking up as the screen door slammed. She was watching a rerun of "Highway To Heaven."

"Find your rabbit?" she asked.

"No."

"Dinner will be ready soon."

"I'm not hungry. I'm going to my room."

"You ain't going trick-or-treat?"

"I don't want to."

"You sick?" She glanced away from the television and looked at him suspiciously. The smell of old beer and the food scraps on the counter brought back Dexter's nausea.

"No. Just got some homework," he managed to lie through quivering lips.

"Homework, like hell. When you ever done homework? Your clothes are dirty. What have you been up to?"

"I fell at school. You know it was raining?"

"And me with laundry on the line," she said. As if it were the sky's fault, and there was nothing a body could do when the whole damned sky was against them. She looked back to the television, took two swallows of beer, and belched. He wondered what she would give out if any trick-or-treaters dared come down their dangerous street and knock on the door.

On the television screen, Michael Landon was sticking his nose into somebody else's business again. Dexter looked at the actor's smug close-up for a moment, then tiptoed to his room. His thoughts suffocated him in the coffin of his bed.

Maybe he should have picked up Tammy Lynn's shoe. Then he could give it back to her, even if he couldn't give back the other things. Like in Cinderella, sort of. But then she would know. And that was like fairy tale love, and Dexter didn't ever want to love anything as long as he lived.

Anyway, Riley had a gun. He thought of Riley pointing the gun at him, that moment in the woods when he thought the tip of Riley's boot would be the last thing he ever saw. The boot, the shoe, the blood. Dexter finally fell asleep to the sound of whatever movie Mom was using for a drinking buddy that night.

He dreamed of Tammy Lynn. She was splayed out beneath him in the clearing, the collar tight around her neck, the leash wrapped around his left fist. She was naked, but her features were formless, milky abstractions. He was holding his knife against her cheek. Her eyes were twin beggars, pools of scream, wet horror. He woke up sweating, his stomach shivery, his eyes moist. He'd wet the bed again.

Rain drummed off the roof. He thought of the blood, watered down and spreading now, soaking into the soil. Her blood sacrifice, the price she paid for love. He didn't get back to sleep.

He dressed just as the rain dwindled. By the time he went outside, the sun was fighting through a smudge of clouds. The air was as thick as syrup, and nobody stirred in the houses along the street. The whole world had a hangover.

Dexter went down the trail. He wasn't sure why. Maybe he wanted to relive the day before, the struggle, the tears, the drops of blood. Maybe he wanted to get the shoe.

Water fell off the green leaves overhead as he wound his way into the woods. His shirt was soaked by the time he reached the clearing. The forest was alive with dripping, flexing limbs, trees drinking and growing, the creek fat and muddy. A fungal, earthy stench hung in the air. He stepped into the clearing.

The ground was scarred with gashes of upturned soil. Brown holes. Empty. Where Dexter had buried the pets.

Blood sacrifice. Works like magic. Especially on Halloween.

Dexter tried to breathe. The shivering in his belly turned into a wooden knot.

Twigs snapped damply behind the stand of laurels where he had hid the day before.

No. Dead things didn't come back to life. That only happened in stupid movies.

Tammy Lynn's shoe was gone. No way would she come back here. It had to be Riley, playing a trick. But how did Riley know where he had buried the animals?

He heard a whimpering gargle that sounded like a cross between a cluck and a growl, maybe a broken meow. The laurels shimmered. Something was moving in there.

"Riley?" he whispered hoarsely.

The gargle.

"Come on out, dickwit," he said, louder.

He saw a flash of fur, streaked and caked with dirt. He fled down the trail. His boots hardly touched the ground, were afraid to touch the ground, the ground that had been poisoned with blood magic. He thought he heard something following as he crossed into the yard, soft padding footfalls or slitherings in the brush, but his heart was hammering so hard in his ears that he couldn't be sure. He burst into the house and locked the door, then leaned with his back against it until he caught his breath.

Something thudded onto the porch, clattering along the wooden boards. Behind that sharp sound, a rattling like claws or thick toenails, came a dragging wet noise.

Clickety-click, sloosh. Clickety-click, sloosh.

It stopped just outside the door.

Dexter couldn't move.

"What the hell's wrong with you?" Mom stood under the archway leading into the kitchen. Her face was pinched, eyes distended, skin splotched. Greasy blades of hair clung to her forehead.

Dexter gasped, swallowed. "The—"

She scowled at him, her fists clenched. He knew this had better be good. "— I was just out running."

"You're going to be the death of me, worrying me like that. Nothing but trouble." She rubbed her temples. Her smell filled the small room, sweetly pungent like a bushel of decaying fruit. Dexter put his ear to the door. The sounds were gone.

"What are you so pale for? You said you wasn't sick."

Dexter shrank away from her.

"Now get up off that floor. Lord knows, I got enough work around here already without putting you in three changes of clothes ever goddamned day."

Dexter slunk past her into the living room.

"Guess I'd better get that laundry in," Mom said to no one in particular. Her hand gripped the doorknob, and Dexter wanted to shout, scream, slap her away. But of course he couldn't. He could only watch with churning bowels as she opened the door and went outside. Dexter followed her as far as the screen door.

The porch was empty.

Of course it was. Monsters were for movies, or dumb stories. He was acting like a fourth grader. Stuff coming back from the dead? Horseshit, as Dad would say.

Still, he didn't go outside the rest of the evening, even though the sky cleared. Mom was in a better mood after the first six-pack. Dexter watched cartoons, then played video games for a while. He tried not to listen for clickety-sloosh.

One of Mom's boyfriends came over. It was the one with the raggedy mustache, the one who called Dexter "Little Man." Mom and the man disappeared into her bedroom, then Dexter heard arguing and glass breaking. The boyfriend left after an hour or so. Mom didn't come back out. Dexter went to bed without supper.

He lay there thinking about magic, about blood sacrifice. About the open graves in the pet cemetery that should have been filled with bones and decaying flesh and mossy fur and shaved whiskers and scales. He tried to erase his memory of the creature in the bushes, the thing that had followed him home. He couldn't sleep, even though he was worn from tension.

His eyes kept traveling to the cold glass between his curtains. The streetlight threw shadows that striped the bed, swaying like live things. He tried to tell himself that it was only the trees getting blown by the wind. Nothing was going to get him, especially not all those animals he'd dismembered. No, those animals had loved him. They would never *hurt* him.

He'd almost calmed himself when he heard the soft click of paws on the windowsill. It was the sound the cats had made when they wanted to be let in. Dexter's Mom wanted them out of the house, because of the hairballs and the stains they left in the corners. But Dexter always let them in at night to curl on top of the blankets at his feet. At least for a week or so, until he got tired of them.

But he didn't have any cats at the moment. So it couldn't be a cat at the window. Dexter pulled the blankets up to his eyes. Something bumped against the glass, moist and dull, like a nose.

No no no not a nose.

He wrapped the pillow around his ears. The noise was replaced by a rapid thumping against the outside wall. Dexter hunched under the blankets and counted down from a hundred, the way he did when he was six and Dad had first told him about the monsters that lived in the closet.

One hundred (no monsters), ninety-nine (no monsters), ninety-eight (no monsters)...

After three times through, he no longer heard the clickings or thumpings. He fell asleep with the blankets twisted around him.

Dexter awoke not knowing where he was. He sat up quickly and looked out the window. Nothing but sky and Sunday sunshine.

Dad picked him up that afternoon. Dexter had to walk down to the corner to meet him. He kept a close eye on the woods, in case anything stirred in the leaves. He thought he heard a scratching sound, but by then he was close enough to get inside the truck.

Dad looked past Dexter to the house. "My own goddamned roof," he muttered under his breath.

"Hi, Dad."

"I suppose she filled you up with all kinds of horseshit about me." His hands were clenched into fists around the steering wheel. Dexter knew what those fists could do. There had to be a way out, a way to calm him. Riley's words came to Dexter out of the blue: *Gotta tell 'em that you love 'em.*

Yeah. Works like magic. He'd seen how that turned out. Got you what you wanted, but somebody had to pay.

"She didn't say nothing."

"Any men been around?"

"Nobody. Just us. We...I miss you."

Dad's fists relaxed and he mussed Dexter's hair. "I miss you, too, boy."

Dexter wanted to ask when Dad was moving back in, but didn't want him to get angry again. Better not to mention Mom, or home, or anything else.

"What say we go down to the dump? Got me a new Ruger to break in." Dexter managed a weak smile as Dad pulled the truck away from the curb.

They spent the day at the landfill, Dexter breaking glass bottles and Dad prowling in the trash for salvage, shooting rats when they showed their pointy faces. Dexter felt no joy when the rodents exploded into red rags. Dad was a good shot.

They ate fastfood hamburgers on the way back in. It was almost dark when Dad dropped him off at the end of the street. Dexter hoped none of Mom's boyfriends were around. He opened the door to hop out, then hesitated, remembering the clickety-sloosh. He had managed to forget, to fool himself out under the clear sky, surrounded by filth and rusty metal and busted furniture. In the daytime, all the nightmares had dissolved into vapor.

Dexter looked toward the house with one hand still on the truck door. Dad must have figured he was reluctant to leave, that a son missed his father, and that no goddamned snotty-eyed bitch had a right to keep a father from his own flesh-and-blood. "It's okay. I'll see you again in a week or so," Dad said.

Dexter searched desperately for something to say, anything to put off that hundred-foot walk across the dark yard. "Dad?"

"What?"

"Do you love Mom?"

Dexter could see only Dad's silhouette against the background of distant streetlights. Crickets chirped in the woods. After a long moment, Dad relaxed and sighed. "Yeah. 'Course I do."

Dexter looked along the street, at the forest that seemed to creep up to the house's foundation. "You ever been scared?"

"We're all scared of something or other. Is something bothering you?"

Dexter shook his head, then realized Dad probably couldn't see him in the dark. "No," he said, then, "Do you believe in magic?"

Dad laughed, his throat thick with spittle. "What kind of horse-shit has she been filling you up with?"

"Nothing. Never mind."

"The bitch."

"Guess I better go, Dad."

"Uh-huh."

"See you." He wanted to tell Dad that he loved him, but he was too scared.

"Say, whatever happened to that little puppy of yours?"

"Got runned over."

"Damn. I'll see Clem about getting you another."

"No, that's okay."

"You sure?"

"Yeah."

"Bye now."

"Yeah."

Dexter stepped away from the truck and watched the tail-lights shrink as Dad roared away. The people in the few neighboring houses were plastered to the television. Blue light flickered from their living room windows. The trees were like tall skeletons with too many bones.

Leaves skittered across the road, scratching at the asphalt. A dog barked a few streets over. At least, it sounded like a dog. A good old red-blooded, living and breathing turd factory. Never hurt nobody, most likely.

He walked into the scraggly yard, reluctant to leave the cone of the last streetlight. He thought about going up the street and cutting across the other end of the yard, but that way was scary, too. The autumn forest hovered on every side. The forest with its clickety-sloosh things.

He tried to whistle as he walked, but his throat was dry, as if he had swallowed a spiderweb. He thought about running, but that was no good. In every stupid movie where dead things come back, they always get you if you run.

So he took long, slow steps. His head bent forward because he thought he could hear better that way. Halfway home. The lights were on in the kitchen, and he headed for the rectangle of light that stretched from the back door across the lawn.

He was twenty feet away from the safety of light when he heard it. Clickety-sloosh. But that wasn't all. The gargle was also mixed in, along with the tortured meow and the rustle of leaves. The noise was coming from behind a forsythia bush near the back steps. The thing was under the porch. In the place where Turd Factory had napped during sunny afternoons.

Dexter stopped.

Run for it? They always get you if you run. But, now that he thought about it, they always get you anyway. Especially if you were the bad guy. And Dexter was the bad guy. Maybe not as bad as Riley. But at least Riley knew about love, which probably protected him from bad things.

Yell for Mom? She was probably dead drunk on the couch. If she did step out on the porch, the thing would disappear. He was sure of that, because the thing was his and only his.

And if he yelled, he knew what would happen. Mom would turn on the porch light and see nothing, not even a stray hair, just a scooped-out dirt place behind the forsythia. And she'd say, "What the hell do you mean, waking up half the neighborhood because you heard something under the porch? They ain't nothing there."

And she'd probably slap him across the face. She'd wait until they were inside, so the neighbors wouldn't call Social Services. Maybe she'd use the buckle-end of the belt, if she was drinking liquor tonight instead of beer.

He took an uncertain step backward. Back to the curb, to the streetlights? Then what? You had to go home sometime. The thing gargled, a raspy mewling. It was waiting.

A monster that could disappear could do anything. Even if he ran to the road, the thing could clickety-sloosh out of the sewer grate, or pop out from behind one of the junk cars that skulked in the roadside weeds. The thing could drop from the limbs of that big red maple at the edge of the lawn. You can't fight blood magic when it builds a monster on Halloween.

He had a third choice. Walk right on up. Keep trying to whistle. Not scared at all. No-sirree. Zip-a-dee-doo-dah.

And that was really the only choice. The thing wasn't going away. Dexter stepped into the rectangle of light and pursed his lips. He was still trying to whistle as he put his foot on the bottom step. Monsters weren't real, were they?

The bush shook, shedding a few of its late yellow flowers. The gargle lengthened into a soughing purr. Dexter tried to keep his eyes on the door, the door that was splintered at the bottom where the puppy and cats had scratched to get inside. The door with its dented brass handle, the door with its duct-taped pane of glass, the door that opened onto the love and safety promised by the white light of home. The door became a blur, a shimmering wedge lost in his tears as the thing moved out from the shadows.

He closed his eyes and waited for the bite, the tearing of his blue jeans and shin meat, the rattle of tooth on bone. He stiffened in anticipation of cold claws to belly, hot saliva on rib cage, rough tongue to that soft place just underneath the chin.

Clickety-sloosh.

His heart skipped a beat and restarted. He was still alive. No pain yet. He tried to breathe. The air tasted like rusty meat.

Maybe it had disappeared. But he could hear it, panting through moist nostrils. Just beneath him. Close enough so that he could feel the wind of its mewling against his leg.

Savoring the kill? Just as Dexter had done, all those afternoons and Saturday mornings spent kneeling in the forest, with his pocket knife and his pets and his frightened lonely tears? He knew that fear was the worst part, the part that made your belly all puke-shivery.

He had to show his fear. That was only fair. He owed them that much. And if he looked scared enough, maybe the thing would have mercy, just rip open that big vein in his neck so he could die fast. Then the thing could clickety-sloosh on back into the woods, drag its pieces to the grave and bury its own bones.

Dexter tried to open his eyes but couldn't. Still the thing mewled and gargled. Waiting was the worst part. You could hold your breath, pray, scream, run. They always get you anyway.

Still he waited.

He blinked. The world was nothing but streaks, a gash of light, a fuzz of gray that was the house, a bigger fuzz of black night. Something nudged against his kneecap. He looked down, his chest hot as a brick oven.

It hadn't disappeared.

Two eyes met his. One round and dark, without a white, hooded by an exotic flap of skin. The other eye was heavy-lidded, yellow and reptilian.

Behind the eyes, lumps of meat sloping into a forehead. Ragged pink where the pieces met, leaking a thin jelly. Part fur, part feather, part scale, part exposed bone. A raw rooster comb dangled behind one misshapen ear.

Beneath the crushed persimmon of a nose were whiskers and wide lips, the lips parted to show teeth of all kinds. Puppy teeth, kitty fangs, fishy nubs of cartilage, orange bits of beak like candy corn.

Hulking out behind the massive dripping head were more slabs of tenderloin, breast and wing, fin and shell. The horrible coalition rippled with maggots and rot and magic.

The lump of head nuzzled against his leg. The juice soaked through his jeans.

Oh God.

He wanated the end to come quickly now, because he had given the thing his fear and that was all he had. He had paid what he owed. But he knew in the dark hutch of his heart that the thing wasn't finished. He opened his eyes again.

The strange eyes stared up into his. Twin beggars.

You had to let them feed. On fear or whatever else they needed.

Again the thing nuzzled, mewling wetly. Behind the shape, something slithered rhythmically against the leaves.

A rope of gray and black and tan fur. A broken tail.

Wagging.

Wagging.

Waiting and wanting.

Forgiving.

Dexter wept without shame. When the thing nuzzled the third time, he reached down with a trembling hand and stroked between the putrid arching ears.

Riley's voice came to him, unbidden, as if from some burning bush or darkening cloud: "Gotta tell 'em that you love 'em."

Dexter knelt, trembling. The thing licked under the soft part of his chin. It didn't matter that the tongue was scaly and flecked with forest dirt. And cold, grave cold, long winter cold.

When you let them love you, you owe them something in return.

He hugged the beast, even as it shuddered toward him, clickety-sloosh with chunks dribbling down. And still the tail whipped the ground, faster now, drumming out its affection.

Suddenly the yard exploded with light.

The back door opened. Mom stood on the porch, one hand on the light switch, the other holding her worn flannel robe closed across her chest. "What the hell's going on out here?"

Dexter looked up from where he was kneeling at the bottom of the steps. His arms were empty and dry.

"Don't just stand there with your jaw hanging down. You was supposed to be here an hour ago." Her voice went up a notch, both louder and higher. "Why, I've got a good mind to—"

She stopped herself, looking across the lawn at the houses down the street. Dexter glanced under the porch. He saw nothing in the thick shadows.

Mom continued, lower, with more menace. "I've got a good mind to take the belt to you."

Dexter stood and rubbed the dirt off his pants.

"Now get your ass in here, and don't make me have to tell you twice."

Dexter looked around quickly at the perimeter of forest, at the black thickets where the thing would hide until Mom was gone. He went up the steps and through the door, past her hot drunken glare and stale breath. He shuffled straight to his room and closed the door. The beating would come or it wouldn't. It didn't matter.

That night, when he heard the scratching at the windowsill and the bump against the glass, he opened the window. The thing crawled inside and onto the bed. It had brought him a gift. Riley's bloody boot. When you loved something, it owed you in return. Maybe it had carried the other one to Tammy Lynn's house, where it might have delivered her lost shoe on Halloween, the night of its birth. To thank her for the gift of blood.

The nightmare creature curled at Dexter's feet, licking at the boot. The thing's stench filled the room, bits of its rotted flesh staining the blankets. Dexter didn't sleep that night, listening to the mewling rasp of the creature's breathing, wondering where the mouth was, knowing that he'd found a friend for life.

And tomorrow, when he got off the bus, the thing would greet him. It would wait until the bus rolled out of sight, then drag itself from the woods and rub against his leg, begging to be stroked. It would lick his face and wait for his hug.

And together they would run deep between the trees, Dexter at one end of the leash, struggling to keep up while the thing clickety-slooshed about and buried its dripping nose in the dirt, first here, then there. Once in a while into the creek, to wet its dangling gills. Stopping only to gaze lovingly at its master, showing those teeth that had done something bad to Riley and could probably do it again.

Maybe if Dexter fed its hunger for affection, it wouldn't have a hunger for other things.

Dexter would give it what it needed, he would feed it all he had. Through autumn's fog and into the December snows, through long spring evenings and into summer's flies. A master and its pet.

You owe them that much.

That's just the way love is.

They always get you anyway.

You'll Never Walk Alone

Daddy said them that eat human flesh will suffer under Hell. I ain't figured that out yet, how there can be a place under Hell. Daddy couldn't hardly describe it hisself. It's just a real bad place, hotter than the regular Hell and probably lonelier, too, since Hell's about full up and nobody's a stranger. Been so much sinning the Devil had to build a basement for the gray people.

It was Saturday when we heard about them. I was watching cartoons and eating a bowl of corn flakes. I like cereal with lots of sugar, so when the flakes are done you can drink down that thick milk at the bottom of the bowl. It come up like a commercial, some square-headed man in a suit sitting at a desk, with that beeping sound like when they tell you a bad storm's coming. Daddy was drinking coffee with his boots off, and he said they wasn't a cloud in the sky and the wind was lazy as a cut cat. So he figured it was just another thing about the Aye-rabs and who cared if they blew each other to Kingdom Come, except then they showed some of that TV that looks like them cop shows, the camera wiggly so you can't half see what they're trying to show you.

Daddy kept the cartoons turned down low because he said the

music hurt his ears, but this time he took the remote from beside my cereal bowl and punched it three or four times with his thumb. The square-headed man was talking faster than they usually do, like a flatlander, acting like he deserved a pat on the head because he was doing such a good job telling about something bad. Then the TV showed somebody in rags moving toward the camera and Daddy said, Lordy, looked like something walked out of one of them suicide bombs, because its face was gray and looked like the meat had melted off the bone.

But the square-headed man said the picture was live from Winston-Salem, that's about two hours from us here in the mountains. The man said it was happening all over, the hospitals was crowded and the governor done called out the National Guard. Then the television switched and it was the President standing at a bunch of microphones, saying something about a new terror threat but how everybody ought to stay calm because you never show fear in the face of the enemy.

Daddy said them damned ragheads must have finally let the bugs out of the bottle. I don't see how bugs could tear up a man's skin that way, to where it looked like he'd stuck his head in a lawn mower and then washed his face with battery acid and grease rags. I saw a dead raccoon once, in the ditch when I was walking home from school, and maggots was squirming in its eye holes and them shiny green dookie flies was swarming around its tail. I reckon that's what kind of bugs Daddy meant, only worse, because these ones get you while you're still breathing.

I was scared then, but it was the kind where you just sort of feel like the ashes in the pan at the bottom of the woodstove. Where you don't know what to be afraid of. At least when you hear something moving in the dark woods, your hands get sweaty and your heart jumps a mite faster and you know which way to run. But looking at the TV, all I could think of was the time I woke up and Momma wasn't making breakfast, and Momma didn't come home from work, and Momma didn't make supper. A kind of scared that fills you up belly first, and you can't figure it out, and you can't take a stick to it like you can that thing in the dark woods. And then there was the next day when Momma still didn't come home, and that's how I felt about the bugs out of the bottle, because it seems like you can't do nothing to stop it. Then I felt bad because the President would probably say I was showing fear in the face of the enemy, and Daddy voted for the President because it was high time for a change.

I asked Daddy what we was going to do, and he said the Lord would show the way. Said he was loading the shotgun just in case, because the Lord helped those that helped themselves. Said he didn't know whether them things could drive a car or not. If they had to walk all the way from the big city, they probably wouldn't get here for three days. If they come here at all.

Daddy told me to go put up the cows. Said the TV man said they liked living flesh, but you can't trust what the TV says half the time because they want to sell you something. I didn't figure how they could sell anything by scaring people like that. But I was awful glad we lived a mile up a dirt road in a little notch in the mountains. It was cold for March, maybe too cold for them bugs. But I wasn't too happy about fetching the cows, because they tend to wander in the mornings and not come in 'til dark. Cows like to spend their days all the same. If you do something new, they stomp and stir and start in with the moos, and I was afraid the moos might bring the bugs or them gray people that eat living flesh.

I about told Daddy I was too scared to fetch them by myself, but he might have got mad because of what the President said and all. Besides, he was busy putting on his boots. So I took my hickory stick from by the door and called Shep. He was probably digging for groundhogs up by the creek and couldn't hear me. I walked out to the fields on the north side, where the grass grows slow and we don't put cows except early spring. Some of the trees was starting to get new leaves, but the woods was mostly brown rot and granite stone. That made me feel a little better, because a bug-bit gray person would have a harder time sneaking up on me.

We was down to only four cows because of the long drought and we had to cull some steers last year or else buy hay. Four is easy to round up, because all you got to do is get one of them moving and the rest will follow. Cows in a herd almost always point their heads in the same direction, like they all know they're bound for the same place sooner or later. Most people think cows are dumb but some things they got a lot of sense about. You hardly ever see a cow in a hurry. I figure they don't worry much, and they probably don't know about being scared, except when you take them to the barn in the middle of the day. Then maybe they remember the blood on the walls and the steaming guts and the smell of raw meat and the jingle of the slaughter chains.

By the time I got them penned up, Shep had come in from wherever and gave out a bark like he'd been helping the whole time. I took him into the house with me. I don't ever do that unless it's come a big snow or when icicles hang from his fur. Daddy was dressed and the shotgun was laying on the kitchen table. I gave Shep the last of my cereal milk. Daddy said the TV said the gray people was walking all over, even in the little towns, but said some of the telephone wires was down so nobody could tell much what was going on where.

I asked Daddy if these was like the End Times of the Bible, like what Preacher Danny Lee Aldridge talked about when the sermon was almost over and the time had come to pass the plate. I always got scared about the End Times, even sitting in the church with all the wood and candles and that soft red cloth on the back of the pews. The End Times was the same as Hell to me. But Preacher Aldridge always wrapped up by saying that the way out of Hell was to walk through the house of the Lord, climb them stairs and let the loving light burn ever little shred of sin out of you. All you had to do was ask, but you had to do it alone. Nobody else could do it for you.

So you got to pray to the Lord. I like to pray in church, where there's lots of people and the Lord has to mind everybody at the same time. It's probably wrong, but I get scared when I try to pray all by myself. I used to pray with Momma and Daddy, then just Daddy, and that's okay because I figured Daddy's louder than me and probably has more to talk about. I just get that sharp rock feeling in my belly every time I think about the Lord looking at nobody but me, when I ain't got nothing to hide behind and my stick is out of reach.

But these ain't the End Times, Daddy said, because the gray people don't have horns and the TV didn't say nothing about a dragon coming up out of the sea. But he said since they eat human flesh they're of the Devil, and said their bodies may be walking around but you better believe their souls are roasting under Hell. Especially if they got bit by the Aye-rab bug. I told him the cattle was put up and he said the chickens would be okay, you can't catch a chicken even when your legs is working right, much less when you're wobbling around like somebody beat the tar out of you with an ax handle.

He said to get in the truck. I made Shep jump up in the truck bed, Daddy come out of the house with a loaf of white bread and some cans of sardines. Had the shotgun, too. He got in the truck and started it and I asked him where we was headed. He said in troubled times you go get closer to the Lord.

I asked him if maybe he thought Momma would be okay. He said it didn't matter none, since the Devil done got her ages ago. Said she was already a gray person before this bug mess even started. Said to waste no prayers on her.

The dirt road was mushy from winter. The road runs by the creek for a while, then crosses a little bridge by the Hodges place. That's where I always caught the school bus, with Johnny Hodges and his sister Raylene. Smoke was coming out of their chimney and I asked Daddy if we ought to stop and tell them about what the TV said. Daddy said they might be gray people already. I tried to picture Johnny with his face all slopped around, or Raylene with bugs eating her soft places. Mister Hodges didn't go to church and Johnny told me he used to beat them sometimes when he drank too much. I wondered if all the people who didn't go to church had turned gray and started eating human flesh.

We passed a few other houses but didn't see nobody, even at the preacher's place. The church was right there where the gravel turned to paved, set up above the road on a little green hill. The graveyard was tucked away to one side, where barbed wire strung off a pasture. The church was made of brick, the windows up high so that people wouldn't look outside during the preaching. Seeing that white cross jabbed up into the sky made me feel not so scared.

We parked the truck around back. Daddy had me carry the food and he carried the shotgun. Said a Bible and a shotgun was all a man needed. I didn't say nothing about a man needed food. I found a little pack of sugar in the truck's ashtray and I hid it in my pocket. We didn't have no Co'-colas.

They keep the church unlocked in case people want to come in and pray. Daddy said people in the big city lock their churches. If they don't, people might come in and sleep or steal the candle holders and hymn books. But this is the mountains, where people all know each other and get along and you don't need to lock every-thing. So we went inside. Daddy made Shep stay out, said it would be disrespecting to the Lord. We locked the door from the inside. I thought somebody else might want to come get close to the Lord in these troubled times, but Daddy said they could knock if they wanted in.

We went up to the front where the pulpit is and Daddy said we might as well get down and give thanks for deliverance. I didn't feel delivered yet but Daddy was a lot smarter about the Bible, so I went on my knees and kept my eyes closed while Daddy said oh Lord it's looking mighty dark but the clouds will part and heaven will knock down them gray people and set things right. I joined in on the amen and said I was hungry.

Daddy opened up the sardines and they stank. I spilled some of the fish juice on the floor. We ate some of the bread. It was gummy and stuck to my teeth. I was tired and tried to lay down in the front pew but it was like sleeping in a rock coffin. I didn't know why people in the big city would want to do such a thing. Daddy started reading from the Bible but the light got bad as the afternoon wore on. The church ain't got electric power.

I asked Daddy how long we was going to stay holed up and he said as long as it took. I wished we had a TV so we could see what was going on. Night finally come, and I was using the bathroom in back when I heard Shep whimpering. I reckon he was lonely out there. Sounded like he was scratching in the dirt out back of the church.

I climbed up on the sink and looked out the little window. Under the moonlight I saw the graveyard, and it looked like somebody had took a shovel to it, tore up the dirt real bad. Somebody was coming up out of one of the holes, and I reckon that's what Shep was whimpering about.

I went and told Daddy what I seen and he said maybe it was the End Times after all. Shep started barking and I begged Daddy to let me open the door. He said the Lord would take care of Shep, but then I heard him bark again and I was trying to open the door when Daddy knocked me away. Said he'd take a look, stepped outside with the shotgun, and the gun went off and Daddy started cussing goddamn right there on the church steps. Shep started moaning and I ran to the door and Shep was crawling toward the woods on his belly like his back was broke. I thought Daddy had shot him and I started to cry but then I seen somebody coming from the woods. Daddy racked another shell into the chamber and hollered but the person just kept coming. Daddy told me to go in and lock the door but I couldn't. I was too scared to be in that big dark church by myself.

Daddy shot high and the pellets scattered through the tops of the trees and still the person kept coming, walking slow with a limp. Another person came out of the trees, then another. They was all headed in the same direction. Straight toward the church.

One of them bent down and got Shep and I never heard such a sound from a dog. Daddy was cussing a blue streak and let loose both barrels and one of the people stood still for just a second, and I could see that gray face turned up toward the moon, the eye holes empty. Then his insides tumbled out but he kept on coming for us and Daddy was pushing me back through the door and we got inside and locked it.

Daddy went up front and I could hear him crying. Except for that, the church was quiet. I thought the gray people might try to knock the door down but maybe they got scared away because of it being a church and all. I went up beside Daddy and waited until he was hisself again. He said he was sorry for showing fear in the face of the enemy and said Oh Lord, give me the strength to do your work. I said Lord, protect Momma wherever she is and Daddy said it was wrong to ask for selfish things.

Daddy said the End Times was a test for the weak. Said you had to stay strong in the Lord. Said it about fifteen hundred times in a row, over and over, in a whisper, and it made me scared.

I was about asleep when Daddy poked me with the gun. Said come here, son, over by the window where I can see you good. The moon was coming through the window and I could hear the gray people walking outside. They was going around in circles, all headed in the same direction.

Daddy asked me if I got bit by one of them bugs. I said don't reckon. He said, well, you're looking a little gray, and I told him I didn't feel nary bit gray. He asked me if I was getting hungry and I said a little. He gave me the rest of the bread and said eat it. I took a bite and he said you didn't say thanks to the Lord. Then he thanked the Lord for both of us.

I asked Daddy if Shep had gone to heaven. He said it depended on whether he was dead before the gray people ate him. Said Shep might have done turned gray hisself and might bite me if he saw me again. I almost asked Daddy to say a prayer for Shep but that sounded like a selfish thing.

I must have finally dozed off because I didn't know where I was when I opened my eyes. Daddy was at the front of the church, in the pulpit where Preacher Aldridge stood of a Sunday. The sun was about up and Daddy had the Bible open and was trying to read in the bad light. Somebody was knocking on the church door.

Daddy said the word was made flesh and dwelt among us. Daddy stopped just like Preacher Aldridge did, like he wanted to catch his breath and make you scared at the same time. Then Daddy got louder and said we beheld His glory, the glory as of the only begotten of the Father, full of grace and truth.

I asked what did that mean and Daddy said the Lord come down among people and nobody saw the signs. Said they treated Him just like any normal person, except then He set off doing miracles and people got scared and nailed Him to the cross. Said it was probably gray people that done it. I asked Daddy if we ought to open the church door and see who was knocking.

Daddy said gray people wasn't fit to set foot in the house of the Lord. I asked what if it's the preacher or the Hodges kids or Opalee Rominger from down the road. Daddy said they're all gray, everybody. Said they was all headed under Hell. Said ever sinner is wicked and blind to their sinning ways. I didn't see how Opalee Rominger could eat living flesh, because she ain't got no teeth.

The knocking stopped and I didn't hear no screams so maybe whoever it was didn't get ate up.

I listened to Daddy read the Bible. The sun come up higher and I wondered about the cows. Did the gray people eat them all? It wasn't like they ain't enough sinners to go around. I didn't for a minute believe that everybody was gray. There had to be others like us. There's a hymn that says you'll never walk alone. I don't reckon the Lord breaks promises like that but I was way too scared to ask. Daddy's eyes were getting bloodshot, like he hadn't slept a wink, and he was whispering to hisself again.

I drank water from the plate that Preacher Aldridge passed around on Sundays. The water tasted like old pennies. Daddy didn't drink nothing. I asked him if he wanted the last can of sardines but he said man can't live by bread alone but by the word of the Lord. I wondered what the Lord's words tasted like. I wondered what people tasted like. I ate the sardines by myself.

That night was quiet, like the gray people had done gone on to wherever they were headed. I woke up in the morning plenty sore and I asked Daddy if we could take a peek out the door. Daddy hadn't moved, stood up there at the pulpit like he was getting ready to let loose with a sermon. He had the shotgun raised toward heaven and I don't reckon he heard me. I asked it louder and he said you can't see the gray people because ever sinner is blind. I said I ain't no sinner but he said you're looking mighty gray to me.

I said I ain't gray, and then he made me prove it. Said get on your knees and beg the Lord to forgive you. He pointed the shotgun at me. I didn't know if he would use it or not, but the way his eye twitched I wasn't taking no chances. I got on my knees but I was scared to close my eyes. When you close your eyes and pray it's just you and the Lord. You're blind but the Lord sees everything. I asked Daddy to pray with me.

Daddy set in to asking the Lord to forgive us our sins and trespasses. I wondered if we was trespassing on the church. It belonged to the Lord, and we was here so we wouldn't get ate up. I didn't say nothing to Daddy about it, though. I added an extra loud amen just so Daddy would know for sure that I wasn't gray.

Later I asked Daddy how come ever sinner is gray. He said the Lord decides such things. He said Momma was a sinner and that's why she was gray all along and her soul was already under Hell. I didn't say nothing to that. Sometimes Daddy said I took after my Momma. I wished I'd took after Daddy instead and been able to pray all by myself.

I said it sounded like the gray people was gone. Daddy said you can't trust the Devil's tricks. Said the only way out was through the Lord. I said I was getting hungry again. Daddy said get some sleep and pray.

I woke up lost in the dark and Daddy was screaming his head off. He was sitting where the moon come through the window and he said look at me, look at my skin. He held up his hands and said I'm gray, I'm gray, I'm gray. Said he was unfit to be in the House of the Lord. He put the shotgun barrel up to the side of his neck and then there was a flash of light and sounded like the world split in half and then something wet slapped against the walls.

I crawled over to him and laid beside him 'til all the warm had leaked out. I was scared and I wanted to pray but without Daddy to help me the Lord would look right into me and that was worse than anything. Then I thought if Daddy was in heaven now, maybe I could say a prayer to him instead and he could pass along my words to the Lord.

The sun come up finally and Daddy didn't look gray at all. He was white. His belly gurgled and the blood around his neck hole turned brown. I went to the door and unlocked it. Since it was Sunday morning, I figured people would be coming to hear the sermon. With more people in the church, I could pray without being so scared.

I stacked up some of the hymn books and stood on them so I could look out the window. They was back. More gray people were walking by, all headed in the same direction. I figured they were going to that place under Hell, just like Daddy said, and it made me happy that Daddy died before he turned gray.

Time passed real slow and the bread was long gone and nobody come to church. I never figured so many people that I used to pray with would end up turning gray. Like church didn't do them no good at all. I thought of all the prayers I said with them and it made me scared, the kind of scared that fills you up belly first. I wondered what the Lord thought about all them sinners, and what kind of words the Lord said back to them when they prayed.

Daddy's fingers had gone stiff and I about had to break them to get the shotgun away. He'd used up the last shell. The door was unlocked but nobody set foot in the church. I was hoping whoever had knocked the other day might come back, but they didn't.

The gray people didn't come in the church. I figured if they was eating live flesh they would get me sooner or later. Except maybe they was afraid about the church and all, or being in plain sight of the Lord. Or maybe they ain't figured out doors yet. I wondered if you go through doors to get under Hell.

Night come again. Daddy was dead cold. I was real hungry and I asked Daddy to tell the Lord about it, but I reckon Daddy would call that a selfish thing and wouldn't pass it on. I kept trying to pray but I was scared. Preacher Aldridge said you got to do it alone, can't nobody do it for you.

Maybe one of them Aye-rab bugs got in while the door was open. Maybe the gray people ain't ate me yet because I ain't live flesh no more. Only the Lord knows. All I know is I can't stay in this church another minute. Daddy's starting to stink and the Lord's looking right at me.

Like I'm already gray.

I don't feel like I am, but Daddy said ever sinner is blind. And it's the kind of hungry that hurts.

Outside the church, the morning is fresh and cold and smells like broken flowers. I hear footsteps in the wet grass. I turn and walk, and I fit right in like they was saving a place for me. I'm one of them, following the ones ahead and leading the ones behind. We're all headed in the same direction. Maybe this entire world is the place under Hell, and we've been here all along.

I ain't scared no more, just hungry. The hungry runs deep. You can't live by bread alone. Sometimes you need meat instead of words.

I don't have to pray no more, out here where it ain't never dark. Where the Lord don't look at you. Where we're all sinners. Where you're born gray, again and again, and the End Times never end.

Where you never walk alone.

PENANCE

It caught Gran next.

Small red sores appeared in the wrinkles of her neck and face. In the candlelight of the kitchen, the sores sparkled like jewels. Father wouldn't look at her anymore. I'm sure he would have locked her in the spare bedroom, except the beds were already occupied by the corpses of Bobby and Mother. The house smelled of corruption and ointment.

Father had started wearing his mask again. He sat in the living room, watching the Web screen, hoping the misery of others would ease his own. At least they hadn't cut our electricity, though our water service had been terminated. I guess they figured that the Penance wasn't transmitted by electrons. But Father made us use the candles anyway. He said the fire was God's purifying light, now that we had been robbed of the sun.

Gran sat at the kitchen table, her eyes glassy, the candle's flame reflecting off her pupils. I dipped a towel in the bowl of gray water, wrung it out, and patted Gran's face.

"Don't waste it, Ruth," she said.

"Shh," I said. "It's no time to be brave."

"The saints may not bring any more."

"Have faith," I said.

The saints hadn't brought food or water in three weeks. Maybe the army had finally wiped them out. Maybe the Penance had caught them. Or perhaps God had called them home.

Gran's eyes welled with tears that she couldn't blink away. I wiped at the fluid that leaked down her face.

"You should be wearing your gloves," she said, her voice raspy.

I kept wiping. I hung the towel over the back of a chair and squeezed some ointment from a rolled-up tube. The gel was cold on my finger. I touched it to Gran's sores, at least the ones that hadn't burst open.

"You're warm," I said.

"The fever." She shivered under her dusty blanket.

"Tell me about the mountains," I said, both of us needing her stories. Gran had grown up in the Appalachians of Virginia. Now the mountains had become a mecca as hundreds, maybe even thousands if that many were left, escaped the city. Some of them were already infected, carrying in their hearts the thing they were fleeing. From the Web news, back before the army had taken control of transmissions, we had learned that people were killing each other there, too. But when Gran lived in the mountains, it was a place of peace.

Gran drew the blanket more tightly across her chest. "We had a little cabin," she said. "In the morning, you could see for miles, the high ridges like islands above the ocean of fog. The air was so clean you could taste it, maple and oak and pine, with just a touch of woodsmoke from the chimney. Your father, he looked so much like Bobby—"

Her voice broke. The tears welled up again at the mention of my brother. I fought back the water that threatened to pool in my own eyes. I reached for the towel, but Gran shook her head and smiled. "The tears don't sting anymore."

The curtain over the doorway parted and Father came into the kitchen. The mask made him look like an insect. His eyes were large and frightening, distorted by the goggles. He went past us without speaking and opened the refrigerator. The buzz and murmur of the Web screen protected us from the awful silence of the room and the world outside.

We watched as he thumbed through the stack of cheeses. He pushed aside the packages that had been opened. He found one he liked, put it in the pocket of his coveralls, and pulled a bottle of wine from the lower shelf. Then he rummaged through the cabinets.

He pulled out a can of tuna. He looked past Gran to me. "Have you touched this?" he said, his voice muffled by the filters of his mask.

I shook my head. Father dropped it in his pocket. He had his own can opener, fork, and knife. No one could touch his utensils. He even slept with them.

"What's on the screen?" I asked, hoping to get him to stay for a moment.

"The army says the war with the saints and scientists is nearly over," he said. "I should have joined the army while I had the chance."

My heart spasmed and then sank in my chest. The extermination of the saints meant there would be no more midnight deliveries. "What will we do for food?" I asked him.

"We shouldn't expect others to spare us God's punishment," he said. I waited for him to deliver another sermon, parroting the Commander-In-Chief's press conferences. About how we had brought the plague among us by our sinning ways, how the world had to be cleansed, how the scientists conspired with Satan to deliver us unto these dark ages.

Instead, Father went back through the curtain, the wine bottle tucked under his arm. He couldn't even spare us a sermon.

"Your father used to go into the woods with his hatchet," Gran continued, as if recalling fond memories at a funeral. Like Father was already dead. "He'd cut me a little pile of twigs and say, 'Here, Mommie, these are for the fire.' I made a big deal of putting them in the fireplace and rubbing my hands together, then blowing into the flames."

She shivered again, either from nostalgia or fever. "I'd say, 'It's a magic fire.' And the next day, frost would be thick on the trees and grass and creek stones. We would put on our mittens and go walk in the woods, the leaves like a crisp carpet under our feet. Our breath made clouds in front of our faces." She glanced at the curtain that hung over the entry. "He believed in magic, back then."

"Blue heaven," I said, trying to make her forget her pain. Gran used to say, "When I die, Lord, take me back to blue heaven."

"Looks like He'll be taking me there soon."

"Do you want to go?" I asked.

Her eyes narrowed and her mouth collapsed into creases. "Only the Lord knows the proper hour."

I felt for her hand. Her skin was like damp tree bark. "No. I mean, do you want to go now?"

"Don't tease an old woman," she said.

I leaned over the table and lowered my voice, even though Father was in the warm cocoon spun by the Web screen and alcohol. "I found a way out."

She looked at me, her eyes cold, dead of hope. "No. I heard the hammers and nails. The soldiers buried us. In here with the Penance."

The Penance had started in the cities, New York, Los Angeles, Miami. We watched on the news, the videos of hospitals and people in ambulances and doctors trying to explain the Penance away. Father would shake his head and say that the sinners had brought God's wrath. When the army closed off the roads leading from Charlotte, my parents shared a prayer of thanks that we had been spared.

But the Penance didn't stop among the highrise buildings, and barbed wire and barricades couldn't hold it back. It reached the foothills where we lived, just as surely as it stormed the beaches and jetted across the oceans. And the army chased it, growing in might along with the Penance, two great careening forces. They both came to Barkersville and hemmed us in.

In the beginning, it was only one house. Megan, from my eleventh grade class, came to school one day with the sores on her face. The school officials sent her home. After school, as I walked down her street on the way to our house, the trucks pulled up. Soldiers in gas masks got out, carrying guns, boards, ladders, and tool belts. They nailed the doors and windows shut, then added a layer of plywood over the boards. Megan's father tried to fight them off, but they hit him with the butts of their rifles and pushed him back inside. Megan screamed as they boarded her window.

I heard her screams every day, even when I crossed to the other side of the street. On the fourth morning, I tried a new route to school, one that took me well out of my way. On those other streets, more than half the houses were boarded up, an "X" spray-painted in red on each barred door. A thin dog rooted in the garbage that covered the sidewalk. The few people that were out looked at me warily, and moved away as I passed their yards.

I ran the rest of the way to school, anxious at being late. Soldiers covered the playgrounds, their shouts the only sound in a place once filled by games and laughter. They were sealing off the building, chaining the doors closed. I hid in the trees and watched as students tried to escape from the upper windows. The soldiers climbed their ladders and hit the kids with hammers. I went home, my stomach aching, my hands trembling.

The next day, Mother came home, her face in her hands. She was a doctor, and we thought she was crying over the misery she witnessed as the Penance devastated her patients. Prayers hadn't helped them. Neither had medicine.

Father pulled her hands apart. She had sores on her face. Father slapped her. "Wicked whore," he said. "You have brought the pestilence among us."

She was packing her clothes when soldiers rolled their trucks into our yard. Father had called them, hoping they would take her away and spare the rest of the family. After all, why should we suffer for her sins?

The soldiers grunted from behind their masks. Father held his arms wide in welcome. He was a big disciple of the Commander-in-Chief by that time. The army was doing God's holy work, only following orders, he said.

They drove their nails even as Father cursed them. He pounded on the door that had been slammed in his face. He kicked at the wood that surrounded and bound us. He picked up his Bible and slammed it against Mother's head. He fell to his knees and wept prayers.

The soldiers drove away. Gran and my younger brother Bobby hid in the bathroom until Father's rage subsided. I helped Mother to her room. She collapsed on the bed.

"I'm going to hell," she said.

"No, you're not."

"I have sinned." She shivered and grabbed my hands.

"We have all sinned," I said. "But God is merciful."

"I helped them," she said. "I worked with the scientists and I prayed for the saints."

"Just try to get some rest. I'll bring you a cold drink."

Her face was raw and red, her eyes wide. "What have I done?" she gasped to the ceiling. "What have I done to deserve this, O Lord?"

God may have forgiven her, but she never forgave herself. She died two weeks later. Then Bobby got the sores.

"What did I do wrong?" Bobby asked. He was ten years old. He was Father's favorite, everybody's favorite. Even mine. But then, he was the son, and I was only the daughter.

"Nothing," I said. "Sometimes even God makes mistakes." God would forgive me this blasphemy, because my intent was pure.

I kept him hidden from Father. By then, Father was so obsessed with the Web reports that he didn't even notice Bobby was sick. When Bobby died, I put him in the spare bedroom with Mother.

Gran stayed in the kitchen most of the time. The saints had chopped out a small hole in the kitchen window, just large enough for Gran and me to send out whispered confessions. Sometimes at night, cheese or canned foods or bottles of water would be shoved back through the opening. Some nights, the streets were filled with the noises of trucks and gunfire. On those nights, no food arrived.

One time, just as the sun was sinking and throwing its red light through the opening, I heard a scratching sound outside the wall. I thought it was a saint. I whispered, "All have sinned and come short of the glory of God."

No one answered. Confessions were usually rewarded with material goods, sustenance, the manna of the damned. I called again. Gran, who was asleep at the table, twitched once and fell still.

"Ruth," came a guarded voice. Saints weren't supposed to use mortal names.

"Who is it?"

"John. From school."

John. I recognized the voice. He sat behind me in Social Studies, quiet and smart, his hair always a little unkempt.

"You can get in trouble," I whispered through the hole, wondering how he had escaped the school. Unless, like me, God had chosen him to be tardy that day.

"I'm a soldier now."

My pulse raced. I pictured him outside the house, in his crisp uniform, a hammer on his belt, a rifle strapped over his shoulder. I wondered which of the nails he'd driven into our doors and windows.

"Has it caught you yet?" he asked. The dying day had made the sky more deeply red. A little of that blood-colored light leaked through the wall.

"No," I whispered. "My brother Bobby died. Mother, too."

"I'm scared."

Soldiers weren't supposed to be scared. They were doing God's work.

"Why are you here?" I asked.

"The Penance is catching some of the soldiers. I heard a rumor today that even the Commander-in-Chief has it. I just wanted to tell somebody I was sorry."

My stomach ached, my face flushed. I wondered whether it was the first rush of fever or just hatred of this unwanted confession. "Don't say these things," I said. "God will strike you."

"Let Him strike," John said breathlessly. Night had fallen, leaking through the hole in the wall like a black oil. A truck sounded on the street, men shouted, and a siren wailed several streets away. I lit another candle and waited near the hole, but I heard no more of John.

Father bathed himself in the light of the Web screen. In the beginning, the videos had been of bodies piled high in the streets as solemn news anchors reported the latest death tolls. Health officials spoke of concentrated efforts to find a cure. Eventually these gave way to army television. Most of the time the Commander-in-Chief occupied the screen, his fist lifted in righteous indignation, his eyes bright with hate, his mouth contorted by his sermons. Father raised his fist in unison with the image.

"Kill them all, and let God sort them out," was one of Father's favorite slogans. I avoided him after he began wearing the mask. Most of the time, I stayed in the kitchen with Gran, the farthest room from the bathroom, where our wastes had fouled the air. We slept in the room that I had shared with Bobby.

One night I heard a tapping, a squeaking of metal and the slight crack of dry wood. I was afraid, because the sound meant change, and all change was for the worse. I prayed the night away, and somehow God spared us. The next morning, as I pressed at the wood that covered the window, anxious for a glimpse of the new sun, one of the boards fell away. Others were loose, too, enough for a person to wriggle through. I could hardly keep myself from bursting through and falling onto the green grass outside, but I was afraid soldiers might be watching.

I waited until evening to tell Gran. Her eyes misted over. When I was through describing my plan, she lowered her head.

"It's our only chance," I whispered.

"It's the Lord's will that we be punished," she said.

"Maybe it's the Lord's will that the boards are loose."

"The wicked can't flee their own wretched hearts."

"Gran, Gran," I said. "Not you, too. Why would God want to punish you?"

"No one is clean. All have come short of the glory of God."

Father gave a shout from the living room, joining in a televised cheer for the Commander-in-Chief.

"We only have enough food left for a week or so," I said. "We'll die in here."

"I'll die anyway. Here, there, what's the difference?"

Her words hung in the air like smoke from a fatal gun. She would die, sweating and shivering, writhing in the sheets, chewing her tongue as the blood poured from her ears and eyes.

God is blind to suffering. We make our prayers anyway.

"In the autumn, the mountains look like a rumpled patchwork quilt," Gran said. "Your grandfather would sit on the porch with his easel and paints. He used oils because he believed that the long drying time made him more patient, more careful."

One of his paintings hung in the living room. It was of a neglected flower garden, bright marigolds and morning glories and tulips fighting the weeds for sunshine. Grandfather had been Jewish. The Commander-in-Chief said the Jews may have brought the pestilence among the faithful. God delivered it, but the Jews spread it. Either the Jews or the Catholics. Oh, yes, and the scientists, as well. Satan's forces were legion.

"I would make him tea," Gran said. "Hot tea. He would blow on top of the cup until it was cool enough to drink. I can still see the funny face he made when he blew, his eyebrows scrunched down and his lips curled."

"Did Father want to be a painter, too?"

"No, but he liked tea," she said. She coughed, and a fleck of blood appeared in the corner of her mouth. "You look a lot like him, you know. When he was your age, I mean."

I couldn't believe my father had ever been my age. "When did he join the Church?"

"When he was your age."

"Is that why you joined?"

She blinked. "I just...joined. Like we were supposed to."

A new sore was erupting, above her right eyebrow. I dabbed at it with the towel. She weakly pushed my hand away.

"In the mountains, you can touch the clouds," she said. "You're closer to God there. Even the rain is sweet. Your father used to catch it on his tongue."

"Thou hast given them blood to drink, for they are worthy," I said, repeating one of Father's slogans.

"Why hasn't the Penance moved into you?" Gran asked.

Who can know the workings of the Almighty? I shrugged. "By the grace of God," I said. "Though I am wicked and surely deserve the Penance as much as anyone."

She seemed satisfied with this, and let her chin droop against her chest.

I stood and went to the refrigerator. I wasn't hungry. I thought of the mountains, of exodus, of flights from persecution. I closed my eyes, shamed by my cowardice and doubt.

Father turned up the volume on the Web screen. The Commander-in-Chief was raving, his voice like thunder, saying "And I heard a great voice out of the temple, saying to the seven angels, 'Go, and pour out the seven vials of the wrath of God upon the earth.'"

I remembered the time I was twelve and Bobby, then six, got a goldfish for his birthday. One morning the fish had floated to the top of the glass bowl, belly-up, lips sucking for life, gills undulating weakly. I took it from the bowl and flushed it down the toilet. When Bobby came in the room, I told him the goldfish had crawled to the river during the night. Heading for bigger water.

I wondered which sin I would pay for, the lie or the killing of a fish.

I turned to face Gran. "I'm sorry for talking about it," I said.

She merely nodded, too weak to argue.

"It's a test of faith," I continued. "I suffered a moment of weakness. I promise to be strong."

"Don't make promises to me," she said. "Make them to the One that matters."

"Please don't tell Father," I said, clasping her hand.

She pursed her pale lips. Father came through the curtain. The sound from the Web screen filled the kitchen as he held the curtain open. The army was singing a hymn. Even though I couldn't see his mouth, I knew Father was moving his lips to the rhythm. His eyes were moist, fogging his goggles.

"Sing," he shouted, the mask vibrating from the force of his voice. "Sing that we may find salvation."

Gran joined in with her thin and sweet alto. "...I once was lost, but now I'm found, was blind..."

I added my voice to the multitudes. "...but now I see."

Father removed his mask, his face wet with tears. The candle's flame bobbed and swayed with our breathing. Beautiful music flooded the house, overpowering the silence of corpses and drowning out the rumble of the army truck rolling down the street. We soared into the second verse, a family united, a nation united, all under God. Father rubbed at his cheek. The first reddening had appeared there, the sores a day or two away.

We sang the hymn, and half a dozen more. Father went back to the Web screen and his Bible, the bottle of wine open on the table beside him. Gran hobbled down the hall to pray over the two bodies, then I heard the door close as she went to bed. I filled my pockets with canned meat, cheese, and crackers.

That night we went through the window. As I pushed the boards away, I wondered if a saint could come disguised as a soldier or if an angel might carry a claw hammer. The Lord worked in mysterious ways.

Gran may have heard the noise, may have been awake in the darkness mouthing her prayers. But she said nothing. Or perhaps she was already dead, growing stiff as her fluids leaked into the mattress.

Bobby was heavy, but no heavier than a wooden cross. He would slow me down, make me an easier target for the soldiers. But my blood is certainly no more precious than that of Him who had gone before.

I headed north, toward the mountains. Sinners have little to lose. We can't run from the Penance. But the sinless surely deserve to rest in peace. Bobby will sleep in a blue heaven, where the dust of his flesh shall mingle with the clouds.

And this I pray.

SEWING CIRCLE

"The only Jew in town," Morris said as Laney pulled into the church parking lot.

He pointed to the stained-glass window cut into the middle of the belfry. It looked expensive, more than a little country church could afford. Jesus smiled down from the window, arms spread in welcome and acceptance.

"The story's about the sewing circle, not the church," Laney said.

"Jesus as a ragpicker. Was that in the Bible?"

"You're too cynical."

"No, I'm just a frustrated idealist."

Morris rubbed his stomach. He'd gone soft from years at a desk, his only exercise the occasional outdoor feature story, usually involving a free meal. He'd given up the crime beat, preferring to do the "little old lady in the holler" stuff, the cute little profile features that offended no one. Still, the fucking quilt beat was the bottom rung on the ladder he'd started climbing back down a decade ago.

"Come on, it'll be fun," Laney said. She was the staff photographer, and true to her trade, she managed to keep a perspective on things. Cautious yet upbeat, biding time, knowing her escape hatch was waiting down the road. For Morris, there was no escape hatch. The booby hatch, maybe.

"'Fun' is the Little League All-Stars, a Lion's Club banquet where they give out a check the size of Texas, a quadriplegic doing a power wheelchair charity run from the mountains to the coast. But this"—he flipped his notebook toward the little Primitive Baptist church, its walls as white as pride in the morning sun— "Even my Grandma would yawn over a sewing circle story."

"You can juice it up," Laney said as she parked. She always drove because she had two kids and needed the mileage reimbursement. All Morris had was a cat who liked to shit in the bathtub.

"That's what I do," he said. "A snappy lead and some filler, then cash my checks."

Though the checks were nothing to write home about. He'd written home about the first one, way back when he was fresh out of journalism school. Mom had responded that it was very nice and all but when was he getting a real job? Dad had no doubt muttered into his gin and turned up the sound to "Gunsmoke." They didn't understand that reporting was just a stepping stone to his real career, that of bestselling novelist and screenwriter for the stars.

They headed into the church alcove, Laney fidgeting with her lenses. Morris had called ahead to set up the appointment. He'd talked briefly to Faith Gordon, who apparently organized the group though she wasn't a seamstress herself. The sewing circle met every Thursday morning, rain, shine, flood, or funeral. Threads of Hope, the group called itself. Apparently it was a chapter of a national organization, and Morris figured he'd browse the Web later to snip a few easy column inches of back story.

The alcove held a couple of collection boxes for rags. Scrawled in black marker on cardboard were the words: "Give your stuff." Morris wondered if that same message was etched into the bottoms of the collection plates that were passed around on Sundays. Give your stuff to God, for hope, for salvation, for the needles of the little old ladies in the meeting room.

"Hello here," came a voice from the darkened hallway. A wizened man emerged into the alcove, hunched over a push broom, his jaw crooked. He leaned against the broom handle and twisted his mouth as if chewing rocks.

"We're from the Journal-Times," Morris said. "We came about the sewing circle."

One of the man's eyes narrowed as he looked over Laney's figure. He chewed faster. "'M'on back," he said, waving the broom handle to the rear of the church. He let the two of them go first, no doubt to sweep up their tracks as he watched Laney's ever-popular rear.

The voices spilled from the small room, three or four conversations going at once. Morris let Laney make the entrance. She had a way of setting people at ease, while Morris usually set them on edge. His style was fine on the local government beat, when you wanted to keep the politicians a little paranoid, but it didn't play well among the common folk in the Appalachian mountain community of Cross Valley.

"Hi, we're with the paper," Laney said. "We talked to Faith Gordon about the circle, and she invited us to come out and do a story."

Five women were gathered around a table, in the midst of various stitches, with yarn, cloth scraps, spools of different-colored threads, and darning needles spread out in front of them.

"You ain't gonna take my picture, are you?" one of them asked, clearly begging to be in the paper. That would probably make her day, Morris thought. The only other way she'd ever make the paper was when her obituary ran. She was probably sixty, but had the look of one who would live to be a hundred. One who knew all about life's troubles, because she'd heard about them from neighbors.

"Only if you want," Laney said. "But a picture makes the story better."

"We just thought the community would be interested in the fine work you ladies are doing," Morris said. That wasn't so bad, even if the false cheer burned his throat like acid reflux.

"If Faith said it was okay, that's good enough for us," said a second woman. She was in her seventies, wrinkled around the eyes, the veins on her hands thick and purple, though her fingers were as strong as a crow's claws. "I'm Alma."

"Hi, Alma," Morris said. He went from one to another, collecting their names for the record, making sure the spelling was correct. You could miss a county budget by a zero, apply the wrong charge in a police brief, and even fail to call the mayor on Arbor Day, and all these mistakes were wiped out with a Page 2 correction. But woe unto the reporter who misspelled a name in a fuzzy family feature.

Alma Potter. Reba Absher. Lillian Moretz. Daisy Eggers. The "other Alma," Alma Moretz, no immediate relation to Lillian, though they may have been cousins five or six times removed.

"Just keep on working while I take some shots," Laney said. She contorted with catlike grace, stooping to table level, composing award-quality photographs. The janitor stood at the door, appreciating her professional ardor. He was chewing so fast that his teeth were probably throwing off sparks behind his eager lips.

"So, how did you ladies meet?" Morris smiled, just to see what it felt like.

"Me and Reba was friends, and we'd get together for a little knitting on Saturdays while our husbands went fishing together," Alma Potter said. "They would go after rock bass, but they always came home with an empty cooler."

"God rest your Pete's soul," Reba said.

"Bless you," Alma said to her.

Morris glanced at his wristwatch. Thirty column inches to go, plus he had to knock out a sidebar on a weekend bluegrass festival. All with the Kelvinator looking over his shoulder. Kelvin Feeney, Journal-Times editor and all-around boy wonder, a guy on the come who didn't care whose backs bricked the path to that corner office at the corporation's flagship paper.

"So, Alma, when did you start sewing?" Morris thought of making a pun on "so" and "sew" and decided to pass.

"Oh, maybe at the age of five," she said. Her eyes stayed focused on the tips of her fingers as she ran the needle through a scrap of yellow cotton. Laney was working the scene, twisting the lens to its longest point, zooming in to get the wrinkled glory of the old woman's face.

"Did you learn from your mother?" Morris asked, scribbling in his notebook. Maybe he could use some of this in the Great American Novel he'd been working on since his freshman year, which had been tainted by a professor who thought Faulkner was the Second Coming and Flannery O'Connor was the Virgin Mary.

"She learnt it from me," Daisy Eggers said, her eyes like wet bugs behind the curve of her glasses. Daisy might have been anywhere between eighty and ninety, her upper lip collapsed as if her dentures were too small. When she spoke, the grayish tip of her tongue protruded, constantly trying to keep her upper false teeth in place.

"Good, we'll get back to that." Morris made a note as Laney's shutter clicked. "Tell me about Threads of Hope."

"You really need to talk to Faith about that," the other Alma said. "She's the one started it. We were all sewing anyway, and figured why not get together on it?"

Reba, who appeared a little less inclined to defer to their absent leader, said, "Threads of Hope gives blankets to sick kids in hospitals. Like the Ronald McDonald House and the Shriner's Hospital. It's all about the kids. But you'd best talk to Faith about that part of it."

Okay, Morris thought. It's not Pulitzer material but at least it has sick kids. Now if I could just work a cute babe and a puppy into the story, I'd hit the Holy Trinity.

"Is it local kids, or someone with a specific type of illness?" Laney asked the obvious question. She was actually better at that than Morris.

"Oh, just ones sick any old way. Faith, she's a nurse at Mercy Hospital, and she comes in about once a month and collects them, takes them off. We'll get a dozen done on a good morning." Reba held up the quilt she was working on and pointed to a scrap of denim. "That come from Doc Watson. You know, the famous flat-picker."

Morris had written about Doc a dozen times. Doc was also up in his golden years, with six Grammys on his trophy case. The musician had tried several times to retire, but every time he did, someone would launch a festival in his honor and he'd feel obliged to perform there.

Lillian spoke for the first time since giving her name. "These scraps have stories in them. They're like pieces of people's lives. And we figure the kids get some of the life out of those pieces."

"And a little hope," the other Alma said.

"Threads of Hope," Daisy said, knitting a fishnet-style afghan. Her knitting needles clicked like chopsticks, pushing and hooking yarn. The janitor came into the room, and though it was cramped, he managed to sweep the tiny scraps off the floor without once brushing against Laney. Morris wrote it all down, and they were back in the office by lunch time. The ladies had been all smiles by the time they left, speculating on how many copies of Friday's edition they were going to buy and which relatives they would call.

The phone call came shortly after eleven in the morning. The edition couldn't have been on the street for more than an hour, and those who received the paper via home delivery probably wouldn't see theirs until late afternoon. Morris dreaded the post-edition phone calls. The tri-weekly had a low circulation, but the reading audience was exacting.

"Journal-Times news desk," Morris answered, in his most aloof voice.

"Are you Morris Stanfield?"

"Yes, ma'am." It was always bad when they guessed your name.

"We have a serious problem."

"Ma'am?" Morris' finger edged toward the phone, planning a quick transfer to the Kelvinator. Serious problems were beyond the capabilities of an ink whore.

"Did you write the Threads of Hope article?"

Sometimes they called to say thanks. Sometimes, but not often.

"About the sewing circle."

"Where did you get your information?"

"From the ladies."

"The ladies." She sounded like a high school English teacher who was upset that a student had opted for the Cliff Notes during the Hawthorne semester. Her voice sounded familiar.

"It was a feature about a group of friends who get together and sew. A people feature."

"You were supposed to call me."

"Are you Faith Gordon?" He had meant to call her, really, but between the domestic dispute that led to a police standoff and the damned bluegrass festival sidebar, Morris had been forced to slam his story out an hour before deadline. The Threads of Hope web site had provided some history on the organization, about how the effort had been started by a seamstress in Kentucky whose son had been diagnosed with a brain tumor. A story of courage and perseverance, a true sob story, fraught with unsung heroes and all that happy bullshit.

"This is Faith. The ladies said you would call."

"I'm sorry. Deadline caught me. What's the problem?" Morris tried to replay the article in his mind. Often, by the time he finished writing one, it was seared into his memory until the next pint of whiskey or the next skull-numbing city council meeting, whichever came first. Writing was all about remembering, while the rest of Morris's life was all about forgetting.

"The headline," Faith Gordon said. "It says 'Local Women Stitch Blankets For The Needy.'" These blankets are for any sick child, not just those of economic difference."

"I don't write the headlines," Morris said.

"But it has your name right under it."

"Yes, ma'am, but the editor wrote that headline. Perhaps you can speak to him."

"It says 'Local Women Stitch Blankets For The Needy' by Morris Stanfield. You've done serious damage to the organization, not to mention insulting the women in the sewing circle. You should be ashamed."

"How did I damage the organization? I don't think many people in our readership have even heard of Threads of Hope."

"Exactly. Your callous disregard for the facts has tainted Threads of Hope for the whole community. And the ladies...poor Alma Potter was in tears."

"I'm really sorry to hear that," Morris said. He couldn't remember if Alma Potter was the "other Alma" or not.

"No wonder people no longer trust the media. If this is any example of how you take the good intentions of an innocent group and twist it into a sensational story—"

"Whoa," Morris said. "If I made a factual error, I'd be glad to run a correction. But I took my information directly from the sewing circle's own words, with some Internet research on the parent organization."

"You didn't talk to me," Faith said.

Morris at last saw the real problem. Faith Gordon's name hadn't appeared until the third or fourth paragraph. She obviously felt she was the real story, the tireless organizer who was practically an entire spool of hope, one who lifted the entire project on her shoulders and inspired everyone who could navigate the eye of a needle to great acts of charity.

"I'll transfer you to my editor," Morris said, and punched the buttons before she could respond. By leaning back in his chair, he could see out his cubicle to the glassed-in office of the Kelvinator. Feeney was checking on stock prices, probably in the middle of an editorial column on the dubious merits of funding public libraries. Morris waited until the editor picked up the phone, then turned his attention to his own computer. He opened his email and found six messages about the Threads of Hope story. Three were from Faith, reiterating her displeasure. Two were from Reba, who was concerned about a misquotation, and the last was from Lillian, who said she thought the article was good until Faith had told her what was wrong. Now, Lillian wrote, she was ashamed to have her name associated with either the Threads of Hope or the Journal-Times, and she was canceling her subscription "right this second."

Morris was in the midst of deleting the messages when the Kelvinator appeared in the mouth of the cubicle.

"Morris," the editor said. He was ten years younger than

Morris, with a personal digital assistant in his shirt pocket. His eyes moved like greased ball bearings.

"Bad headline, huh?"

"No, it was problems in your copy."

"What problems?"

"Faith Gordon has a list. You can talk to her about them when you see her."

"See her?"

"Write a follow-up. That's the only way to fix the mess you've made."

"There's no fucking mess. I didn't say anything about the blankets being for needy children."

"You must have, or I wouldn't have put it in the headline. Anyway, the easiest way to handle this is to interview Faith. And use a tape recorder this time, so you won't misquote her."

"But it was just a chummy little feature—"

"It's gotten bigger than that. I had a call from the Threads of Hope's national office. Apparently Faith Gordon has been blowing smoke up their asses, too."

"So let them sue for libel."

The Kelvinator tossed a sticky note onto Morris' cluttered desk. "Two o'clock today at the church. Polish it up for Monday's paper."

"Can Laney come with me?"

"We already have enough photos. She has to cover a flower show at the mall."

Morris crumpled the note as the Kelvinator returned to his office. He wished there were enough threads to make a noose. A noose of hopelessness, by which to hang himself before he had to write another quilt story.

The church sat in a valley and a fog hung over it, rising from the river that ran beside the road. The church parking lot was empty. That seemed odd, even for a Friday afternoon. He thought he was supposed to meet the entire sewing circle. Maybe he had a solo showdown with the legendary Faith Gordon. He shuddered, opened the dashboard, and retrieved the pint of Henry McKenna and a vial of Xanax. Substances that provided his own threads of hope, or at least stuffed cotton wadding between him and his anxiety and despair.

He stuck one of the tranquilizers on his tongue and toasted the stained-glass Jesus. "Here's to you, Big Guy."

Belly warmed, Morris entered the quiet church. He had been raised Baptist but had recovered quickly, and his only religious experience since then had been a foray into the Unitarian church in a half-assed attempt to meet women. Still, the polished oak of the foyer, the sermon hall with its carefully arranged pews, and the crushed velvet drapes invoked feelings of solemnity, as if he were actually in the presence of something mystical and important. He stepped carefully, afraid to break the hush.

"Mr. Stanfield."

He turned, recognizing the shrill, strident voice of Faith Gordon. He had expected a beefy, shoulder-heavy woman with a broad face and hands that could strangle an ox. Instead, she was diminutive, even pretty in a severe way. Her cheeks were lined from years of not smiling. She was about Morris' age but had none of his gray.

Morris attempted a boyish grin, knowing this was a time to turn on the charm, even if he came off like Clint Eastwood miscast in a comedy. "Miss Gordon. I'm sorry my story disappointed you."

"It's not me I'm worried about. It's the ladies in the circle. They were so excited about being in the paper until I told them about your errors."

"We can make it right."

"You can never make it right. The damage is already done. Feelings have been hurt. And what about the children who received blankets from Threads of Hope? How will they feel when told they are 'needy'?"

Morris dropped his grin. He wanted to scream at her, tell her that a fucking space-filler in the back pages of a dinky local rag didn't cause empires to rise or fall, and, truth be told, didn't sell a single goddamned car for the dealer whose ad ran right beside it. A newspaper was fucking fishwrap, a dinosaur walking in the shadow of the Internet that was too dumb to know it was going extinct. The only people who'd read the piece of brainless crap had been the members of the sewing circle.

"I didn't write that 'needy' part," Morris said. "My editor put that in. He thought it was more of an eye-grabber."

"The article has your name on it," Faith said. "You've damaged all the children who have been blessed by Threads of Hope. God can't forgive those who don't accept their sins."

"God doesn't have anything to do with it."

"If you can't apologize to the Lord, you can at least apologize to the circle." She stood to the side and motioned down the hallway, indicating that Morris should go first.

He resigned himself to go on and get his "mission of contrition" over with, then hurry back to the office and type it up with Henry McKenna as his co-author. He was halfway to the meeting room when he felt a prick in the back of his neck. At first he thought he'd been bitten by a spider, and he reached to wipe the creature away. The janitor came out of the meeting room, eyes bright, jaws making gravel.

"Let's get him upstairs," Faith said.

At first, Morris thought Faith wanted him to help subdue the janitor, who looked as if he'd escaped from a facility for the criminally insane. But the janitor didn't flee. Instead, he dropped his push broom and approached Morris. After a couple of steps, there were two of him, and Morris's head felt as if it were stuffed with wet pillows, the silent walls drumming in wooden echoes. He spun awkwardly, and Faith held up an empty hypodermic needle, the tip gleaming with one drop of clear liquid.

A kaleidoscope played behind his eyelids as he rose from the depths of a stupor. He'd experimented with a number of chemicals in his college days, but he could never recall suffering such a sledgehammer to the brain. The kaleidoscope slowly came into focus and he realized his eyes were open. He tried to move his head.

The kaleidoscope that had heralded his return to consciousness turned out to be a stained-glass window. Jesus stood there, arms spread, catching the dying sunlight. Morris recognized it as the same window that adorned the steeple of the church. The room appeared to be an attic of some kind, and a bell rope ran the length of one wall and disappeared through a small opening in the ceiling.

He must have fainted. Heat, stress, and a good dose of whiskey on an empty stomach. Not to mention the trank. And maybe a touch of the flu had crept up on him.

Snick.

Snick, snick.

As groggy as he was, it took him a moment to place the sound. Scissors.

The members of the sewing circle were gathered around him, stitching, darning, cutting scraps of cloth. He looked from face to face, trying to focus. Both Almas were there, though Morris had forgotten the names of the others. No, Reba, that was it. The chatty one. And Lillian. And one, wasn't she named after a flower? Rose? Violet? No, Daisy, that was it. Daisy.

He tried to smile but couldn't. His lips were too numb.

"Looks like Mr. Big-Time Writer is awake," Reba said, without a trace of her earlier humor.

"A shame he can't be troubled to get a little thing right," the other Alma said. "Now, what would happen if we left a few loose threads in one of our blankets just because we didn't care enough to do it right?"

"Why, that would be like having no hope," Daisy said. "Worse, it would be like giving up hope on the children."

"Oh, but we know how needy they are," the first Alma said. "Because we read about it in the paper."

Morris tried again to lift his head. The women weren't looking at him. They concentrated on their work, snipping, stitching, working threads and needles and yarn. Morris' stomach roiled, and he was afraid he was going to vomit in the presence of these women before he could lift himself and make it to a bathroom. Flu, for sure.

"Don't try to talk none," Reba said. "You done enough harm with your words already."

Lillian giggled like a schoolgirl. "You tied that knot off right, didn't you, Reba? I know how much pride you take in your work."

"Wouldn't want to go disappointing nobody. Unlike some people."

A door opened somewhere beyond Morris' range of vision. The women stopped working and looked in that direction, their faces rapt.

"How's our latest charity project coming along?" Faith asked.

"Right fair," the other Alma said. "Not such good material to work with, but I think we can shape it up some."

"Well, after all, they say we help the needy," Faith said. "In fact, I think I read so in the Journal-Times."

Morris couldn't help himself. Sick or not, he was going to tell them all to fuck off. So what if he lost his job? He could paint houses, drop fry baskets, go on welfare. At least he'd no longer have to pretend to give a damn about little old ladies making sacrifices solely because of their own selfish need to feel useful.

He tried to speak, but his lips didn't move. Not much, anyway.

"Mr. Stanfield, Reba has been sewing for fifty-nine years, as you know, since you reported it in your article. That was one fact you reported correctly. So you can rest assured her stitches are much stronger than the flesh of your lips."

Stitches? Lips?

He screamed, but the sound stuck at the top of his vibrating vocal cords. Faith came into view. She leaned over him, appraising the handiwork. "A silent tongue speaks no evil," she said.

"And doesn't put down the good work of others," Reba said, looking to Faith for approval.

"That's right," Faith said. "I'm sorry we're having to take time from our true work. Several children won't get blankets this week because of Mr. Stanfield. But this task is perhaps just as important in the Lord's eyes. This is a true charity case."

Morris summoned all his effort and craned his neck. His clothes were sewn to what looked like the fabric pad of a mattress. He squirmed but could only move his arms and legs a few inches. He flexed his fingers, trying to make a fist.

"Alma, how was that tatting on his hands?" Faith asked.

Alma Potter beamed with satisfaction at being recognized by the circle's leader. "I done proud, Faith. Them fingers won't be typing no more lies for a while."

Morris felt his eyes bulging from their sockets. The first tingle of pain danced across his lips.

"I'm sorry, Mr. Stanfield," Faith said. "I don't have any more morphine. The hospital's supply is closely monitored. I could only risk stealing a few doses. But my sin is one the Lord is willing to forgive because it serves a greater good."

The women were busy around him, their needles descending and lifting, the threads stretching and looping. The other Alma was busy down by his feet, her gnarled hands tugging at his toes. Lillian brought a scrap of cloth to his face, but Faith held up a hand.

For the first time, Faith smiled. "Not yet, Lillian. We can close his eyes later. For now, let him look upon good works. Let him know us by our deeds, not by his words."

Lillian looked disappointed. Faith put a gentle hand on the old woman's shoulder.

"A good blanket takes care and patience," Faith said. "Hope takes patience. All we can do is our part, and let the Lord take care of the rest."

"Just like with the sick children," Lillian said.

"Yes. They're sick, but never needy. As long as one person has hope enough for them all, they are never in need."

Morris tried to communicate with his eyes, to lie and tell Faith that he now understood, that sick children were never needy no matter what the Kelvinator said, but his eyes were too cold and lost to the world of light and understanding. He was a cynic and had nothing inside but desperation. He gazed at the stained-glass Jesus, but no hope could be found in that amber face as the sunlight died outside.

The gauze of morphine slipped a little, and now he could feel the sharp stings as the needles entered his arms, legs, and torso. Reba was stitching up his inseam, her face a quivering mask of concentration as she worked toward his groin. Daisy's tongue pressed against her uppers as she pushed and tugged in tiny little motions.

Silver needles flashed in the glow of the lone gas lamp by which the sewing circle now toiled. From outside, the plate-glass image must have flickered in all the colors of salvation.

But from the inside, the image had gone dark with the night. Summoning his remaining strength, Morris ripped the flesh of his lips free of their stitches and screamed toward the high white cross above.

"Look, his eyelids twitched," came a voice.

"There, there," Lillian said, as if on the other side of a thick curtain. "You just rest easy now."

"Where—" Morris was in the sewing room downstairs, flat on his back on the table, surrounded by piles of rags. They must have carried him here after they—

He brought a wobbly hand to his mouth and felt his lips. They were chapped but otherwise whole.

"I think he's thirsty," said Faith, who knelt over him, patting his forehead with a soft swatch of linen. She turned to the janitor, who stood in the doorway. "Bruce, would you get him a cup of water, please?"

As the janitor shuffled off, Faith again settled her kind, healing eyes on him. "You fainted. A big, strong fellow like you."

"Must be—" The words were thick on his tongue. He flexed his fingers, remembering the sharp tingle of needles sliding through his skin, the taut tug of thread in his flesh. A dream. Nothing but a crazy, drug-stoked nightmare. "Must be the heat," he managed.

"It's okay," Faith said. Gone was her severe and chiding tone. She now spoke in her gentle nurse's voice. "We'll take care of you. You just have a chill. Rest easy and wait for the ambulance."

"Ambulance? No, I'm fine, really, I just need—" He tried to sit up, but his head felt like a wet sack of towels.

"Your pulse is weak," Faith said. "I'm concerned you might go into shock."

"That means we need to cover him up," the other Alma said.

Faith smiled, the expression of all saints and martyrs. "I guess we should use the special blanket," she said.

"Blanket?" Morris blinked lint from his eyes.

"We made it just for you. We were going to give it to you in appreciation for writing the story and let you enjoy it in the comfort of your own bed. But perhaps this is more fitting."

"Fitting," Daisy said with a hen's cackle. "That's as funny as Santa in a manger scene."

Lillian approached the table, a blanket folded across her chest. Unlike the other quilts, this one was white, though the pieces were ragged, the stitches loose, the cloth stained and spotted. "We done our best work on this one," she said. "We know a sick soul when we see one."

"Threads of Hope sometimes come unraveled," Faith said. Her sweet tone, and her soft touch as she felt his wrist for a pulse, was far more unnerving than her previous bullying.

"That's right," Reba said. "Sometimes hope is not enough."

"And kids die and go on to heaven," Lillian said. "The Lord accepts them whole and pure, but their pain and suffering has to go somewhere. Nothing's worse than laying there knowing you're going to die any day, when by rights you ought to have your whole life in front of you."

Lillian helped Reba unfold the patchwork blanket. Morris saw the white scraps of sheet were actually varying shades of gray, cut at crazy angles and knotted together as if built in the dark by mad, clumsy hands.

"There's another side to our work," Faith said. "One we don't publicize. If it had a name, it might be called 'Threads of Despair.'"

"I like 'Threads of the Dead,'" Reba said, in her high, lilting voice. Her remark drew a couple of snickers from the old women gathered around the table. Morris didn't like the way Reba's eyes glittered.

"I'll write the story however you want it, and let you proof it before I turn it in to the editor," he said, his throat parched.

"Cover him up," Faith commanded. "I'd hate to see him go into shock."

Morris once again tried to lift himself, but he was too woozy. Maybe he really did need an ambulance. And a thorough check-up.

He was having a nervous breakdown. And these fine women, whom he'd insulted and belittled, were compassionate enough to help him in his time of need. Faith was right, he was the needy one, not those sick children.

As they stretched the mottled blanket over him, preparing to settle it across his body, Morris saw the words "Mercy Hospital Morgue" stamped in black on one corner.

Sheets from the hospital?

The cloth settled over him with a whisper, wrinkled hands smoothing and spreading it on each side. His limbs were weak, his mouth slack, as if the blanket had sapped the last of his strength. Though his skin was clammy, sweat oozed from his pores like newly hatched maggots crawling from the soft meat of a corpse. He was being wrapped in fabric even colder than his soul.

Threads from the dead, from those who had lost hope.

Sheets that would give back all that had gone into them.

A handmade blanket stitched not in the attic of the heart but in the dark basement of the disappointed.

"The ambulance will be here in twenty minutes," Faith said. "Until then, cherish the despair you deserve."

She tugged the blanket up to his chin, and then, with a final, benevolent look into his frightened eyes, she drew it over his face.

SCARECROW BOY

The sun raised a sleepy eye over the north Georgia hills. Short-leafed pines shivered here and there in the breeze, surrounded by the black bones of oak. Ground mist rose and waltzed away from the light. A stream cut a silver gash in the belly of the valley on its way to the Chattahoochee, the only thing in a hurry on the late-autumn morning. Inside a warped barn, the scarecrow boy rose from its dreams of brown fields and barbwire.

Jerp rubbed his eyes to wipe away the glare of dawn as he walked with his grandpa to the barn. The grass crunched under his boots and his breath painted the thick vapor in the air. A banty rooster bugled a reveille. Wrens fluttered from under the tin eaves of the barn, on their way to scratch earthworms from the hard ground. The sky was ribbed with clouds, a thin threat of snow.

Jerp glanced at the second-story windows of the barn. No scarecrow boy yet. But Jerp knew it was in there somewhere, flitting between cracks with a sound like dry paper crumpling. But maybe it only came alive at night, when the darkness kissed its moon-white face.

"Quit your daydreaming, boy. Got chores to do." Grandpa

247

roped a stream of tobacco juice onto the ground. Steam drifted from his spit and he shifted the bucket from one gloved hand to the other.

Jerp wanted to tell Grandpa again about the scarecrow boy. About how it smiled at him when he was alone in the barn, how it danced from its nail on the wall, swinging its ragged limbs as if caught in a December crosswind. About how Jerp got the feeling that the scarecrow boy wanted something, a thing that only Jerp could give it. But Grandpa would say, "Got no time for such foolishness."

Grandpa held open the barnyard gate and waited until Jerp followed him inside, then closed the gate as carefully as if he were performing a ritual.

"Always close up behind you. We do things right around here." Those were the same words he had said every morning and night when they came down to do chores.

Grandpa passed the bucket to Jerp and removed his gloves. Jerp watched as the big-knuckled hands slammed the hasp into place. The noise echoed across the hill, maybe waking the scarecrow boy.

The milk pail banged against Jerp's knee as he followed Grandpa across the barnyard. A sow grunted under her breath in one of the side pens, mistaking the sound for the arrival of the slop bucket. She rolled over in the marsh of her own waste and glared at Jerp. Jerp wasn't scared of her. He was more worried about the scarecrow boy who would be waiting in rafters or cribs or dark corners for Jerp to step within reach.

Jerp followed Grandpa to the front of the barn. Its rough gray planks were split from decades of harsh weather and ten-penny nail heads stuck out like little brown eyes. Grandpa slid open the heavy door, which hung from wheels that rolled across a steel track overhead. They ducked under the oily ropes that had been dipped in chemicals and stretched across the barn opening. The horse and cows liked to rub their backs against the ropes and the chemicals were supposed to keep the flies away, but the flies were like the sun, reliable and stubborn.

"Gonna be a real corker of a day, Jerp." Grandpa crinkled his eyes, the closest he ever came to smiling. "Maybe we can get some work done around here."

"Yes, sir," Jerp said, checking the barn windows once more for any sign of the scarecrow boy. The windows were empty.

The barn air smelled of hay and dust, manure and animal hair. The cows mooed from their stalls, in a dull hurry to be turned out. Grandpa took a three-legged stool down from the wall and carried it to the milk cow's stall. He sat on the stool and reached underneath the cow and began tugging up and down as if picking fruit. Jerp held the pail so that the cow couldn't kick it over, watching the shadows for the scarecrow boy until at last the pail was full.

"Fetch some ears of corn for the chickens, and I'll meet you back at the house," Grandpa said. He was going to leave Jerp alone in the barn. No, not quite alone.

"But what about—" Jerp knew he was going to sound like a whimpering little city boy. He gulped and finished, "What about breakfast?"

"We see to the animals first. You know that." Grandpa juddered his head as he drew up to spit again. Jerp nodded and turned, walking to the corncrib with feet as heavy as International Harvesters. He heard Grandpa teasing the sow out in the barnyard. Jerp put a trembling hand on the latch.

He turned the latch and the door creaked open. Rats and their shadows scurried for the corners, their rustling making them sound as big as bobcats. He looked under the stairs that led to the hayloft, searching the darkness for movement. At first he saw only rotted pieces of harness and a broken cross-saw blade, its teeth reddened with age. Then he saw the scarecrow sitting among the sun-bleached husks. A smile stitched itself across the faded face. The scarecrow was looking at Jerp as if one of them was a mirror, with eyes as flat as old coins.

It was the boy in the barn, the one he had tried to tell Grandpa about. The one he had seen many times from his bedroom window, through the fog his breath had made on the glass. The scarecrow boy that had swayed like a sheet on a clothesline, its skin glowing sickly in the dark loft. The scarecrow boy that had stared from the barn window as if knowing it was being watched. The scarecrow boy that looked as if it were waiting.

But it's not real, Jerp told himself as he reached down to the grooved skin of the corn husks. *The scarecrow boy is not there if you don't see it.*

Jerp tried not to look under the stairs, even though the sweat was coming now and his eyes strained toward the corners of their sockets and the sunlight wasn't pouring fast enough through the cracks between the siding planks.

Had it moved? No, it was only a pile of old crumbling rags. Rotten cloth and straw never hurt nobody, just like Grandpa had said. Even though Jerp had seen the scythe of its smile. He gathered an armful of corn to his chest and ducked back, slamming the crib door shut with his foot and elbowing the latch into place.

Jerp's heart hammered in his ears as he shucked the corn and rubbed the grains loose with his thumbs. The kernels fell like golden teeth, and the chickens gathered around his feet, pecking at the grommets of his boots. He was trying to tell himself he *hadn't* seen the boy in the barn. That the scarecrow boy *wasn't* wearing a ragged flannel shirt and jeans with holes in the knees. It *didn't* have skin as white as raw milk and eyes that glimmered with a hunger that even biscuits and hamfat gravy wouldn't ease, nor was its hair as black as a crow nor its teeth as green as stained copper. It *hadn't* sat there through the frozen night, chattering until whatever served as its bones worked themselves loose.

It had to be a straw puppet, tossed in the corner until growing season. Only weeds and fabric. Only a scarecrow. But Grandpa didn't use scarecrows.

"Scarecrows are for the birds," Grandpa had said. He used pie pans on strings and shotgun blasts and bait laced with battery acid to drive away the magpies and crows. He said every scarecrow he'd ever put out had been covered in droppings by the end of the afternoon. As far as Grandpa was concerned, all a scarecrow did was provide a shady picnic area for the little thieves.

Jerp wasn't going to think about the scarecrow boy in the barn. He had more chores to do, and he didn't want Grandpa to give him the *look*, the one where he raised one white eyebrow and furrowed his forehead and twitched the corner of his mouth a little. It was a look of disappointment, his wordless way of saying *Jerp, you've come up short, can't cut the mustard, maybe you really oughta be in Atlanta with your parents, where you can be just another big-city sissy and everybody can call you "Jerald."*

Jerp would rather run through a barn full of thin, silent scarecrow boys than to have Grandpa give him the look.

So Jerp pretended to forget the scarecrow boy as he curried the mare and turned it out for the day, then gathered the eggs that the game hens had squirreled away in their dusty nests. He checked on the two boars to see if they had enough water and dumped a bucketful of mashed grain and sorghum into their trough. Grandpa didn't name any of the animals. He said he didn't think it was right that people gave names to things that they were going to eat.

"What's good for the goose is good for the gander," Grandpa had said, without bothering to explain what that meant. Jerp thought that maybe he meant everything died just the same.

Death was part of life on the farm. Thanksgiving brought a blessing to all but the turkey. Hens who went barren because their eggs were stolen soon steamed on the table, stunted legs in the air. Hogs and cattle found a hundred different uses in the kitchen, baked, broiled, fried, or barbecued.

"God bless this bounty on our table," Grandpa said before each meal. Jerp thought maybe he should do the prayers while the animals were still alive. The way he had done for Grandma.

Jerp had peeked once during the dinner prayer, and saw Grandpa looking out the window to the barn at the same moment he added the part that went, "And, please, dear Lord, spare us from evil."

Jerp shivered with the memory of that word, *evil*, and the way Grandpa's voice had cracked just a little as he said it. Jerp put away the currying brush and feed bucket, but the chill continued down his spine. Because he heard a soughing, scratchy sound from the hayloft above. He looked up just as a few strands of straw fell through the cracks in the floorboards. He hurried out of the barn, careful to latch the gate just as he had promised Grandma before she died.

Jerp had sat with her one night, when her spark of life was fading rapidly. She looked at him with burning, fevered eyes, looked past and through him to the window, to the long shadows of the barn.

"There's a season for ever thing," she had gurgled. "The gate..."

Jerp thought she meant the Pearly Gates. He waited for her to say more. But she closed her eyes to the lamplight and slept.

Now Grandma was dead but the scarecrow boy was alive. Last year's piglet had grown plump and earned its place in the kitchen while the scarecrow boy still had its own moldy bristles. The cornfield was a dry graveyard, with not a morsel for the birds to scavenge, but the scarecrow boy still played silent sentinel. In seasons of change, seasons of slaughter, seasons of harvest, the scarecrow boy had patiently held its ground.

As Jerp reached the farmhouse at the top of a slight rise of meadow, Jerp turned and looked back at the barn. It sagged silently to one side, making a crooked face. The two loading bays of the loft were deep eyes and the barn entrance was a hungry mouth with a hay-strewn tongue and stall-posts for teeth. In a high lonely window, Jerp saw the scarecrow boy staring back at him through the chickenwire screen. Jerp's heart clenched as he went inside the farmhouse.

Grandpa was pouring milk into a gallon glass jar so he could tell when the cream was separated.

"Grandpa, do barns have souls?" Jerp asked. Skyscrapers didn't have souls, airports didn't have souls, but maybe barns were different.

Grandpa turned and gave a look that wasn't *the* look, but it was a look that could be its cousin, one that said *I swear to Thee, what'll you think of next? A boy who dawdles in daydreams ain't much good on a farm.*

"Barns have animals and haybales and feedbags and potato barrels and a mighty load of cow patties. But I don't know about souls. That's for them who breathe on God's green earth, and them that's gone on to heaven," Grandpa said, his voice as smoky as a brushfire in an orchard.

"Don't animals go to heaven, too? And if they do, won't God need barns to put them in when the nights get cold? And won't God need somebody to watch over the livestock and the gardens?"

Grandpa finished straining the milk through cheesecloth and screwed the lid tight on the jar. "No need for food where people don't need to eat, Jerp. Up there, the Lord provides. Here, we have to help ourselves."

He said it in a way that Jerp thought meant *No wonder you couldn't stay out of trouble back home, what with these kinds of darn-fool notions.* But he only added, "Now, how about some scrambled eggs before we work up some tobacco?"

They had a filling breakfast, then went back to the barn. Grandpa opened the door to the corncrib and started up the stairs. Jerp peeked in from the doorway, hoping that Grandpa had seen the scarecrow boy while at the same time hoping the scarecrow boy didn't really exist. Daylight was now breaking through the window and flooding the corncrib, and a thousand specks of dust were spinning in the air. Then Jerp remembered that the scarecrow boy had been upstairs, where Grandpa was now. Jerp heard Grandpa's boots moving across the hayloft floor, causing needles of hay to fall to the packed ground below. Jerp held his breath and hurried up the stairs.

One side of the loft was filled with dried tobacco stalks, speared on poles and hung upside down. The smell of the burley leaf was heady and sweet. Grandpa sat at the makeshift workbench he had made from a piece of plywood and two haybales. He pulled the lower leaves from one of the stalks until he had as much as his hand could hold, then wound a leaf around one end until the tobacco fanned out like a peacock's tail. He tossed the tied bundle into a wide basket, continuing the routine that had occupied them for the past week.

"Tops for cigarettes, bottoms for cigars," Grandpa said, motioning for Jerp to sit down. They bundled in silence for a while, the air around them thick as snuff. When they finished the pile, Jerp went to take another pole from the rack. Each pole held about ten stalks of tobacco and had been too heavy for Jerp to lift back when the leaves were green and sticky and full of grasshoppers. But now the stalks had dried and Jerp could lift them by reaching from his tiptoes and sliding until the pole fell down into his arms.

Jerp put his hands between a row of stalks and parted them like curtains, trying to see how much more they had to do before they could load up the bed of the red Chevy truck and drive to the warehouse in town. His hands were already cracked and rough and his fingers ached. He looked down the long rows that meant days' more work. Something crackled among the brown leaves. The scarecrow boy was standing among the stalks, staring at Jerp with eyes as dark and unreflecting as tobacco juice.

Jerp froze, his hands gripping two stalks as if they were prison bars. The scarecrow boy didn't say a word, but its mouth turned up in a smile, stretching its pale skin even tighter across the limp bones of its face. It motioned for Jerp to step forward, slowly waving one flanneled arm. The scarecrow boy's fingers wiggled stiffly, like white artificial worms.

Jerp could only shake his head back and forth. His throat felt like a boar's head had been shoved in it. He sucked for air and drew only dust. Suddenly his limbs unlocked and he ran to Grandpa.

"What is it now, boy?" Grandpa said, and didn't say, but didn't have to, *I thought you were finally learning how to work, finally getting some use out of those hands God gave you, hands you were wasting on piano keys and poetry and shoplifting, hands that couldn't make a tough enough fist to keep the bullies away.*

Jerp said nothing, just looked at the knot-holed floor.

"We're wasting good daylight," Grandpa said, and Jerp heard between the words, *They burn them lights twenty-four hours a day in the city, but out here we work at God's pace. Out here we ain't got time for made-up monsters and scary stories. Busy hands touch no evil.*

Jerp swallowed a fistful of grainy air.

"Well, sit down and I'll get it myself," Grandpa said, and he really meant *And this weekend, it's back to the fancy boarding school that my son spends a fortune on, the school where the teachers make too much money to complain about a no-account troublemaker like you. And from now on, you can eat ham that's wrapped in cellophane.*

"No, Grandpa, I'll bring it," he burst out, hoping his voice didn't sound as airless as it felt. "I just wanted to let you know that we're almost finished and we'll soon get it to market."

Grandpa nearly smiled, showing the yellowed stumps of his few remaining teeth before he caught himself. "Good boy. What ye sow, so shall ye reap," he said, trying to quote from a book he had never learned to read.

Jerp went back among the tobacco and closed his eyes and hauled down a pole. He was carrying it to the workbench when suddenly he was hurtling into space.

He had fallen through one of the square holes that Grandpa used to toss hay down to the cattle. The pole was longer than the hay-chute and caught on the edges, bending like a bow but holding Jerp's weight.

He heard Grandpa yelling as if they were miles apart. He kicked his legs, trying to find purchase in the empty air. Crumbs of tobacco leaves trickled down the back of his shirt. His hands, toughened by a season in the fields, held onto the pole until his body stopped swaying.

"Hold on here, Jerp. You okay, boy?" Grandpa's voice came from somewhere above.

Jerp felt as if his arms had been ripped from his shoulder sockets, the way they had felt when he grabbed the electric fence to see how strong the shock was. He looked down at the barn floor fifteen feet below. The scarecrow boy was standing there, grinning like a turtle eating saw-briars even though its eyes were cold and dead.

"Lordamighty, it's a wonder you ain't broke your neck," Grandpa yelled. Boots drummed down the loft stairs, then the crib door banged shut. Then Grandpa was underneath him, telling him to let go. The scarecrow boy was gone.

Jerp relaxed his hands, and the balls of his feet drove into the dirt floor. Pain shot through his ankles. Grandpa caught him before he fell over.

"You sure you're okay?" Grandpa asked, holding Jerp's shoulders.

Jerp nodded numbly. Accidents happened on a farm. Timber fell on legs, snapping them like dry twigs. Horses kicked out blindly, causing concussions or worse. Plows and harrows sometimes turned more than red clay, sometimes making furrows in flesh and blood.

And accidents happened in the city. Gunmen drove by and filled the street with random hot lead. Drug dealers knifed rib cages because someone looked like someone else through angel-dusted eyes. Airliners sheared off rooftops and spread carnage like confetti. Misunderstood boys were labeled maladjusted and sent to juvenile hall where they learned nothing except how to be real criminals instead of amateurs.

"I'm sorry, Grandpa, I just lost my step," Jerp said as his wind returned. "I'm all right now. Let's get back to work."

Work was the answer. Work would keep evil away. Work would keep thoughts and daydreams and made-up monsters away. Work would make Grandpa happy.

"You sure?" Grandpa asked, and this time there was no threat in the words, only real concern and tenderness. Jerp nodded again and walked to the corncrib door, trying to hide his limp. They went back up to the loft and Grandpa lifted the pole that spanned the hay-chute.

He let out a liquid whistle and said, "Boy, lucky you fell just right. This thing mighta speared you like a frog on a gig."

The scarecrow boy could have made it happen that way, if it had wanted. But Jerp would work harder now.

They bundled tobacco the rest of the day, until the pile of sheaves was taller than Jerp. Grandpa complained about having a headache, and by the time they had cooked and eaten supper, the headache had turned into a fever. As night rose like a cliff made of coal, Jerp built a fire and Grandpa sat by the hearth, a shawl across his knees.

He looked miserable in his helplessness. "Jerp, I ain't up to doing chores tonight. You think you can handle them?" he said, his voice as chalky as his face.

"Sure, Grandpa." Jerp was anxious to make up for dropping

that egg basket, forgetting to slop the hogs that day two weeks ago, and burning the cabbage bed by broadcasting too much fertilizer. "I know what to do."

"Don't forget to put up the cows."

Put up the cows. In the barn. With scarecrow boy riding herd.

"Something wrong, boy? You ain't afeared of the dark, are you?"

Dark wasn't bad. Dark was only black, suffocating stillness. Dark didn't walk. Dark didn't *smile*.

"No, of course you ain't. And remember to latch the gate when you're done," Grandpa said, his attention wandering back to the fire which reflected off his rheumy eyes.

Jerp put on his coat, his fingers shaking as he fumbled with the zipper. He took a flashlight from the ledge by the front door and went out into the night, under the black sky where stars were strewn like white jackstones. Crickets chirped across the low hills. Jerp's flashlight cut a weak circle in the darkness, and he followed the circle to the gate.

The cows had come in on their own, following the twitching tail of the mare who was smart enough to know where food and shelter could be found. They were milling outside the pen, rubbing against the split locust rails. Jerp walked through the herd, grateful for the warmth the animals radiated. He lifted the latch and they spilled into the barnyard, annoying the sow into a round of grunting. Jerp slid back the barn door and the animals tottered inside. So far, so good.

But now he had to go to the hayloft. Now he had to go through the corncrib and up the stairs and across the loft that was littered with square black holes. Now he had to meet the scarecrow boy on its home turf.

He almost turned and ran back up the hill to the light and safety of the farmhouse, almost let his legs betray him by becoming a whirling windmill of fear. But then he pictured Grandpa asking if all the animals were put up and fed and the chores done proper. And Jerp heard the words that Grandpa had been waiting to say.

I was hoping to leave this farm to you, to let you carry on the tradition that your father abandoned. I was hoping someday the soil would lay claim to you, because busy hands touch no evil. But if the dirt's not in you, you can't plant there.

Jerp squinted in the moonlight that spilled into the barn. He kicked a horse chip across the ground. He took a pitchfork from the wall and walked to the corncrib. He would be part of the farm, not a big-city sissy.

Jerp banged the wooden handle on the door to warn the rats and the scarecrow boy that he was coming and had work to do. Taking a deep taste of air, he slammed the door open so hard that the sweet potatoes rolled around in their bins. He ran up the steps with one hand clenched around the pitchfork.

The haybales were stacked like bricks on the far end of the loft. He tiptoed through the tobacco that hung like long sleeping bats, around the hole he had fallen through earlier, and past the workbench. He was among the hay now, walking down an aisle between the silent stacks. Jerp turned the corner and there was scarecrow boy, sitting on a bale and grinning at him, a straw jabbed between its teeth.

Jerp held the pitchfork in front of him. If the scarecrow boy was stuffed with straw, Jerp was ready to pierce its flesh and shred its muscles and rake its insides out. If the boy had a ragball heart, Jerp would make the heart stop beating. Jerp's own heart was racing like that of a crow that had eaten poisoned corn.

The scarecrow boy looked at Jerp with eyes that were beyond life, eyes that neither flinched nor twinkled in the flashlight's glare. Eyes that were as black as good bottom soil, black as manure. Eyes that had seen drought and flood, lush and fallow fields, harvests both meager and bountiful. Eyes that were seeds, begging to be planted and given a chance to take root, to grow and bloom and go to seed, to spread on the winds and in the bellies of birds, to propagate among the loess and loam and alluvial soils of the world.

"You've been waiting for me," Jerp said. "Always."

The scarecrow boy nodded, its head wobbling on its shoulders like an apple tied to a kite.

Suddenly Jerp knew whose farm this was. It had never been

recorded on a deed down at the county seat, but some laws were unwritten and universal. Rights of ownership went to the possessor.

And Jerp belonged here, belonged to the farm and to the scarecrow boy.

The scarecrow boy spread its musty arms as if to hug Jerp. Jerp let the flashlight drop to the floor as the scarecrow boy rose like smoke and drifted through the tines of the pitchfork. Jerp tried to draw back, but he felt as if he had a splintery stake up his spine. His arms went limp and he itched, he itched, his hands were dusty and his mouth was dry. The pitchfork fell onto the planks, but the clatter was muffled, as if he were hearing it through layers of cloth. Jerp tried to stretch the threads of his neck, but he could only stare straight ahead at the boy in front of him.

At the boy with the smile that curved like a blackberry thorn. At the boy who had stolen his face and meat and white bones. At the boy who was wearing his scuffed lace-up boots. At the boy who was looking down at his hands—*no, MY hands*, his cobwebbed mind screamed—as if the hands were a new pair of work gloves that needed to be broken in.

Then Jerp knew. He had forgotten to latch the gate behind him. Even though Grandpa had told him a thousand times. But Jerp had been so afraid. It wasn't his fault, was it?

Jerp tried to open his mouth, to scream, to tell the boy to get out of his skin, but Jerp's tongue was an old sock. He strained to flap the rags of his arms, but he felt himself falling into the loose hay. He choked on the cotton and chaff and sweetly sick odor of his own dry-rot. And still he *saw*, with eyes that were tickled by tobacco dust and stung by tears that would never fall.

Jerp watched as the boy now wearing Jerp's clothes bent to lift the pitchfork. The boy tried out its stolen skin, stretched its face into new smiles. Then the boy who had borrowed Jerp's body stepped between the haybales and was gone. Minutes or years later, the barn door slid open.

Jerp tried his limbs and found they worked, but they were much too light and boneless. He dragged himself to the window and pressed his sawdust head against the chickenwire. Jerp looked out over the moist fields that would now and always beckon him, he listened to the breezes that would laugh till the cows came home, he sniffed the meadows that would haunt his endless days. He wondered how long it would be before the next season of change. Already he ached from waiting.

Jerp looked down into the barnyard and saw the boy who wore his flesh walking toward the farmhouse, the pitchfork glinting under the moon, perhaps on his way to punish someone who had shirked the evening chores.

The boy remembered to latch the gate.

LAST WRITES

Ah, the vanity of the living.

Just look at him.

He sits on the upper floor and surveys the flat sweep of ocean. The sea is weak, exhausted from a night of stretching, yet he watches as if some catastrophe will occur at any moment. True, ships have sunk here in sight of shore on the calmest of summer days, but not on this man's watch. All he knows is what the logbook has told him and what he has gleaned from the tales of those who sent him here.

He will not learn, and he has time ahead of him. His eyes may become bleary and strained, he will grow lonely, he will think things that no normal man should. Yet, when his term is over, he will rejoin the sweeping tide of the living and give this place little thought. He will leave this place, and that is why I hate him. That is why I must become a part of him, invade his thoughts and dreams. We each seek to become immortal, and I must live on through him.

He imagines himself a lighthouse keeper, yet he keeps nothing. He comes and he goes, like the others. And still I shall remain. I am the real keeper here.

He fancies he knows of solitude. Sitting there in his bamboo chair, with his lantern and bottle of spirits. The labels have changed over the years, grown more colorful, but the bottom of the bottle still speaks the same words. The speakers of several languages have sat in that chair: Portuguese, Italian, Dutch, but mostly English and Spanish. Yet the language is the same to me. Theirs is the language of the living.

This one is handsomer than some of the others. He has side-burns clipped close to the lobe, beard trimmed in a fashion I haven't seen before. He is young. They get younger every year. Or perhaps I am older. Please, merciful God, let me be older.

The object on the table beside him emits a purring sound, like that of a cat stuck in a sewage drain. The man puts the object to his ear as if it were a conch and speaks.

"Hello, Norfolk Lighthouse."

He pauses, listening. If it were a conch instead of the strange object, he would be hearing the roar of the ocean. Or the blood rushing through his head. Sometimes those two things are the same.

"Hi, Maleah," he says, his face changing instantly, lifting into a bright and open expression.

Maleah. A pretty name. It sounds of Hawaii, that Pacific island region of which sailors sometimes speak. She must be as beautiful as her name.

I hate her, for she occupies him.

I go to the window, stick my head in a sea breeze ripe with the scream of gulls, but I can't drown out his words.

"I miss you, too," he says. "But it's only for a year. And I'll get a lot of writing done while I'm here."

His other hand, the one not holding the non-conch, goes to the bottle. He nods, sips, glances at the window. At me.

I rattle the shutters. Perhaps I am getting older. I don't bang them with the same enthusiasm of a couple of centuries ago. Still, paint sloughs off and bits of stucco dust fall to the beach far below.

"Maleah," he says into the conch-thing. A telephone, they have called it. "Something weird is happening."

Now I am "something weird." I would sigh if I had breath. But I must do this the hard way. Just like always.

I knock on the door to the upper chamber. I stand on the winding staircase, the yawning gap of darkness that leads to a pale, gleaming light far below.

The door swings open, the strong stench of spirits marking his breath, and I see his stricken face—as stricken as mine, surely, and then I fall again, far, far, far. As I fall, I smile. He has forgotten Maleah and thinks of me.

Sooner or later, they all dream only of me. To the last.

I wasn't always like this. When I was alive, I walked the beach in search of shark's teeth and pretty shells. In bare feet, dawn fast and pink on the horizon, the water licking at my ankles with a gentle, foaming tongue. The lighthouse was a marker, a means to measure the distance I had walked from the cottage I shared with my doting, deaf parents.

Usually, I turned back when the lighthouse window was clearly visible, though on foggy mornings I might not see the towering structure until I was nearly upon it. On those days, a single bright lantern would burn in the uppermost window, serving as a guide for ships that might be daring the narrow passage. I was a ship myself, a vessel with an empty hull, as lost as any rudderless cutter.

On the day I died, I decided to keep walking, though the tide had run out and my parents would be waiting for me to sweep sand from the floors, cook mackerel, and air the mildewed blankets. I loathed the smell of fish. It permeated the walls, and driftwood smoke would leak through the fireplace stones and sting my eyes. That morning, I couldn't bear the claustrophobic cottage. The day was warm and pleasant, with only a few thin strips of clouds in the blue sky. My feet carried me farther along the shore than I had been in years, to the north, toward the lighthouse that had been built before my birth. My passion for solitude could scarcely have been more gratified.

My father told me strange tales surrounding the lighthouse— how men who kept the light burning through the dark hours somehow lost some of their own light, so that when their year of duty was over, their eyes were dry and hollow, their faces lacking in emotion, their tongues slow to speak. Through the years, several ships had run aground in the shallows, while others had cracked their spines on the rocky outcroppings to the west. Perhaps the memories of those failures haunted the lighthouse keepers, though not every man had witnessed a tragedy. Perhaps it was merely the lengthy solitude that turned them into dull, haggard beasts.

The lighthouse towered before me that day, bright as sand as it stretched higher and higher into the sky with my every step. It was capped with copper that had long ago turned dull green. The masonry that from a distance had seemed solid revealed itself to be covered with spidery cracks, iron bands girding the base. As I grew nearer, I detected rust on the hardware of the single oaken door set in the rounded base of the structure.

The door had a large metal knocker in the center. The keyhole in the door handle was like the black eye of a dead shark. Sand skirled in the breeze around the base of the door, and cool, fetid air oozed from the cracks between the oak planks. I touched the wood, wondering about the man behind. I tapped the door and a hollow echo sounded inside.

In the little fishing village where my parents were born, two miles from the lighthouse, the people often spoke of lighthouse keepers who were only seen in daylight, on those rare occasions when they replenished supplies. The keepers were an odd lot, unkempt and wild-eyed, given to excess whiskey. The keeper position rotated by the calendar year, though sometimes stories emerged of those who had been unable to endure the loneliness and turned up raving in the streets, shouting about shipwrecks and sea monsters and Neptune with a forked trident riding in on the backs of deformed porpoises.

I thought perhaps one of those madmen was inside that morning, high above me, far removed from the smell of mackerel. What strange tales he might share. And I, at eighteen, was as much at a loss for company as any man who had ever consigned himself to that upper chamber. I lifted the knocker and brought it down hard against the strike plate. The only sound in reply was the reverberation inside the base of the lighthouse, the whispering of the surf, and the distant cry of a gull.

I knocked again, looking back toward the point where my parents' house lay. Desperation fueled my hand as I worked the iron ring. I think I even started to weep, but I can't be sure, because the sea air was salty and that was centuries ago. But at last there came a turning in the works of the door, and it creaked open.

I found myself facing a man of dark countenance, with black, haunted eyes and a large, pale forehead. He was perhaps twenty, though his eyes looked far older than that, as if he had witnessed tragedies in abundance. His hair was swept away from his brow in a wild manner, like a tangled tuft of sea oats. He wore a vest and a white shirt, both stained and rumpled. The smell of drink hung about him like a mist.

"Do you know how many steps I had to climb?" he said.

I gave him my sweetest smile, though I'd had little practice in that art. Despite his grave expression, he was handsome.

"I live around the point," I said, "Since we're neighbors—"

"I have no need of neighbors," he said. "I wish to be alone." But I caught him staring past my shoulder at the shoreline. The beach was empty, for the coral was sharp and discouraged bathers, and the currents here were too rough for putting out fishing boats.

"I was wondering if I could see the view from up there," I said, leaning my head back to look at the windows far above. "I've lived here all my life but I scarcely know what the place looks like."

"I have my duties," he said. "I've no time for guided tours."

"Please, sir, I will only be a moment. Just one look. And I came all this way." I smoothed the lap of my dress, a gesture I had seen women use in church when speaking to men they wished to flatter.

He seemed to reflect for an instant, and his eyes grew softer. "Hmm. You remind me of someone I once knew. Perhaps I can spare some time. But you must promise to be careful. These stairs are wretched."

"I will take care, sir." As I followed him inside, I couldn't help smiling a little. Perhaps I had an untapped gift for getting my way.

It is something I have perfected over the years. Something I grew better at after I died.

The base of the lighthouse was hollow, with a well perhaps forty feet deep. The metal stairs wound up into the gloom, and I could see why he thought them treacherous. He had left an oil lantern by the foot of the stairs, and carried it while he returned to close the door. The lantern threw long, flickering shadows up the curved wall of the lighthouse.

"Come along," he said, offering his hand as he mounted the stairs.

"I think I shall hold the rail," I said, believing myself coy.

He held the lantern below his face, and in his position above me, the flame made the dark creases in his face even more somber. "Very well. Let me know if you tire."

We navigated upwards, his shoes thundering on the narrow metal steps. I followed close behind, watching my feet. He turned once to check on me, and seemed satisfied that I could keep my balance. We were perhaps halfway up when he paused, breathing hard. I was in better shape due to the great distances I had to walk to the village. He held the lantern high, and I glanced down at the great black space below. I gasped despite myself, and a smile came to his lips. It wasn't a cruel smile, but a playful one.

"It's difficult the first few times, but it gets easier," he said.

"You haven't told me your name," I said.

"Poe," he said. "From Baltimore. And yours?"

I wasn't prepared to tell him yet. I was still wary of what the villagers might think if he went around reporting that I had visited him alone. Word would also get back to my parents, and while I resented their control of me, I still loved them and wished them no additional worries on my behalf.

"Mary," I said, the first name that came to mind. Only later, after my death, would he know my true name.

"Mary. One of my favorites."

We continued our climb and eventually reached a small trap door at the top. While I didn't count them that morning, in subsequent years I have made note of each step. There are 136, all of them narrow and slow and worn by thousands of footsteps. Not mine, though. Since that morning, I don't use them. Now, I float.

He went first, then helped me up with a strong hand. Poe's watch chamber was sparsely furnished. A table and a chair were on one end of the round room, a logbook of some type on the table, a quill pen and inkwell beside it. Papers were piled beneath the logbook, and a collapsed telescope lay across the open pages of the book. A bunk sat low to the floor at the other end of the room, a walnut trunk at its foot, presumably to contain his clothes. A cabinet stood near the trunk, filled with bread, dried meat and fish, apples, and several rows of corked bottles filled with amber liquid. A chamber pot, covered indiscreetly with a board, was off to the side. Empty bottles were scattered beneath the bunk, and the cramped room had the same spirited aroma that surrounded the man, combined with the cloying stench of the chamber pot.

Poe waved one florid hand to the three windows facing the seaside. "There's your view," he said, then sat in the chair by the logbook.

The flat, gray water stretched for miles, the horizon farther than I had ever seen it. The ocean seemed to curve, and distant full-sheeted masts protruded from the water like tiny clusters of white flowers. The shoreline stretched in either direction, the north sweeping more gently, the south broken by crags and cays. The natural breakwater of which ships' captains were afraid was black and sharp, gleaming like wet teeth. I took in the view for some minutes, not remarking.

"One gets bored with it after a while," Poe said. He uncorked one of the bottles and poured some of the liquor into a glass. He drank without offering me any.

"Are you not a lover of the sea?" I said. "I would have thought someone taking a post such as this—"

"—must be as mad as a hatter," he said, looking glumly into his glass. "Four months here, and I've barely even started."

"I don't understand," I said.

He gestured toward the papers on the table. "My work."

"You keep a record of the currents, tides, and ships?"

"Not that work. I meant my writing."

"You are a writer, then?"

"Yes. I used to be a newspaper reporter. But I'm driven to write of false things. I thought with a change of scenery, and blessed isolation . . ."

"You have plenty of both here, I imagine. I know something of isolation myself."

He gave a grim smile, as if his loneliness were the deepest in all the world and weighed most heavily on his shoulders. He drank more liquor, in gulps instead of sips, and refilled his glass. My legs were trembling from the long climb, but the only place to sit was his bed. I had never been in a man's bed.

"Isolation is the devil's tool," Poe said. "I want to concentrate on my work, but one hears things in this damnable cylinder. The rush of high tide sounds like voices in the chamber below, like the soft cries of those who have been pulled under the water. Think of all those ships lying on the ocean floor yonder, and the white bones of those who went down with them. Where do you suppose they go?"

For the first time, I had an inkling of the man's instability. His brooding good looks became sharper and fiercer, his eyes flashing with a morose anger. Beyond the windows, the clouds had gathered and grown darker as if to match Poe's mood. A squall was pushing in from the sea, and the cutters spread across the sea had taken down their sails as the wind increased.

"A storm is blowing in," I said. "Shouldn't you light the lamps?"

He said nothing, just wiped at his chin.

"The current shifts here with these spring storms," I said. "Surely you were told that by your employer."

"Damned De Grat. He should have known I could never tolerate this place—or my own company—for an entire year."

Wanting to pull him from his mood, not yet ready to trouble him to lead me back down the stairs, I asked what he was writing.

"It's about a shipwreck."

"Shipwreck?"

"A ghost ship. With a morbid crew."

I laughed. "One hears plenty of those tales. I found a paper in a corked bottle once, washed up on the beach."

His eyebrows arched. "What did it say?"

"The water had gotten to it."

"It always does," he said, with the air of one who had floated many futile messages.

"Can I hear the story?"

"It's no good," he said. He tapped the rumpled pages beneath the logbook. "This may be the last thing I ever write."

"Have you been published?" I asked.

A smile slithered across his moist lips. "Some poems."

"Please, read me one."

"It's not fit for ladies," he said, and I wondered how much of his gallantry was due to drunkenness. He closed the logbook and passed it to me. I opened it to the first page. I'd had some schooling in the village, but could read little. He had started entries on January first. His handwriting was florid and bold, the words scrawled with an intensity that matched his features.

He took it from me. "'January two,'" he read. "'I have passed this day in a species of ecstasy that I find impossible to describe. My passion for solitude could scarcely have been more thoroughly gratified. I do not say satisfied; for I believe I should never be satiated with such delight as I have experienced today. The wind lulled about daybreak, and by the afternoon the sea had gone down materially. Nothing to be seen, with the telescope even, but ocean and sky, with an occasional gull.'"

"That's lovely," I say. I know nothing of poetry.

"'January three,'" he continued. "'A dead calm all day. Towards evening the sea looked very much like glass. A few seaweeds came in sight; but besides them absolutely nothing all day, not even the slightest speck of cloud.'"

"Much like this morning, only now the wind is picking up and there's a swell rising."

He closed the book and stared out at the sea for a moment. "What do you know of murder?" he asked, appraising me, his eyes gleaming.

"Very little," I said. "I can't imagine such a horrid thing."

"I can," he said. "Far too easily. The mind of man is a foul, corrupt thing. And when a man is alone with his thoughts . . ."

He drained his glass again, refilled it, spilling a few drops on the table. "But forgive me," he said, louder. "I forget my manners. You are a guest and I have made you stand."

He rose unsteadily from the chair and sat on the bunk, indicating with his glass that I was to take the chair. I hesitated, afraid to linger but also wary of his wrath. I sensed he could be set off with but the slightest provocation, and I began to regret my bold adventure. The sky outside had grown even darker, and though it was scarcely noon, the ocean and sky merged on the horizon into a single bruised color, clouds whipping like rags on a line. The wind screamed at the gaps around the windows, and from below came the dull roar that the man imagined were the voices of the dead.

I shivered, though the room was warm. "I must be getting home," I said. "My parents are waiting, and I dare not get caught out in this storm."

"Why don't you stay until it blows over?" he said, leaning back on the bunk a little. Men who worked with shipping had a certain reputation, and I suspected this man was no different. Though part of me had longed for some romance resulting from my encounter with a lighthouse keeper, I didn't want to suffer the rough attentions of an animal. The desire for solitude in itself did not make a man sensitive.

"They'll be expecting me," I said. I took a tentative step toward the trap door, loathe to negotiate those many steps again without a lantern.

Poe grabbed my arm, and his eyes were dead as coal. "I can't be alone anymore," he said. "Don't you hear them?"

I tried to pull away, but his was the grip of a lunatic. "Please," I implored, silently cursing my recklessness in coming here. A barren life on a lonely strip of shore was better than no life at all, and the excitement I had craved was now full upon me, but I wanted it no more.

"The voices," he said with a hiss, his face clenched, sweat clinging to that high, broad forehead. "With every storm they come, the souls of the shipwrecked and lost at sea."

As the wind picked up, I thought I could hear them, but perhaps it was only the roaring heartbeat in my ears. I wrenched free, desperate and afraid. He grabbed at me again, and I dodged away. He howled, the mad sound blending with the wind until it filled the watch chamber.

"Don't leave me," he shouted, diving toward me. I stepped backward, into the space of the open trap door, falling to the top step and then into the yawning black abyss, toward those tormented voices at the base of the lighthouse.

I stayed with Poe for the remainder of his term. He disposed of my body, of course, weighed me down by slipping scrap iron into my dress, and set me out to sea in the early morning dark of high tide. I came back with the tide the next night, watched as he brooded with his bottles and occasionally scrawled barely legible words on his papers. I read his logbook over his shoulder, what I could of it.

I waited until he fell into a restless sleep before I began whispering. Poe was right, those voices in the well of the lighthouse were of the dead, and I both imitated and joined them. Poe tossed in his sleep, sweated like driftwood, and finally woke. "Who's there?" he asked.

I told him my name, as I told all of them my name in the years and centuries to come. He finished his story, wrote poetry, and drank to forget me, though he could not forget the one who was his constant companion. He had come to the lighthouse to be alone, but in the end, that was the last thing I allowed him. He read to me from his journal: "It is strange that I never observed, until this moment, how dreary a sound that word has: 'Alone.'"

And though Poe left at the end of the year, I imagine I haunted him for the remainder of his days. I longed to be the last thing of which he ever wrote.

The sun has risen on a new year. The watch chamber has changed little, though now the lights are electric. I learned from the living as my days ran together, as the lighthouse keepers became park rangers and oceanographic researchers and meteorologists. They brought computers, radars, radios, and televisions, sounds and pictures that compete with the eternal beauty beyond the windows. The ships have changed, no longer using sails, some hovering over the water as if on cushions of air. However, the sea has changed little, and I have changed even less.

In recent years, the occasional paranormal investigator appears, laden with equipment, but they are not as interesting because they too willingly believe. This year, a woman occupies the watch chamber. Over the last century, women have become more common, though usually the chamber is still operated by sole sentinels. I prefer it that way. They end up lonely while I always have company.

I go to her now, my dress like a sheet of torn vapor, my hair trailing, my fingers scarcely visible and cold. I tap on the window, whisper like the wind, aching to know my new companion.

She looks up from the computer and frowns at the sunset on the horizon. She doesn't yet understand that I am the horizon, the point between the dead and the living. Where, as Poe said on one of those long nights we spent together, the moon never beams without bringing him dreams. All of them dream of me sooner or later. I grow more solid with the sinking of the sun, and I smile as I drift into the chamber.

She pushes back in her chair, the wheels squeaking like frightened rats. She doesn't believe her eyes. They never do.

"Who are you?" she says.

I almost call myself "Mary," but that deception rang hollow centuries ago. As I told Poe, I want to be remembered as my true self, not as another.

"My name is Annabel Lee," I say.

I'll be with her until the end of both of our days. As with Poe, my first and always, she will make me immortal.

FROM THE ASHES

Looking back over old work is like looking at photographs: you see that younger, more innocent, and more foolish version of yourself and wonder how you ever got this far, and how you never really understood much of what was shaping your life at the time.

Writers love their own words. They have to. They spend much of their time isolated, hunched over a keyboard, squinting at a screen until their eyes burn and their spines scream and their wrists stiffen in protest. And all they have to show for the sacrifice is a scattering of glyphs that sometimes seems to have no meaning in any language. To then assume that barrage of symbols will take on a comprehensive narrative and satisfying arc is truly an act of arrogance.

But writers go one step further–we expect people to not only read the words, to not only piece them together into a coherent story, but we demand adoration for our act. And, occasionally, a little bit of cold coin.

The only time I will voluntarily reread an old story is when I am revising it or proofing it for a book like the one you hold in your hands. Because my first instinct is to correct all the flaws that are now so obvious to the wiser and more battle-scarred version of myself, and the second is to cringe and fling the offensive prose into the recycling heap. Sure, there was youthful vigor aplenty in the tales, a little brashness and vanity, and a barely hidden glee in the process of stacking words as if they were a child's alphabet blocks. But just as the parent must come in and clean up what the petulant child has kicked over, the writer must look at his older work with nothing less than total dismay.

There is one saving grace, though. These stories saved my life and helped me reach this little scenic turnout in the journey.

I wrote most of these stories when I was struggling with alcoholism, depression, fatherhood, divorce, selfishness, fear, and other personal trauma, all of it self-inflicted. And all I could do was scream onto the page in much the same way pre-morphine amputees screamed into the pillows in the field hospitals of bygone wars. Hear me, don't hear me.

With a little time under my belt, and a little acceptance, the pain seems like such a waste. I would gladly have traded a little peace for all the work I've managed to pile up over the years. But perhaps these stories played a part in reaching my new station. Indeed, Dark Regions publisher Joe Morey and I kicked around the title of "Growing Pains" for the collection. Like the fetus in "The Christening," I had to kick and squirm and squeal to be born. I had to fight for it, even though the fight was only against myself.

As a result we have this collection, largely written over the years 2000 to 2006, as documentation of that period of my life when I could easily have gone the other way–into the darkness and despair that I so often ridicule others for embracing as *poseur* stage costume. Perhaps there's a lesson in the cumulative pile of burnt offerings, but that old photograph is as much gray as it is black and white.

So here's a little color commentary to flesh out the fantasy.

Timing Chains of the Heart: This was one of my first published stories, appearing in the short-lived Internet magazine E-Scape in 1998. I believe it was inspired by some of those old EC horror comics of the "Tales of the Crypt" sort, and a story that stuck with me about someone driving a hearse and the coffin ripping open in an accident, with the corpse ending up behind the wheel. I've also developed a small *ouvre* of transformative horror, in which the reader–and sometimes the author–isn't sure whether the haunting is real or only occurring in the mind of the protagonist. Instead of delivering on the expected crash, I prefer the continued horror of the endless, open road. After all, the scariest part of hell is the allegation that it lasts forever.

Dog Person: This was inspired by a true story. My friend Al Carson was talking about his dog's expensive medical problems and how he decided to have Sally "put to sleep" instead of spending thousands of dollars. We discussed a fictional version of the tale and, in his version, there were two shots–first was the mercy killing of the dog, then the suicidal shot. I went with the version here, where the guy loves his dog so much that he just can't face life without her. And, of course, the treacherous wife gets the fruit of her hateful labors. Originally published in Cemetery Dance Magazine #56 in 2006 and selected by editor Ellen Datlow for inclusion in *The Year's Best Fantasy & Horror.*

The October Girls: Written under the original title of "Playmates" in 2001, I wrote this for a promotional e-book that fellow authors Brandon Massey and Jon Merz were distributing. The idea of a dead best friend is not uncommon or new, but I like the chilly flavor of the dead friend's jealousy. In the end, however, our sympathy shifts to the girl who must live a wretched childhood rather than the one whose pain has ended. I'm currently developing this as a book series, with the characters more grown up and firmly in the early 20's. Unfortunately, even young grown-ups are more dishonest than children, so this may be the closest we get to the truth.

Murdermouth: I'd toyed around with carnivals and circuses before, especially with zombies, and I've penned a few first-person zombie tales. To me, suffering bottomless, vacuous hunger is more horrifying than actually being pursued by such creatures, and I still prefer the old-school zombies that plod along with total patience and determination instead of darting around like wolves, sometimes weilding firearms. In much of my work, I'm attempting to figure out the nature of love. As with the real thing, sometimes I just get a little squishy in the process. Published in the anthology *The Book Of All Flesh* in 2001.

Sung Li: Every author needs to drag out at least one creepy-doll tale, and this is mine. The subtext of child abuse is a little too facile and gross, but the doll and the knife were drawn from my real life, and again we have a bit of ambiguity about the reality of the supernatural occurrences. I write without outlining, so I often don't know the ending until I get there. And sometimes not even then. Originally published in At The Brink of Madness #3 in 1999.

Silver Run: Mark Twain is one of my favorite writers, and his blend of cynicism, observation of human nature, and yarn-spinning skill are tough to mimic, but I gave it a try here, albeit with more of a mountaineer flair. The story was written for *Legends of the Mountain State*, based on folklore of West Virginia and published in 2007. I was in Charleston for the West Virginia Book Festival when I read an article about haunted train tunnels, and the rest is history. The view on women depicted herein is wholly fictional and not inspired by the author's relations, or lack thereof, with the fairer gender.

In The Family: This was written before the "Six Feet Under" television series, proof that undertaker families are kind of strangely appealing. However, they often have great senses of humor, as you can imagine. This story isn't too funny, though, and has a bit of a Norman Bates flavor and I'm not sure the science is too valid. My plan is to be cremated myself, as I don't really trust anyone playing with my internal organs, especially if they're getting paid by the hour. First appearance in The Third Alternative #41 in 2005.

The Night Is An Ally: I dug the old "Weird War" comics that usually had short scripts with a twist ending, and I'd also read a book called *Ordinary Men: Reserve Police Battalion 101 and the Final Solution in Poland*. I was fascinated by the psychological process in which "ordinary men" evolved into cold-blooded killers, and I have no more answers today than I did then. And I believe it's frigteningly easy for such events to replicate themselves repeatedly in the human future. This appeared in the Mike Heffernan-helmed anthology *A Dark And Deadly Valley* in 2007.

Work in Progress: I studied art in college and have this secret little fantasy of becoming a painter in my old age. Or maybe I just think it's cool that Van Gogh whacked off his ear and mailed it to his sweetheart. Proof that guys will do anything for sex. But it could have been worse, if he had chosen a different organ...which is another story in itself, but I'm not writing it. Published in Crimewave #9 in 2006.

The Endless Bivouac: I'd researched the horrors of the Andersonville prison camp in which Union soldiers died by the tens of thousands, and this original story is actually a mirror version of a story I'd written a decade ago. This time around, I explored the horror from the guard's point of view rather than the spirit of the prisoner he'd killed. At the end we find the enemies have set aside their weapons. The war is over. Or is it?

She Climbs A Winding Stair: This story spun itself from an image of a ghost woman looking out on the sea, waiting and waiting for her seafaring love. I'd done some research on Portsmouth Island off the North Carolina coast, which was abandoned with buildings intact and is now a part of the National Park system. Ghost towns aren't necessarily limited to the Old West. Originally published in The Book of Dark Wisdom #9.

Watermelon: I'm almost embarrassed to admit this is autobiographical, but if you've read the book, then you've caught me with my pants down, anyway. One night, while drunk, I yanked a watermelon from the fridge and beat the holy hell out of it, ramming my fist inside and yanking out the pink pulp. I wasn't even that angry. But I imagined that was the sort of diffuse outlet that prevented some greater atrocity somewhere else. And as with the protagonist here, you suspect worse things down the road, life goes on, and hell lasts forever. Appeared in Cemetery Dance #51 in 2005.

The Meek: This story had an odd evolution, as it was originally intended for an Australian anthology that ultimately collapsed. Publishing ventures seem to give rise to more disease, bankruptcy, depression, divorces, and computer problems than all other human endeavors combined, at least to judge from all the excuses offered up by people with bigger dreams than abilities. But that's why I'm a writer, because I need only a piece of paper and pen, and these days a laptop. At any rate, here's another "carnivorous ruminant" tale with religious overtones, later visited more in depth in my novel *The Farm*. Originally published in the limited-edition CD anthology Extremes II in 2001, a hybrid format that also contained three of my original rock songs that can be heard on my Web site.

The Rocking Chair: Another of my "haunted pregnancy" tales, this one allowed me to explore bizarre family relationships and double crosses as well. I'm not completely sure I nailed my intentions with this one, because I wanted a clear ambiguity about the chair, not a typical "Surprise–it's a haunted rocker!" surprise ending as expected. Shock endings rarely work on modern audiences, and if that's all you got, then the story is weak anyway. So I'm sticking with the interpretation that Grandma did in the baby because she suspected it wasn't blood kin. This is its first appearance anywhere.

The Weight of Silence: While anticipating the birth of my daughter, I had a horrid run of "sinister pregnancy" stories, most of which were centered around conniving, cold-hearted mothers who didn't really want to be mothers. And double crosses are among my favorite fictional tools, especially where romance is involved. Put it all together and you get a story that probably won't be found on the table of a waiting room in the maternity ward. Originally published in the *Corpse Blossoms* anthology in 2005.

The Hounds of Love: This is one of my favorite stories, and again I'm plumbing the well of love and attachment. Sometimes I wonder if love is simply possession, and if you love something, you have an obligation to it. I was afraid this one was a little too gruesome but I vowed not to back down a bit, even though it got rejected a few times. Most serial killers start out as animal torturers, so perhaps this strange critter's love is enough to keep little Dexter on the straight and narrow. Published in *The Book of More Flesh* in 2002.

You'll Never Walk Alone: This is the third of my stories to appear in James Lowder's Flesh zombie series, in the 2004 *Book of Final Flesh*, and I co-opted religion yet again, as well as that old inspirational show tune "You'll Never Walk Alone." I also went back to the mountains with this one, for though most of my novels are set in the Appalachians, my stories travel all over the place and often with strange company. Some things are far scarier than walking alone, I can assure you.

Penance: This set-up was inspired by the Black Plague-era habit of nailing people inside their own houses to prevent them from infecting others. Of course, such an apocalyptic situation practically begs a religious overtone, and I'm always happy to oblige. I hope I don't come off as preachy, because I certainly don't have any answers, and I try to offer uplifting moments in the horror, like those golden shafts of sunlight that sometimes break through a gathering storm. I'm generally an optimist, though I don't blame people who don't believe it. Appeared in Black October #3 in 2002.

Sewing Circle: Original to this collection and nspired by a true incident in which I wrote what we in the journalism trade call a "fluff piece" about a local quilting group. The leader of the group, who wasn't present and was barely mentioned in the article, harassed me endlessly about a minor error, to the point that I decided she was vengeful that I hadn't made her the centerpiece of the article. Since the group met at a church, it was easy to spin the idea to its most absurd and extreme conclusion.

Scarecrow Boy: This story went through numerous rewrites and I loved the "country" flavor of it, though it took a while to develop a satisfactory narrative arc. One editor said it was too much like the old horror-movie trick of "Don't open the gate, you *know* better than to open the gate," and then the character conveniently opens the gate. But sometimes we don't listen to reason, or we get absent minded, or maybe we just grab at whatever means necessary in order to gain eternal life. Published in Chiaroscuro at Chizine.com, in 2001.

Last Writes: This is one of only two co-writing projects I've ever been involved in, and the first in which the collaborator was dead. Sometimes I think if I actually had to collaborate, the other guy would be dead before we made it through the third chapter. But luckily Edgar Alan Poe is timelessly cool and, best of all, doesn't need a cut of the royalties. I liked the idea of having Poe as a character in his own story, since the original fragment that inspired the project was written in first person. From *Poe's Lighthouse* in 2006.

Thanks for scattering my ashes in the wind, and for helping my whispers linger. In many ways, my spirit is a phoenix risen from these ashes and I look forward to sharing many more adventures and tales with you. God willing and the Tao being receptive, I will. I am. We are. It is.

Scott Nicholson
August 2008

Scott Nicholson is the author of seven Appalachian thrillers, including T*he Skull Ring* and *They Hunger*. He is also a screenwriter and graphic novelist, creating the comic series *Grave Conditions*. His first novel *The Red Church* was a Bram Stoker Award finalist and alternate selection of The Mystery Guild. He studied creative writing at the University of North Carolina and Appalachian State University and has been active in Mystery Writers of America, Horror Writers Association, and International Thriller Writers.

Nicholson's hobbies include organic gardening, songwriting, guitar playing, fishing, and swimming. He is also a freelance editor and hosts an annual paranormal conference and writing retreats. He lives in the Blue Ridge Mountains of North Carolina.

His Web site is www.hauntedcomputer.com.